VICIOUS CIRCLE

VICIOUS CIRCLE

Douglas Clark

PERENNIAL LIBRARY

Harper & Row, Publishers
New York, Cambridge, Philadelphia, San Francisco
London, Mexico City, São Paulo, Singapore, Sydney

First PERENNIAL LIBRARY edition published 1985.

Library of Congress Cataloging-in-Publication Data

Clark, Douglas.
   Vicious circle.
   I. Title.
PR6053.L294V5   1985   823'.914   85-42559
ISBN 0-06-080778-4 (pbk.)

85 86 87 88 89 OPM 10 9 8 7 6 5 4 3 2 1

For my sisters

VICIOUS CIRCLE

— 1 —

Young Mrs Marian Whincap peered anxiously at the big turkey in the oven before worriedly basting it for the umpteenth time with the fat from round the potatoes with which it was cooking. Then she pushed the tin back on its shelf, straightened up and turned the gas down to the lowest possible flame before closing the door. As she put the oven glove down, her husband, Adam, appeared in the kitchen doorway. Seeing the frown of worry on her face, he stepped forward and kissed her forehead. It was slightly damp with perspiration from her labours in the heat of the kitchen. Her response was fretful. "Darling, your father is really too bad."

"I know, my sweet, but he has been called out to an emergency. It's not as if he was just playing us up."

"Where's he gone?"

"Heaven knows. It's Christmas Day, so the surgery is closed. Dad, as senior partner, is on duty. I don't really know whether that's because he expects fewer calls today and has chosen the easiest of the holiday stints or whether he considers that it's the job of the senior bloke to make himself available on the day of days." He paused a moment to hold her by the shoulders, at arm's length, and to smile at her encouragingly. "You know these doctors, Marian. They never divulge

1

who they're going to see or why. It's part of the mystique."

She smiled a little in acknowledgement of his efforts. "Your mother doesn't know, even. All she could tell me was that he said she was to come here in her own car and he would join her as soon as possible. But that was at half-past eleven. It's twenty-past one now."

"Don't worry, sweetheart."

"How can you say that? This is our first Christmas. Our first party like this. We've got nine other guests in the sitting room and the dinner's nearly ruined. The turkey's getting hard and the sausages are cooked to a frazzle."

Adam appreciated her concern. It was to be the best Christmas party ever. Marian had taken enormous trouble over the marketing and preparations and, like every newly-married girl faced with her first, big, in-law occasion, she was suffering from near-nervous debility lest the whole affair should become a social disaster. He made a sudden decision.

"Serve lunch, Marian. Go on, serve it up. I'll get back to entertain our guests and I'll bring them through as soon as you're ready, whether dad is here or not."

"Oh, Adam! Your father promised to carve."

"I know, sweetie. But doctors are not their own masters. You know that. And as for carving . . . well, I'll have to get my hand in sooner or later. We can't invite him over every time you cook a bird."

She smiled again. "I'm sorry. Let's both join the others. We can give him another five minutes, I suppose."

"Sure?"

She nodded. "Is my hair all right? It seems to go all anyhow in the heat and steam."

"It's terrific. As wavy as the big dipper at Battersea."

"Thanks. It doesn't smell of boiled sprouts, too, does it?"

"Not so's anybody would notice. More of sage and onion stuffing, I'd say."

She pretended to chase him, outraged, through to the big sitting room where the lighted Christmas tree, the holly, vases of yellow chrysanthemums and smaller pots of freesias, together with serried groups of upstanding cards, gave a background of colour to the jollity of the gathering.

There were to be twelve of them for lunch, including Marian and Adam. The choice of guests was a bit lop-sided as to families, but they were all old friends of each other from long before the marriage of their young host and hostess.

On Adam's side, his father who had not yet arrived, Dr David Whincap, a GP in Croxley, the county town, seven miles away. Adam's mother, Janet Whincap. His married sister Gwen and her husband Tony Kisiel. Tony's parents, Josef and Alice Kisiel. And finally, Adam's aunt, Janet Whincap's sister, Flora, with her husband, Robert Bennett, solicitor and coroner of the Croxley District.

On Marian's side, outweighed heavily by her husband's relatives, were her parents, Detective Chief Superintendent Theo Rainford of the County Police and his wife Margarethe. Marian's grandmother, Margarethe's mother, Mrs Elke Carlow, German-born and a widow, had been invited together with her widowed sister, Frau Mimi Hillger, who lived with her. But Elke had preferred to refuse the invitation and Mimi, very much under her sister's thumb, had been obliged to refuse, too.

So, counting host and hostess there were eleven people present, all waiting for the twelfth to arrive.

"Don't worry, darling," said Margarethe Rainford to her daughter. "Every housewife that ever lived has had some sort of disaster—major or minor—happen to her Christmas dinner. You're getting yours over early in

3

your married life and it really is very little—to be half an hour late at table."

"But it took so much arranging and fiddling to get everything done for the same time in just one oven. I hadn't a spare shelf for the roast potatoes, and..."

"Drinkies!" said Robert Bennett, interrupting Marian's tale of woe to hand her a sherry.

"I've already had two, Uncle Bob."

"Save your confessions for when they might do you some good, my dear. You need no excuse today. This is the first time Flora and I have been in your house and we're both as jealous as hell."

Marian smiled with pleasure. "It's all due to Adam, really."

"Who sewed those pretty curtains?"

Marian laughed. "No, silly. I meant he found Helewou and did it up and he's made a lot of the furniture himself."

"I know, my love. And I take my hat off to him. Not only for his skill and craftmanship, but also for his courage in flouting...not the wishes of his parents, exactly...but the traditional ways of his family by going out to do what he most wanted to do. To design and build! To create beauty and make it useful."

"Exactly what I've been saying for a long time," said Theo Rainford. He had come up behind his daughter and had consequently heard most of what Bennett had been saying. "I told Marian that if she keeps young Adam a good house, feeds him wisely and well and keeps his books straight she'll be doing a far better job than she would be doing by just going out to pound a typewriter in some office."

"Couldn't agree more," said Bennett. "That way they're both independent but mutually supporting—if that's a possibility."

"We'll let it ride," said Rainford. "When you solicitors get querying things, Bob, you never know when to stop and something everybody understands perfectly in the beginning becomes so convoluted nobody can recognize it in the end. Like that game we're all due to play later on—passing a message I think it's called. The original always gets fouled up in that, too."

"I was going to offer you a refill, Theo," said Bennett. "But after that little bit of calumny I don't think I'll bother—in case I get your order mixed and bring you vodka instead of gin."

"I'll get them both," said Marian, taking their glasses and leaving them alone.

"You know, Theo," said Bennett. "I find it particularly offensive in our present day society that some artist like Adam, who can produce pieces to compare with those of Hepplewhite and Chippendale, should be obliged to spend his valuable time filling in income tax and VAT forms and keeping rubbishy account books just to satisfy an army of unproductive, prodnose bureaucrats."

"Oh, Uncle Bob..." Marian had arrived with their drinks.

"I'm right, girlie. Ask your father. Both he and I are on the fringes of bureaucracy and we should know."

"I meant that bit about Adam. I know he's clever and creative, but Hepplewhite and Chippendale!"

"There is no doubt about it," said Tony Kisiel, joining in the conversation. "Today's really good stuff—like Adam's—will measure up with the best of the old stuff. Antiques, besides good work, have got age on their side. Adam is producing good work—better. His handwork *must* be better because he has comparable skill with the old masters, but he also has better tools, better glues, even better lights to work by. All his pieces need is age to put them in the same class as those of his eminent predecessors."

"I didn't realize you knew about such things, Tony," said Bennett. "A man of parts, eh?"

"He's an enthusiastic amateur, Uncle Bob," said Gwen Kisiel. "He only got the bug a year or two ago."

"You collect, do you?" said Rainford.

"Not really. But I browse, examine, visit, read—all the bits I can afford to do short of collecting."

"Interesting. I think that particular bug is catching. I'm thinking of asking Adam for a job when I retire."

"Your son-in-law would be your boss," said Bennett. "Would that be a good situation—in both senses of the word?"

"Why not?" The policeman shrugged. "Adam told me a few days ago that he will want to start his own deliveries fairly soon if things go on as they are doing. Cartage is devilish expensive and he's had one or two pieces held up, gone astray and even bruised."

"That must be a damn nuisance for him."

"Wastes time. He reckons on getting a secondhand van."

"You ought to be able to help him there, with your connections."

Rainford nodded. "And I could drive the van for him—up to London or Southampton docks. He's beginning to export now, you know. In a small way, of course, but special orders are starting to come in from quite far afield. I could nurse the bits to see they came to no harm. I might even be able to build the crates and pack them. That would save him a lot of time for more gainful employment."

"You seem to have got it all thought out," smiled Bennett. "It sounds an ideal set-up for a chap who'll already be on a decent pension."

"That's the idea."

"Good," said Josef Kisiel who had joined them to hear most of what Rainford had said. "That is good, because I remember that only two years or three years ago maybe you were going about collecting old furniture for nothing."

"Who? Me?" asked Rainford in surprise.

"No, no! Not you," said Kisiel whose voice was still so heavily accented that at times it was difficult for those unaccustomed to it to understand.

"You said you," laughed Rainford.

"I meant your beautiful Marian and her husband, the talented Adam."

Marian laughed at her father's apparent amazement. "That's really how Adam got started, daddy. We picked up old furniture which he carefully took to pieces."

"For the wood, you mean?"

"We got a lot of it for nothing. Some from Mr and Mrs Kisiel. People actually thanked Adam for taking those big old pieces away, because nobody would buy them."

"And he is still using the wood?" asked Kisiel.

"Bits of it. And he still scrounges any that comes his way. But he has to buy a lot of the new woods that are coming in. It's very expensive."

"Which reminds me, " said Rainford, addressing his daughter. "Your grandmother Carlow said she would like Adam to call in and mend her gate-leg table."

"Not again!"

"You mean he's mended it once already?"

"Twice. The same leg both times."

"Doesn't say much for his work, does it?"

Marian replied, crossly: "Adam wants to renew the leg, but she won't let him. She insists it would devalue the table which isn't worth anything in the first place."

"Don't get aerated, love. How does the silly old thing keep on breaking it?"

"She uses it as a sewing table. Plonks a heavy old hand-machine on it and winds away for dear life making curtains and turning sides to middle with old sheets. The table is so unsteady the joints won't take it. It was meant for playing patience on or holding a tea tray."

"She's a stubborn old woman," admitted Rainford.

"You should hear what Adam calls her. You do realize, don't you, daddy, that he can't afford to spend his time doing and re-doing free work for gran?"

Rainford nodded. Josef Kisiel snorted.

"What's got into you, Josef?"

"That woman. The old German. She would not come here today because I am here. No?"

"Now, Josef," counselled Rainford.

"It is the truth, Theo. I know it. Ask your Marian."

"Maybe," replied the young hostess, anxious to smooth over even the slightest ripple of acrimony among her guests, but then spoiled her effort by adding, "But if gran had agreed to come to the party, you wouldn't have agreed to come, would you, Mr Kisiel? You wouldn't accept the invitation until Gwen and Tony assured you gran wouldn't be here, would you?"

Josef shook his head so emphatically that his great shock of grey hair waved about in its efforts to keep up. He was about to reinforce this unmistakable gesture with words when a car hooter sounded outside.

"Here's dad, darling," called Adam from his spot across the room near the window where the rest of the party was grouped. "Do you want me to help you serve?"

"As long as you can get your father through to start carving…"

"Right."

Helewou was a building almost as intriguing as its name suggested it might be. The old Middle English name meant nothing more than End Wall, being cobbled from the two words hele and wough. But it did indicate that there had been a building on this same spot, aligned in just the same way, for centuries. The barn, for this is what the house was, had been built end-on to the track which, though now a road used frequently by all manner of traffic, had obviously at one time carried nothing more than foot travellers, livestock and infrequent horsemen. Some farmer in those early days had made use of the small area of flat land barely a hundred feet each way and lying between the track and a scarp twenty or thirty feet high. Here he had built his barns and sheds where they were easier to get at than his own house, which still stood, a hundred and fifty yards along the road. Here the track had dropped steeply down its re-entrant and the only site for the house was well above it, easily accessible now by motor cars using a tarmac drive, but impossible for wains and cattle in the old days before bulldozers were available.

Now there were just two successors to the original buildings. Helewou itself, a big barn, end-on to the road, tall, well-roofed and gabled. Behind the main building, added as an afterthought in the shape of a long, stone-built lean-to, was a stable for a good many pairs of draught horses. This conglomerate was the main block that Adam Whincap had turned into his home. The second building stood at right angles to Helewou, between the house and the scarp, close up under the cliff. It, too, was big, and though still somewhat tumbledown was built of stone like Helewou. Whincap was using it as his workshop.

There was little ground space to spare at this level for a garden. What there was had been turned into a concrete hard to serve house and workshop, leaving no more than a few feet of narrow border for flowers. But at the end of the workshop, still there from long ago, was a flight of steps cut into the face of the scarp and roughly bricked. It led up to the garden proper—a plot on top of the scarp, hedged off from the surrounding fields and no bigger than the area occupied by the buildings and their surrounds.

Time and money had not been on Adam Whincap's side, so he had decided to ignore the lean-to stable completely for the time being. He would be able to turn to it and incorporate it into his home later on when he had the necessary resources. Meanwhile it served very well as a domestic lumber room.

The lower floor of Helewou had been split into two, lengthwise. At the front, on the corner nearest the blind end wall, an original two-piece barn door had been hung to lead into a small room which served as half-office, half-hallway. The floor was brick. Out of it, to the right, another more traditional door hung over a shallow step up into the sitting room which Adam had floored with timber. This room was big and long, with a window half-way down its length in the embrasure where the great double barn door had formerly hung. Another, smaller window at the end looked across the narrow gap to the workshop. Opposite the main window, in the newly-built dividing wall, was a brick fireplace with an old-fashioned kitchen range: a high standing firegrate with a deep ash-pit, a boiler to the left and an oven to the right, embellished with cast-iron curlicues and brassware and fronted by a wrought-iron club fender with corner seats. Adam had picked up the old range for little or nothing, and had installed it with a hot-water boiler behind it to serve bathroom and kitchen.

To the left of the fireplace was the door into the dining room. At the end of this room and behind the hallway were the stairs— a new flight made by Adam. He had constructed them without risers or any form of blocking in, because they rose across the only window in the room—the one he had put into the wall to pair the door into the hallway. The other end of the long room had been cut off and turned into a kitchen, so there was no natural light from that direction while, behind the as-yet unpierced back wall, was the lean-to which, at the moment, could only be entered from outside.

But even in its partially completed state, Helewou was a welcoming home and a credit to the industrious young couple who had planned and converted it. Robert Bennett had been right when, on this his first visit, he had suggested that it would be—indeed already was—a property to rouse jealousy in anyone disposed towards living in such a building.

The upstairs was far from complete. Originally, like many such barns, Helewou had been built with a hayloft with ran half the total length. Adam's first task, before building the stairs, had been to extend this vast shelf to cover the whole building. This was its upstairs where only one room was fit for habitation. The remainder had not even been partitioned off except the bathroom which had been installed over the kitchen. And there the project hung fire waiting for Adam and Marian to collect a little more money with which to buy materials for building.

Dr David Whincap, no stranger to his son's house, and as enthusiastic about its progress as Adam and Marian themselves, hung coat and cap up on the pegs in the hallway and entered the sitting room to a series of welcoming calls and Christmas greetings. Adam handed him a glass of dry sherry and ushered him through to the kitchen.

"Yes, I must make my apologies to my hostess."

"Apologies can wait. Marian wants you to start carving."

"In that case..." Whincap stopped to take a gulp of the sherry. As he moved on again, he said: "I suppose I'm in hot water all round."

"Make yourself useful, dad, and we'll try to forgive you."

"Many apologies, my dear," said Whincap, setting down his glass of sherry. As he picked up the carving knife and prepared to whet it on the steel he continued: "But you know how it is. As senior partner I'm on duty on Christmas Day."

Marian, braving the knife, stood on tiptoe to kiss him and then turned her attention to taking the roast potatoes out of the pan with a fish slice. "I know you have to be available, daddy, but I can't help feeling it is most inconsiderate of people to fall ill on Christmas Day. Particularly at lunch time."

"They don't choose to, sweetheart," said Adam, putting a stack of dinner plates down close to where his father was tackling the turkey with all the skill of a one-time surgeon.

"This one did, I fancy." A thin slice of breast backed by crisp skin was overturned neatly on to the top plate. "I'd like a tablespoon for the stuffing, please, Adam."

"Oh? What happened? Or can't you say?" asked his son, scrabbling among the cooking utensils in a drawer.

The doctor turned to his daughter-in-law. "It was your grandmother, my dear."

"Gran Carlow? She must have called you out deliberately. She knew you were due to come here."

"Not a false errand." Another plate was given its portion of turkey and a well-cooked sausage. "She needed my attention."

"Really needed attention? Goodness, she hasn't done anything... anything silly, has she? She's always getting up to her tricks."

"Silly?" The doctor eased out the merrythought so that the breast carving could continue without hindrance. "Silly? Stupid, I'd say. Really stupid and stubborn. That's what she is."

"That's the umpteenth time I've heard her described like that this morning." Marian turned to her husband. "Get them into the dining room, darling, and then come back to carry the plates in." As Adam left to do her bidding, she started to strain the sprouts. "What did gran do, daddy? Are you saying she tried to make herself ill?"

"Yes."

"To commit suicide?"

"No, poppet. She's too smart an old witch for that.

12

But she did take a rather large overdose of her medicine."

"Isn't that an attempt to commit suicide? If it wasn't a mistake?"

"No mistake, my dear." Whincap looked over his array of plates, deciding which one could best take a thigh without becoming overloaded. "She's done it before."

"Overdosed herself?"

"Never to quite the same degree as today..."

"So she *was* trying to commit suicide, if it wasn't a mistake. It was a deliberate attempt..."

"Deliberate, certainly. But with no intention of killing herself." He put the knife and fork down. "I've run out of space for laying out the plates. I'll carry some through. Is everybody sitting anywhere?"

The matter rested there. the food was carried through and all the jollity of the meal drove the business of Mrs Carlow from their minds. Crackers were pulled and paper hats were worn. The cooking was pronounced to be first class and Robert Bennett proposed a humorous toast to host and hostess. But as soon as the lunch had been cleared away and most of the party were reclining, half-asleep, in the sitting room, waiting for the Queen's speech, Marian recalled the earlier conversation. She was washing up at the time. Adam and his father were helping her, the latter—in his own words—paying penance for delaying the party earlier.

"Daddy, would you say or did you mean that Gran Carlow is one of those cases we're always hearing about nowadays? Somebody who is crying out for help and attracting attention?"

"By a bit of suicidal brinkmanship?" added Adam.

"That's a bit—that's pitching it a bit high, darling."

"It's true," expostulated her husband, taking up a handful of wet forks from the draining board and pro-

13

ceeding to dry them one by one. "As I understand it, there are more suicides attempted with the intention of failing than of being successful. Isn't that so, dad?"

Dr Whincap, who was putting away the tableware, replied: "So we're told."

"That's pretty non-committal."

Whincap turned to face the two young people. "This isn't the first time Elke Carlow has played this little trick on me."

"She's done it before? We didn't know," said Marian, pushing a stray strand of hair back with the gauntlet of one of her rubber gloves. "At least we knew she had played pranks, but not that she'd gone to these lengths."

"The trouble is," said the doctor, "I can't decide whether she is playing the game Adam has just described, or..."

"Or what, daddy?" asked Marian, turning on the hot tap to rinse a Pyrex dish.

"I shouldn't really be telling you all this," said Whincap. "It's probably the sherry and table wine talking, but as you, Marian, and, therefore, your parents and grandmother are, in a certain sense, a part of the family now, I don't think I ought to hide the fact that from a family doctor's point of view, Gran Carlow is a self-willed, arrogant old girl..."

"You can say that again, dad," interrupted Adam with great feeling.

"... who thinks she can decide for herself how much of her prescribed medicine she can take and when."

"Silly old fool," grunted Adam.

"As you must know, she has a heart condition for which I prescribe digoxin—better known to you perhaps as digitalis. She's in the habit of deciding that she won't take any for a few days—if she's feeling fairly well—then, when she thinks she's a bit off-colour, she takes all those she has missed in the preceding few days." Whincap picked up the Pyrex dish which Adam

14

had by now dried and laid aside. "In other words, she's often in the habit of overdosing herself. And that, with her particular medicine, is tantamount to poisoning herself."

"Does she make herself sick?"

"Literally—otherwise she wouldn't still be with us. Luckily she gets rid of a good part of it."

"And that was what you were called out for this morning?" asked Marian.

"Your great-aunt Mimi rang me—as usual."

"You said that, dad," accused Adam, "as though you suspected there were some sort of ulterior motive behind the call . . . and the incident."

"Not on Mimi's part. She's a decent old dear. But . . . yes . . . I think Elke was playing up. She wouldn't come here, today, would she, because Josef Kisiel had agreed to come?"

"Oh, dear," sighed Marian. "And I tried so hard to be diplomatic and to ask Gran before Josef and Alice. But she asked if any of the Kisiel family would be here and I had to say that Gwen and Tony had been invited. After all, Gwen is Adam's sister."

"Just as I thought," said the doctor. "Elke refused so you had no qualms about asking Josef and Alice."

"It's Marian's house and party," said Adam. "She can ask whom she likes, and if Elke doesn't like the guest list, that's just too bad."

Whincap nodded his agreement. "On no account must you young people allow family squabbles to interfere with your lives. But actually, old Elke wanted to come, according to Mimi. Mimi herself told me she too wanted to be here. She has no feud with the Kisiels, and tried to persuade her sister, without any luck. Elke dug her toes in."

"A typical case of cutting off your nose," said Marian.

"So I believe."

"And then," said Adam quietly, "in an effort to spoil

the party, she overdosed herself to stop you coming here and to try and get Marian and her mother to drop everything and rush to her bedside. That really would have put paid to our Christmas arrangements, wouldn't it?"

"I think that's what she hoped for, son."

"But you stopped her little game, dad?"

"Yes. I waited there until I was sure there was absolutely no need for Margarethe and Marian to be worried."

Marian turned and kissed him.

"What's that for?"

"To say I'm sorry for saying you were a nuisance for being late for lunch."

"I see. Very nice, too. But you ought to know, Marian, that your grandmother took far more of her digoxin than she has done on previous occasions. I regard that as proof that she had recognized that she can stage these incidents as a means of playing us all up."

Marian had emptied the washing up bowl and mopped down the draining board. Now she stripped off her rubber gloves. "Let's go through and join the others," she said wearily. "It's almost time for the Queen."

Her husband put an arm round her. "Come on, sweetheart. Time to be merry. It's all been great, so far, and you looked smashing in a paper hat."

She smiled at him. "Come on then or we shall miss the broadcast."

After the royal message, at that time when Christmas seems to hang fire for a while, particularly when there are no children to entertain and the prospect of tea with mince pies and iced cake is vile, and there is no inclination or need to do anything before the jollifications of the evening begin in earnest, Dr David Whincap joined Margarethe Rainford and her husband

16

who were snoozily sharing the large three-seater settee.

"Your old mum, Margarethe..."

"What about her, David?"

"She's a pain in the neck," murmured her husband sleepily. "Let's forget her."

"I'd like to, but I daren't," said Whincap. "I tell you what. You go to sleep, Theo, and dream of lots of nice criminal cases all running smoothly towards convictions while I have a quiet word with your missus."

Rainford sat up slowly. "Daren't forget her? What do you mean? When a bloke like you says he daren't do something, Dave, my nose begins to twitch."

"Like a rabbit's," retorted his wife, who was still wearing a paper crown with a large red circle stuck on it. She turned to Whincap. "What's happened, David?"

"I was late for lunch because your Aunt Mimi called me..." The doctor proceeded to give Margarethe the same account as he had given her daughter earlier. Rainford and his wife listened intently until he had finished.

"What did you have to do for her?" asked Margarethe.

"She was vomiting, so that helped. I cleaned her out completely and that, fortunately, seemed to do the trick, though at one time I thought I'd have to call an ambulance and have her admitted."

"Why didn't you?" asked the Chief Superintendent.

"For several reasons. It would have meant the ruination of this party..."

"Which you think was her prime intention?"

"Because you would have had to go to the hospital, Margarethe."

"She's my mother, David."

"Quite. Theo, here, would have felt incumbent upon him to go with you and Marian would have felt it her duty to go, too."

"And Adam and Uncle Tom Cobley an' all," grumbled Rainford. "And you think that's why she took a bigger overdose today than she ever has done on previous occasions?"

"I'm certain of it. And besides ruining a party here, it would have ruined a ward party at the hospital—not only for doctors and nurses, but for other patients, too. Then there would have been the scandal..."

"Surely not," said Theo. "One old woman taking an overdose wouldn't cause a scandal these days."

"I wasn't thinking of it from Elke's point of view," replied Whincap. "But from Margarethe's and Marian's. Can't you just hear the tongues wagging? Daughter and granddaughter having a slap up Christmas party. Gran not there, not invited, obviously. Takes an overdose and tries to kill herself because she feels unwanted."

"Come off it, Dave," said Rainford. "She was invited."

"I know, Theo. But others don't. The story would get about and the mud would stick."

"I can see that," said Margarethe. "So that's why you didn't send her to hospital. It was very thoughtful of you, David."

"That and the fact that I managed to get her right myself," grinned Whincap. "Don't overlook my masterly handling of the case."

"And that is why you were so late for lunch, I suppose."

"Just so. But what I have to tell you, Margarethe—and this is really the object of this conversation— is that I have removed every digoxin tablet from your mother's house. Mimi and I searched every room."

"But won't mother need her medicine?"

"To kill herself with?" asked her husband scathingly.

"Don't worry, my dear," said Whincap. "It's quite

long-acting stuff so there'll still be some working away there—a safe amount, I trust. And in any case I should have had to withdraw the digoxin to let the effect of the overdose subside. However, you're quite right. She will be needing the stuff. I shall have to put her back on it sooner rather than later."

"And your worry is you think she'll do it all again at some time when she feels she can again put a spanner in somebody's works?"

David Whincap grimaced. "That's my worry, certainly. What do I do, knowing the little games she plays? Do I just shrug off the fact that she may go too far and kill herself?"

Rainford grunted to show he really had no answer and then added: "As a doctor you can't ignore the fact that you know she is potentially suicidal."

"Not only as a doctor. Nobody can just shrug if off. But as a doctor I have to tackle the problem. I daren't let her have a supply of her tablets, but I can't write a prescription every day for just one tablet."

"Can't Aunt Mimi keep them?" asked Margarethe.

"Mimi is no match for her sister. You know your mother dominates her. If I were to entrust the tablets to Mimi, Elke would bully her into letting her have them."

"True enough," agreed Rainford. "Mimi's a gentle old dear and scared stiff of Elke. So there's only one thing for it, Dave."

"Oh, yes? And what's that?"

"You'll have to send your nurse in every day with just enough digoxin for the daily dose. Nursey sees the old hausfrau knocks it back good and proper, and you can rest assured she's not laying up a store of trouble for you in the future."

Whincap shook his head. "No go, Theo, and you know it. The NHS can't afford to send my practice nurse to your mother-in-law's house every day just to see she complies with the dosage instructions on a bottle of pills."

"It would have to afford it if the old so-and-so needed an injection every day instead of a tablet."

"Daily nursing calls are a short-term expedient. An alternative to being in hospital."

"Because it's cheaper, you mean?"

"For whatever reason, but usually because the patient prefers being at home and can be satisfactorily maintained there. I'm not going to claim that Elke Carlow should rightly be in hospital, therefore I'm not prepared to provide an alternative for a nonexistent need."

Rainford said: "That's good thinking, Dave. Cogent and...er...economic. I like it. But it hasn't provided the answer."

Whincap looked at Margarethe. "Could you...?" he began.

"Hang on, hang on," said Rainford. "Are you about to suggest that Maggie should visit her mother daily to give her the pill?"

"It amounts to that."

"That's playing right into the old girl's hands," snorted Rainford. "Talk about managing to upset other people's lives! What if Margarethe couldn't go one day? Had a cold or wanted an awayday or something like that?"

"Probably Marian...."

"She's overworked as it is."

"On the odd occasion?"

"It's no good," expostulated Rainford. "You know Elke. She'll presume. Her type always does. She'll sulk if Maggie doesn't go or if she's a bit late. Then we'll have rows, won't we? And Elke will play burnt-down with poor old Mimi who'll be given a hell of a time

20

just because the silly old witch won't obey doctor's orders."

"Couldn't you...isn't there something else you could give her instead of digoxin?" asked Margarethe.

"Less dangerous, you mean? No. There are a number of alternatives to digoxin, of course, but we should have to take the same precautions even if I changed her to one of them. They're all much of a muchness when it comes to hoarding them into doses big enough to be dangerous."

"Then I shall have to help," said Margarethe.

"Good. But I take Theo's point about Elke starting to presume. I'm going to suggest that my nurse goes in twice a week—not necessarily on the same days each week. I'm sure Marian will agree to go in once a week."

"That leaves me with four days. It's not too bad because I go fairly close to my mother's house most days either to shop or to do my meals-on-wheels stint."

"Fine. Now for the mechanics of the business. I shall give you the prescriptions and you will keep the tablets, Margarethe. The others—Marian and my nurse—will have to come to you before every visit they make."

"So that the dose isn't duplicated by mistake?" asked Rainford.

"That is most important. A misunderstanding could arise. I'd like Margarethe to keep a little list, day by day, just for safety's sake. The big thing is to see that Elke puts the tablet into her mouth and then actually swallows it."

"She's capable of deception," agreed Rainford. "She'd palm the bloody tablet as lief as look at you."

"We must try to avoid that at all costs."

"Avoid what, David?" Robert Bennett, having slept in a neighbouring armchair, was now awake and stretching.

"Nothing to bother you with, Bob."

"Try me."

"Margarethe's mother hasn't been complying with the dosage instructions on her medicine, so we're just discussing ways and means of making sure she toes the line."

"I see." Bennett opened his mouth and shut it again with a grimace of disgust. "You know that cigar I had after lunch has left a really nasty aftertaste."

"You can't complain," said Rainford. "You supplied them."

"That's the only reason why I can complain."

Margarethe got to her feet. "Adam and Marian have gone for a walk with Tony and Gwen. But I'm sure Marian wouldn't mind if I were to make you a cup of tea, just to de-fur that tongue."

"Just the ticket," said Bennett.

"Good idea, love," said her husband. "Strong and dark and lots of it."

"If you want some, come and help get it."

"I can't. You know I'm afraid of that bottle-gas stove."

"Liar," said his wife. "You know the ordinary gas stove was put in last week when the Gas Board brought the town supply in. You even promised to take a few days' leave to help Adam put the central heating in next month."

"Central heating soon, eh?" asked Bennett.

"As if you didn't know, Bob," said Rainford, getting to his feet. "Marian told me you'd given them a cheque for a hundred and fifty quid as a Christmas present specifically to help pay for the radiators and piping lying in the lean-to."

"Shut your trap, copper, and get the tea. What Flora and I gave them doesn't amount to a Chief Super giving up several days of his holiday to act as handyman."

"They're my kids," said Rainford simply.

* * *

Dr Whincap's scheme worked admirably for about six weeks—until a day in early February when Marian, taking her turn, called on her grandmother to administer the daily pill.

Up till then, Elke Carlow had apparently enjoyed the arrangement by which one or other of the three women visited her each day. It had seemed to cause her, if not pleasure, at least some sort of satisfaction to see a face other than her sister's each day. Privately, Marian thought it amused the old lady to have so many others dancing to her tune. And so it came as something of a shock when the granddaughter realized that by now the newness had worn off and, as her father had forseen, the elderly patient had started to presume. It became apparent to Marian that Elke, having won the battle for attention so far, now proposed a spoiling action. She fired the opening shots at three o'clock that day, which was the time the young wife could best get away after having given her husband lunch.

"I shall come, liebling, to live among you."

Not grasping the burden of this statement, Marian replied: "But you do live among us, gran. Everybody is round about you, here in the village or in the town. That's only a few miles away, and..."

"With you, liebling."

"I don't understand, gran."

"With you and your man. Your Adam. In your barn house."

"Oh, you want to come and see us and the house. But of course. I shall get Adam to fetch you and Great Aunt Mimi one Sunday as soon as the weather gets a little warmer."

"He shall fetch me tomorrow."

"Not tomorrow, gran. You know Adam has to work all day."

"Then you shall come to fetch me, liebling."

"What for, gran?"

"To live in your house. I shall pack my belongings tonight. Mimi will send on what I do not take."

Marian stared at her grandmother. In her middle seventies, Elke Carlow was still a tall, imperious woman. There was nothing frail about her. The skin of the arrogant face was uniformly wrinkled and no longer held any colour other than that of old ivory. With no trace of make-up, it seemed more powerful than would have been the case had it been reduced to a doll's likeness by tomatoes of rouge on the cheeks and ill-applied mascara round the eyes. The hair was grey, but still thick and long and plaited into the bun she had worn since a girl. She wore skirts and striped shirt-blouses with leg-of-mutton sleeves and little turndown collars up to the neck, where she always wore a cameo brooch.

"To live in our house? With Adam and me? You mean you would like to stay for a few days?"

"I mean to live with you. You have a fine, big house. The doctor has told me so. Your mother and your father, the policeman, they tell me you have big rooms and lots of them."

"That's true I suppose, but…"

"And you have no children."

"Not yet, gran, no."

"Why then, you have the space for your grand-mother. It is right that the old should be so respected. In Germany, we honoured our elders. Do you not honour me, my liebling?"

"Of course I honour you, gran, but…"

"Then there is no more to be said about it. The matter is settled. I shall come and sit in front of your great stove which the doctor tells me is like those we used to have in Prussia, which were fed with timber from the forests, and which…"

"There won't be any fire to sit against, gran. At least

not often," protested Marian wildly. "Adam has put in central heating so that I won't have to light fires and clean grates. Besides, our stove burns coal, and coal is very expensive."

"Your man does his work in wood, does he not?"

"You know perfectly well he does, gran."

"Then we shall not need coal. We shall have wooden fires, like in Germany."

"Wood fires, gran," said Marian distractedly. "Not wooden ones."

"You English! You do not know your own language. Do you say woollen mills or wool mills?"

"Woollen mills."

"Then we will have wooden fires, not wood ones."

"Gran you can't ... I mean I must talk to Adam about this. And what will Aunt Mimi do? You can't leave her here on her own."

"She will not be on her own. She will later come to live with you in your barn house, also, to look after me."

Marian's heart sank. She could foresee nothing but trouble looming ahead. She knew that she, herself, would never countenance her grandmother living in Helewou. She was not just sure, but certain beyond measure, that Adam would veto the idea without a second thought. He wouldn't even bother to embellish his refusal with a second word. It would be so emphatic as to merit the monosyllable alone—no. But she also knew her German grandmother to be as pig-headed and stubborn as only a Prussian can be. Once she had set her mind on something she wanted, Father Peter himself would be hard pushed to head her off. She would brush aside, as of no account, any refusal of Adam's. And that would lead to bad feeling all round. Elke Carlow believed that the young were put on earth to serve the old, and now she herself was elderly she was determined to get her fair share of attention from those who were, in her book, in duty bound to supply it.

Mimi was not present to hear the conversation. She had gone shopping. There was no one Marian could appeal to for help in driving sense into her grandmother's head. Angry and frustrated, she left the house and drove over to see her mother.

Margarethe showed little surprise on hearing her daughter's story. In fact it was Marian who was surprised when her mother's only reaction seemed to be to ask the question: "She's still on about that, is she?"

"You mean gran has already mentioned her plan to you."

"She has. Twice." Margarethe was making a cup of tea, and plopped a second scoop of leaves into the pot as if to emphasize the number of occasions on which her mother had mentioned the plan. "I thought I'd scotched it the second time, but apparently I didn't. But I really did stress that she couldn't wish herself upon you and Adam." Margarethe poured water from the boiling kettle into the pot. "Apart from the fact that you and Adam are too busy to have her, it's just not on for new young marrieds to have old people sharing the love nest."

"Especially old grumpies like gran."

Margarethe stood with both hands round the bowl of the pot as if to warm them. "You know, darling, she tried the same thing on with me a few years ago. But your father soon put a stop to it."

"How?" Marian poured milk into the two cups.

"He told her," said Margarethe, giving the pot a little jiggle to get the tea swirling around inside preparatory to pouring. "He told her that our house was a police house—which it wasn't, of course—and that the police authorities would not allow us to make permanent lodgers of any sort, whether they were family or not. It was before we moved here, but I think she still believes we live in police property and, being what she is, she has a great respect for authority—the police in particular—and has never tried it on with us again." Margarethe poured a cup of tea for her daughter and smiled. "You know, dear, I think she only agreed to my marrying a lowly policeman in the first place because of her inborn regard for state institutions."

"What am I doing to do about it, mum?"

"Sit yourself down on that stool and drink this." Mrs Rainford handed her daughter the cup of tea and drew up one of the breakfast bar stools for herself.

"First, you must take a firm stand. On no account must you agree to your grandmother coming to stay in your house for even one night because once she was in she would stay. No matter what hard-luck story she tells you or however much wheedling she does, refuse, refuse, refuse. It is most important that you yourself should adopt this attitude so that you are never in the slightest danger of being misunderstood or bringing pressure to bear on Adam to take her."

"He knows her. He wouldn't take her."

"Not even if his nice new wife coaxed him? Darling, men find it difficult to refuse such things to the women they love. You must never be guilty of using his affection for you for this purpose, because I assure you that if ever gran came to live in your house, it would be the end of your happy marriage. I would go so far as to say you would lose Adam. She would drive him out."

"So you think I'd better not tell him?"

"You must tell him. You will need his strength and support. Tell him what she has proposed and leave him in no doubt that no matter what happens you expect him to remain firm and to refuse to have her over the threshold for anything more than a cup of tea. Then you'll find everything will turn out all right. And perhaps your grandmother will forget this obsession, though I doubt it."

"I hope she does."

"Another cup? The pot will stand it."

"Yes, please. I'm in need of a stimulant or sustenance or something after all this."

That evening, when Marian told her husband of her visits to Elke and Margarethe, Adam accepted the news very calmly.

"I thought you'd be angry, Adam."

"No need to be angry, precious. The answer is simple. I'm surprised you haven't thought of it."

"Simple?" She gazed at her husband in amazement. "Tell me."

"Bedrooms," he said. "We've only got one built, and that's ours. I've been looking for an excuse not to start on the others for a bit. Partly because I can't afford the time and chiefly because the timber and plasterboard are going to cost the earth and I haven't recovered from installing the heating yet. Now I've got an even better reason for holding off."

Marian decided it was time she joined her clever husband in his chair. She moved across to him and perched on his knee. "I'll explain to gran next time I go."

"I'll tell her."

"Oh?"

"Don't worry. I shan't kick up a fuss. Just a reasonable but firm explanation—in case she won't see reason. But I think it's my job rather than yours. I can say you approached me to have her here but that I've vetoed it because of the bedroom problem."

She kissed his forehead. Her mother had suggested that is she were to consult Adam the problem would be solved. It appeared mother was right.

* * *

But Adam, innately courteous and kind, had made one serious miscalculation in his estimate of Elke Carlow's character and, consequently, of her reaction to his reasonable explanation. When he called on her and pointed out that it was impossible to house her at Helewou because of the shortage of bedrooms she did not— would not—accept it as a refusal to have her, but rather as a promise. A promise that as soon as the bedrooms were built, he and Marian would take her in. And from that assumption it was but a short step to start bringing pressure on Marian to have her husband start work on the necessary rooms.

This new campaign on Elke's part started early in March. Marian, despite her resolve, began to find it increasingly difficult to beat off the insistent demands. Part of the trouble was that Marian herself and, indeed, her parents, believed Adam's legitimate excuse could reasonably be interpreted as a promise: if Elke couldn't move in because there was no room for her, as soon as there was room she could move in. But the girl did her utmost to head off her grandmother without telling the elderly woman straight out that she wasn't wanted and couldn't be tolerated in Helewou. In vain she stated time and again that she and Adam could not yet afford the necessary materials. They had done wonderfully well to get so far, now there must be a pause whilst finances built up.

"Your man must work hard to earn the money."

"Adam works very hard. And we can't have it both ways. If he is to earn the money to buy things for the house, he cannot afford to take time off to build bedrooms. He is building a business..."

"A thriving business I am told by the doctor."

"Maybe. But to keep it thriving he has to work all the hours that God sends. Even I am helping him now. I do some of the sandpapering and clearing up the workshop as well as the paper work and..."

"He should employ a man."

"That takes money. Besides, any man Adam employs must be a craftsman, and they don't grow on trees."

"You should go out to work again yourself."

The conversation came to an abrupt end at that point. Marian, at last out of patience, flung out of her grandmother's house and hurried to speak to her mother.

"I'm not going there again," she declared. "I shall tell Daddy Whincap that his nurse will just have to do an extra day."

"We'll see what we can do, dear."

"You'd better, mum, because if I have to go there again I'll strangle the old besom."

"Marian! Don't talk like that. Your grandmother is an old lady."

"She's only in her seventies. That's comparatively young these days. She's in full command of all her faculties so she must know what she's doing. And in my book that means she's a mischief-making old cat."

"Steady, steady, steady," said her father, coming into the room from elsewhere in the house. "I've been writing in the dining room so I've been close enough to hear something of what you've been saying to your mother, my love, and I reckon you're playing the old girl's game."

"How do you make that out, daddy?"

"You're letting her get you rattled," replied Rainford heavily. "And that's just what she's setting out to do. She's half-way to success, you know, if she can upset your equilibrium. Once she knows she's got you off balance she'll start playing some other sort of game to get you completely down."

"What sort of game, daddy?"

Rainford picked up an ashtray from the coffee table and went over to his easy chair. "I dunno, love. I haven't got her sort of mind. But I can tell you this. Ever since

I've known her she's been a trouble maker. And long before that from all accounts. If she hadn't put so many people's backs up, she'd be having scads of visitors at that house of hers. As it is, people leave her severely alone. After her husband died, Mimi had to come over here to…"

"Had to?"

"Because nobody else could abide Elke. You'll still find people round here who'll tell you what a blessed relief it was during the war when she was carted off under Regulation Eighteen B. They say your grandfather, old Dick Carlow, was a new man during those years. He always was a nice chap, but Elke had repressed him. When she'd gone, he joined the Home Guard and became one of the lads—on parade and then into the pub for a pint. But it all had to stop when she got back." He turned to his wife. "I'm right, aren't I, my dear?"

"He was a lovely man," said Margarethe. "I can remember that time—just. Father's sister, Auntie Winnie, looked after us. But he died soon after the war."

"Too soon," said Rainford to his daughter. "And you won't need three shots at guessing the main reason why."

"Theo!"

"It's right, Maggie. Everybody has always said so."

"Gossip. You, a senior policeman, shouldn't pay attention to gossip."

"That's just where you're wrong, my love. We cops get most of our information from gossip. And I know for a fact that more than one of his friends urged your father to divorce her."

"Father was too nice a man to do that."

"I know. Besides, it wasn't so easy to divorce in those days and I don't suppose old Elke, for all her other faults, ever went off the rails with another man.

31

She'd never have been able to find another daft enough after your father."

"Theo, this has gone far enough. After all, she is my mother."

"Maggie, I declare to you that I spend most of my waking hours wondering how a woman like her could have produced a daughter as good and lovely as you. Thank heaven she was safely locked away during some of your formative years." He lit a cigarette and then turned to Marian. "Don't let her into your house, girl, but don't let her see she's got you down. Remember her type thrives on getting others at a disadvantage. Don't let her see she's made any impression on you."

"You mean I should go on taking that damned pill to her one day a week?"

"I do, love. She'll keep on at you as sure as houses, but you've cracked it now. You've withstood the first attack. You're primed—or innoculated—against any further onslaughts. If you stop going she'll think she's got you on the run. Don't give her the satisfaction of thinking she's won even one inch of ground."

"I must say I'd made up my mind not to go there again, but if you think I should..."

"Your father's right, dear. His way of putting it is a bit graphic, but that comes of being a policeman. At first they're taught that awful stereotyped way of reporting and then, later, when they finally revolt against it, they go too far the other way."

Marian laughed. "Sometimes I think daddy's quite funny."

"Only sometimes?" asked the Detective Chief Superintendent in mock sorrow. "And me known throughout the division as the Permanent Hoot."

Gwen Kisiel was not unaware of the situation. She was Adam's sister and was very friendly with both him and Marian. Elke Carlow was in no way related to her either by marriage or by blood, and until she had married Tony Kisiel a year or two earlier, she had known little of the German woman. But the Kisiel family had grown up with not only a knowledge of her nearby presence but also with an inborn hatred of her.

Josef Kisiel's hatred of Elke had not carried over to her daughter, Margarethe, nor to Margarethe's husband, Theo, with whom Josef was on amicable, if not close, terms. But he had felt a twinge of regret, nonetheless, when it became clear that his daughter-in-law's brother, Adam, was to marry Elke's granddaughter. He liked Marian, but he regretted the link that was being forged, however tenuous, between himself and Elke. His future grandchildren would be blood relations of her stock should Adam and Marian provide them with cousins. And that rankled. In one of his more intemperate moments he had gone so far as to voice the hope that either Gwen or Marian should not have children. Nor would he have been surprised to learn that Elke Carlow was of like mind. In fact, when he heard from Gwen of Elke's intention to wish herself upon the young Whincaps he immediately jumped to the conclusion that her object in doing so was to break up the marriage in order to sever any existing link between herself and him and to ensure that no future bonds were forged by the birth of a further, connecting, generation. It took Gwen a long time to explain the reason Elke had given Marian for wishing to move into Helewou, and though eventually he pretended to accept his daughter-in-law's explanation, he was not basically diverted from his own interpretation of the events.

He stuck to his original belief, and said so to Dr David Whincap when the two of them met at Tony and Gwen's home at Easter time.

"Don't agree with you, Josef," said Dr Whincap after hearing what the Pole had to say. "She's an old besom—a born mischief-maker without a doubt—and she's trying to play Marian up. But that's as far as it goes in my opinion. By paying too much attention to it we shall encourage her in her nonsense."

Josef eyed the glass of whisky he was holding. "She will not know my feelings," he said quietly. "I do not communicate with her." Though a quiet statement, it was uttered with disdain and loathing.

"Maybe not, old boy, but feelings have a nasty habit of communicating themselves without any words from us. Attitudes, glances in the street, even silences themselves convey meanings that don't have to be spoken."

"Gwenny tells me the old frau pays no attention to Margarethe or Marian. That means her skin is thick. A pig's hide. She could not sense—what is the word?—an innuendo?"

"One senses innuendoes with the mind, Josef, not the skin."

"What is the difference? She is a Prussian. A Boche."

"You still have a great hatred of her, Josef. For your own peace of mind you should rid yourself of the feeling. You are a happy, prosperous man. You cultivate the earth and grow beautiful flowers. Surely that is enough to lessen your feelings of hatred?"

"My friend, were she anybody else, I should be ashamed of what I wish for her. But because she is what she is, I have no feelings of disgust with myself for wishing her dead. Sometimes I have prayed for it."

"Steady, Josef, steady. Have your drink. Go on, see it off and I'll get you another."

"I mean what I have said."

"Nonsense. You're a good, kind man. You cannot really expect me to believe what you have just said." But as he spoke, the doctor knew in his heart—because Kisiel was so honest and straightforward a man—that the Pole really did mean what he had said.

A little later, when the two older men had changed the subject of conversation and were discussing the merits and otherwise of holidays abroad, Janet Whincap and Alice Kisiel came into the sitting room.

"What's to do?" asked Whincap, rising to his feet. "Has the Good Friday baked cod flipped out of the dish or the parsley sauce gone lumpy?"

"No," replied his wife. "Gwen has it all in hand. And Adam has arrived with Marian."

"Is it they we were waiting for?" asked Kisiel.

Alice nodded. "They're out in the kitchen with Gwen and Tony, drinking a soothing sherry."

"Soothing?" asked Whincap.

"Soothing," repeated Alice. "They were a bit steamed up when they arrived."

"Who? Adam and Marian?"

"Don't worry, David," counselled Janet. "It's something Marian's grandmother has done."

"Not again," groaned Whincap. "That woman is the bane of everybody's life. What's she done this time?"

"Adam says a carpenter arrived at Helewou just as they were about to set out to come here."

"A carpenter? To see Adam? What did he want? A job?"

"He thought he'd got one," said Alice.

"I do not understand," said Kisiel. "Is Adam taking on more staff?"

"No, Josef," replied Janet. "Elke had sent him round."

"Now *I'm* lost," said Whincap. "Elke sent a carpenter round to see Adam on Good Friday?"

"Evidently the poor man couldn't make it at any other time," said Janet.

"Stop, stop!" pleaded Whincap. "Just tell me *why* the man went to Helewou. Forget that it's Good Friday."

"He went because Elke sent him."

Whincap struck his forehead with the heel of his hand. "Right. For what reason did Elke send him to Helewou?"

"To measure up the timber and other materials for building the other bedrooms."

"She *what?* Are you saying she sent a carpenter round there—to a craftsman like Adam—without any reference whatsoever to either of the householders?"

"Yes. A bit high-handed, wasn't it?"

"Why should she do that?" asked Kisiel. "To make an impertinence or to cause trouble?"

"According to the carpenter, Elke said that Adam had neither the time nor the money to do the job so, as she was keen to move in with them, she had decided to pay for the job to be done herself."

"Bloody sauce," said Whincap.

"It would be worse than that," said Kisiel. "After she has moved in she will present Adam with the bill."

"No, no," said Whincap. "Adam must have sent the man away with a flea in his ear."

"He sent him away, certainly," said Janet. "But the carpenter had come along in all good faith. He had put himself out to come and measure up on Good Friday. Elke had nagged him into doing it on his day off."

"That I can believe."

"Besides, Adam knew the man slightly. He couldn't be too cross with him for trying to do Marian's grandmother a favour, could he?"

"I suppose not. But I hope Adam told the chap to send Elke a bill for time wasted."

"I imagine he did. But, please, don't go on about it at lunchtime. Marian is a bit upset about it and..."

"Don't worry, my dear. I'll steer clear of the subject." He turned to Kisiel. "I apologize, Josef. A few minutes ago you told me you had, on occasion, prayed for Elke Carlow's death, and I told you you were talking nonsense. Now I'm not so sure."

Kisiel shrugged. "It will come," he said quietly. "Sooner or later. I hope it will be sooner."

— 2 —

That particular prayer of Josef Kisiel was answered a week or two later, on the first day of May. Elke Carlow, that evening, died a nasty death from what David Whincap could only diagnose as an overdose of digitalis.

Frau Mimi Hillger called Whincap's surgery shortly after six to say that her sister was ill. The receptionist took the call.

"Can you tell me what seems to be the matter, Mrs Hillger?"

Mimi Hillger had learned her English in Germany. She spoke it far more correctly than her sister and her voice was lighter with none of the guttural character of Elke's.

"She is sick. By that I mean she is vomiting."

"I see. Are you sure it is not simply a bilious attack and that she does not really need the doctor to call?"

"That is what I thought at first, so I have waited for it to finish. It is more than two hours since she started. But now she has pain as well as vomiting."

"Where is the pain?"

"In her stomach. And now also she says she is seeing coloured lights."

"Coloured lights? That sounds like a liver upset."

"Whatever is the matter she is in great distress and

37

I think her mind is becoming confused. I should like the doctor to come now."

"Dr Whincap is coming to the end of his surgery. I will see he gets your message immediately he finishes with his last patient."

"Thank you. I think it would be best if you were to ask him to hurry."

"I shall," said the receptionist rather airily. She had heard too many urgent requests which had turned out to be false alarms to pay much attention to Mimi's plea. Besides, Mrs Carlow had cried wolf on previous occasions. Dr Whincap had rushed out to see her more than once, only to find the need less pressing than he had been led to believe. Or so the receptionist thought, believing that she knew all that went on in the practice and unaware that the doctors did not discuss with her, for instance, the tendency of some patients to attempt suicide. "I shall tell Dr Whincap. If he thinks it is necessary to visit you he may come tonight. If not, I expect it will be tomorrow morning after surgery."

"If that is so," said Mimi determinedly, "please make sure you note the time of this telephone call. I have done so, because the matter is so urgent."

The receptionist had never before been asked by a patient to log the time of a call, although it was her custom to do so with all calls. Dr Whincap insisted on it in case there should ever be a subsequent legal query. Mimi's request jolted the receptionist a little—frightened her, even. So David Whincap had scarcely opened his consulting room door to let out the last patient before Mimi's message was being passed on to him a little breathlessly.

The receptionist thanked her lucky stars she had not delayed. From the way the doctor shot out of the surgery and into the car she would have said he was almost expecting an emergency at the Carlow house.

It was just after twenty-five minutes to seven when

David reached the house. He noted the time automatically as he hurried to the front door. Like most doctors who have categorized a patient as a potential suicide, Whincap was taking all the precautions he could—almost subconsciously—to protect himself should the need for an inquiry arise. Like a coroner's inquest on a suicide. Not that Whincap believed Elke Carlow was desirous of killing herself deliberately, but she had already travelled some way along that road—even if only by accident. Notably on Christmas Day. But the fact that he considered her previous attempts to have been non-deliberate, or certainly without the intention of killing herself, made this present situation worse in Whincap's view because he believed that his patient could not have taken an overdose of digoxin. He had been at pains to close that path to her, and very thankful he was that he had rationed the tablets and had arranged for them to be administered at the rate of one only each day by responsible people such as Margarethe, Marian and his own practice nurse. In essence, his belief, as he entered the house, was that he would most likely be faced with trying to identify some other toxic substance which Elke had managed to discover for herself.

Familiar with the layout of the house, Whincap found his way up to Elke Carlow's bedroom. Mimi Hillger was there, wearing a plastic apron, holding a bottle of pine disinfectant in one hand and a floorcloth in the other. The bucket of water at her feet testified to her recent occupation.

She said nothing to him. Her silence and his own first glance at the figure on the bed filled him with the realization that this time he was probably too late.

In response to his questioning, he learned from Mimi that Elke had vomited for nearly two hours. His nose told him this was no exaggeration. Despite Mimi's efforts, the stench clung to the walls of the room and everything in it, scarcely diminished by a generous use of the pine fluid.

Accepting that his patient was in an advanced state of poisoning, Whincap knew he could do little. But he had to do what he could. He examined Elke. There was excessive rapidity of the heart's action—the ventricular tachycardia with marked irregularity that is the hallmark of a late stage in digitalis poisoning. This amazed him. He had been so certain that digoxin could not have been the toxic agent. He looked for other, confirmatory signs—the extrasystoles, coupled rhythm, and atrial tachycardia with block. He realized—with bewilderment—that they were all there, all the pathognomonics of digitalis poisoning. By the time he had determined this, administered a syringe of morphine sulphate as a remedy for the vomiting and then tried to get Elke to accept an oral dose of potassium chloride to normalize the ventricular irregularities and slow the tachycardia, it was all over.

But Whincap continued the fight. Although he was satisfied Elke was dead from cardiac failure, he asked Mimi for blankets to prevent loss of body heat and then enquired whether the refrigerator had a supply of ice. He wanted a bag of ice over the heart. Though he knew this was not a measure likely to be helpful, it was one recommended by certain authorities and so he was not prepared to forgo it in these circumstances where there was nothing to lose and everything to gain by trying it.

He did his best. But after a few minutes of watching and feeling for a tell-tale thread of pulse, he turned to Mimi. "Where is the tablet bottle, Mrs Hillger?" he asked heavily.

"There is no bottle, doctor."

"What did she have them wrapped in? A tissue perhaps or a bag? Handkerchief?"

"I have not seen any tablets, doctor. There were

none. Ever since you yourself took the last of them away on Christmas Day she has been given them one at a time just as you arranged that she should."

"By Margarethe, Marian and my nurse? Never by anyone else?"

"Never."

"She always took them properly—swallowed them? Didn't store them away somewhere? I mean she didn't just pretend to take them?"

"I wasn't always here at her medicine times, but when I was, Elke always swallowed her tablet. With water."

"Did she have a tablet today?"

"From your nurse at two o'clock."

"What did she have to eat and drink after that?"

"We had tea soon after half-past three."

"What did you have to eat?"

"Brown bread and butter and gingerbread."

Whincap thanked Mimi for the information and then asked her to help him search for a supply of tablets or a receptacle in which they could have been kept. They spent a quarter of an hour searching drawers, the bathroom medicine cabinet and waste bins, but without success.

"She must have taken them all," said Whincap at last. "Though what the devil she kept them in beats me."

"I cannot help you, doctor."

Whincap shrugged. They were on the upstairs landing. "Is there a key to the bedroom door?"

"In the lock, doctor."

"Ah, yes. Now, Mrs Hillger, I shall have to lock the room." As he pocketed the key he asked: "When did your sister begin to feel unwell?"

He ushered her downstairs as they spoke.

"Immediately after we had finished tea. At least, that is when she complained. She may have been feeling

41

a little unwell before that and hoped that the cup of tea would make her feel better."

"You think so?"

"I think perhaps."

"Why?"

"Because we usually had our tea a little later than we had today, but Elke asked for it early."

"I see. But it was about four o'clock when your sister felt ill enough to mention it?"

"Yes."

They had reached the hall of the house. Whincap asked: "Could I see the tea dishes and the food?"

"The remains of the food, yes. It is in the kitchen." She led the way there. "But I washed up. I said to Elke she should go to lie down while I cleared away. I did not know then it was serious. It was only when I heard her groaning... before that I had treated it like an ordinary bilious attack."

"For how long?"

"From about half past four when she started to vomit until I telephoned your surgery soon after six o'clock."

"That seems to have been a long delay."

Mimi shrugged. "I was busy with Elke. Cleaning her and the bed and the room. Clean sheets, up and down stairs for buckets and cloths...the time just passed."

"Of course. Well, Mrs Hillger, I'm sure you must realize that I cannot sign a death certificate in these circumstances. I am legally bound to inform the coroner that I suspect your sister to have died of poisoning."

"I understand, doctor. The formalities must be obeyed."

"Obeyed? Ah, yes. Complied with is what we usually say. Same thing, really. They are mandatory. Now, if I may use your phone, I will call Margarethe."

"She must be told her mother has died, of course."

42

"I also want her to come here to keep you company until we can make some proper arrangements for you."

"I can stay in the house."

"I think it would be better if you were not alone here tonight."

Whincap drove straight to the home of his brother-in-law, Robert Bennett. By the time he arrived it was almost eight o'clock.

"David, my dear chap, what brings you here?"

"Could I come in, please, Bob?"

"Of course."

"I'd like to use the phone first off if I may. Just to tell Janet where I am."

"Go ahead. I'll get you a drink."

"Thanks. I could do with one."

After making his call, Whincap joined Bennett in the sitting room. "Gin and tonic, David," said Robert, handing him the glass. "All right for you?"

"Perfect," replied Whincap, accepting the drink gratefully.

"Have you eaten yet?"

"I haven't been home since evening surgery."

"That means you haven't. Flora's just about to serve up. She said she's laying a place for you in case you can stay."

"That's very kind of Flora. If I'm not putting you out..."

"Delighted to have you." Bennett opened the sitting room door and raised his voice. "Darling, David's staying for supper. Water the soup down to make it go round." He came back into the room. "Dave, I can see you're in a bit of a stew about something. Seeing you've come here, I'm taking the attitude that you want to talk to me about something. If I'm wrong and it's none of my business, tell me to keep my big nose out of it."

"It is your business, Bob, and it's official."

43

"Ah! An unnatural death, I presume."

Whincap nodded.

"Who? Anybody I'm likely to know of?"

"Elke Carlow."

"Good Lord! The old dear tried to poison herself at Christmas time, didn't she? Has she managed it this time?"

Whincap lay back in his chair and paused as though choosing his words before replying. "I don't think it's as simple as that, Bob, although obviously it will be for you, in your official capacity, to decide."

"You mean it's a case for my officer to make preliminary enquiries?"

Whincap sat up. "I'd better tell you the whole story, Bob. As you know, Elke Carlow had a heart condition for which I was prescribing a digitalis preparation—digoxin tablets. The dosage of digoxin varies between half a tablet up to two a day, according to what the doctor thinks the patient needs. I'd got Elke on one tablet a day. But she was a headstrong old woman and, far from doing as I ordered, she developed the habit of doing what she thought best."

"I gathered from the conversation at Christmas that she'd been mucking about with the dose."

"And how! She'd miss taking her tablet for days on end, then she'd take a whole heap together to catch up."

"I remember you telling me this at Adam's party." He got to his feet. "Let me get you a refill." He took the doctor's glass. "But I also seem to remember that you made some foolproof arrangement whereby various of the old girl's relatives and your nurse were going to call in daily and administer the right dose."

"That's exactly what I did, and the whole business worked perfectly."

"So she couldn't have died from an overdose of digitalis. That, at least, is something."

44

"But she did," said Whincap accepting his glass. "Or at least I think she did."

Bennett said: "You're too old a hand at your doctoring, Bob, to make a gross error on an occasion like this. So, chum, she must have had a hidden supply of the pills."

"No, Bob, she didn't. I made absolutely sure of that at Christmas time. Her sister swears there have been no tablets concealed in the house as far as she knows, and I couldn't find any container. Furthermore, I've kept my eye on the amounts I've prescribed for her daily dose and on the arrangements for administering the tablets. So has my nurse, and she's no fool."

Bennett pursed his lips. There was a silence between the two men which lasted until Flora Bennett joined them. "I rang Janet to say we were going to feed you here as I supposed you had neglected to tell her."

"David didn't know he was staying for scoff when he rang," replied her husband. "Besides, he's a worried man, and worried men are forgetful."

"Worried, David? Is it Janet? Or the family? Can we help?"

"Official problem for me, Flo," said her husband. "Crowner's Quest stuff."

"Oh, I see. Is that all? Come along then. Chicken casserole. Is that all right for you, David?"

"Couldn't be better, thank you."

They discussed the problem during the meal.

"There's no doubt about it," said Whincap in answer to a question, "that for certain heart conditions there is nothing to equal digitalis. That's why I had Elke on it."

"What does it do, specifically?" asked Bennett, gently levering a large piece of pinky-white chicken breast from its bone. "In not too-technical terms."

"It increases the force of contraction of the heart without increasing its oxygen consumption. Harder, remember, not faster. It's like a person gripping a sponge very tightly and then letting it out again as opposed to gripping it loosely before letting it go. The speed of the action could remain the same in both cases."

"I've understood that bit," Flora said.

"Then you can see why digitalis is used in congestive heart failure—when the heart is not making contractions positive enough to keep the works going properly."

"That was Elke's trouble?"

"She had a little auricular fibrillation and fortunately digitalis helps there, too, in that it does tend to slow the heart rate in such cases."

Flora went on to ask: "How does it become fatally poisonous? I know that sounds a silly question..."

"No, no," protested her husband. "Not silly at all. It's the sort of question we should all be asking all the time. Why are poisons poisonous?"

"Silly ass. There are lots of medicines in use which might make you very ill if you were to take too much of them, but so often people do recover from overdoses if they're pumped out, don't they, David?"

"Not while we're at table, pet, please," begged her husband. "I know stomach pumps and their varied gastric harvests are a source of unending delight to David, but to me they're just..."

"Filthy beast!" scolded Flora.

"You were upsetting me."

"There's nothing upsetting about it," said Whincap, "so eat your nice string beans and baked potato."

"I'll get you," threatened Bennett. "Next time you're in my court I'll ruin your reputation by making hints about your unsocial behaviour."

"Such as?"

"Like that large piece of carrot that has suddenly sprouted on your tie and...yes...there's a morsel of onion in the runnel of gravy, too."

"Thanks, Bob. I know you're trying to cheer me up, but I'd rather talk the problem through."

"You're that worried by it?"

"Scared stiff," admitted Whincap.

"So's Bob," said Flora. "He always starts acting the fool when he's worried. Trying to camouflage his feelings to protect me, but I can see through his antics."

"Nice!" said Bennett. "Silly ass, filthy beast and now acting the fool! All in the space of about two minutes! You can see what I have had to put up with from your sister-in-law these many years, David."

"Keep quiet and pass me your plate if you've finished."

Bennett did as he was told and then turned to Whincap. "We've established that we're both worried men. So shall we continue the discussion? Flo asked you something about digitalis being a poison."

The doctor turned to his sister-in-law who was serving helpings of fresh fruit salad. "To answer your question, Flora, it is necessary to bore you a little by pointing out that the cardiac glycosides—that's digitalis and other like substances—have very little beneficial effect on the heart until they are present in the body in a concentration near to that which produces toxic effect. It's a fine dividing line, so a doctor has to control the dosage carefully."

"That explains why you made such specific arrangements for dosing Mrs Carlow after that episode on Christmas Day."

"Quite so. The daily maintenance dose is quite small after the initial degree of digitalization has been achieved by higher doses at the beginning of treatment. So you see, I was already keeping Elke on the verge of the poison level, if you like to put it that way. Very little more would send her over the limit—as it did last Christmas—while a bigger dose still would prove fatal. As it has done this evening."

"I think I understand that, David," said his sister-in-law, passing him his fruit salad. "And I can see now why you're so worried. If, as you claim, there were no extra tablets in the house, those she got hold of to kill herself with could only have come from one source— or so it would seem."

"Right," said Whincap heavily. "The supply that Margarethe kept for her mother."

"And so Margarethe, Marian or your nurse could somehow—not knowingly, of course—be the means by which Elke got hold of what she needed."

"If only I could be certain of that."

"Of what?"

"That bit about their not knowing. If only I could be sure that Elke deceived one or even all of them."

"David! You're not suggesting that any one of them would co-operate with her willingly? To help her to take her own life? Never!"

Whincap sat silent. Bennett himself filled the gap in the conversation after the silence had grown embarrassingly long. "What I think you are suggesting, David, is that Elke Carlow so frightened herself by the overdose she took at Christmas, when she was nearly a goner, that you don't believe she would try again. Am I right?"

Whincap nodded. "That is exactly what I think."

"Rubbish, David," retorted Flora. "If you had really believed that you wouldn't have made those complicated arrangements for ensuring she only got one tablet at a time."

"I had to play for safety, Flora."

"Knowing the precautions to be unnecessary?"

"Thinking them to be so, but not totally sure."

"David, think for pity's sake. You're virtually accusing Margarethe, Marian or your nurse of... well, criminal activity. And you're doing it in front of Robert, knowing full well that, as coroner, he will have to investigate the case."

"If that is how it seems to you, Flora, I've given you and, presumably, Robert, the wrong impression. I trust my practice nurse implicitly. Nobody could be better or straighter. Marian is married to my son. I regard her as a daughter, a loved daughter. And as for Margarethe, well she is a friend of long standing, besides being Marian's mother. Would I, could I, accuse any of those three of criminal behaviour? I would stake my life that when we come to count and account for the pills in Margarethe's bottle we shall find them to be all present and correct."

"Then why ... ?"

"My dear," said Robert Bennett gently, "can't you see? What David is trying to tell me is that we are all in a hell of a mess, but he's been putting it diplomatically."

"Us? *We* are in a mess? How can we be involved? Except through our relationship with David and Janet, of course."

"Sweetheart, I am the coroner. David, quite rightly, has reported to me a death for which he feels unable to issue a certificate. He has come directly to me—which is a common and permissible habit between doctors and coroners in such cases, because it saves all the rigmarole of having the registrar act as go-between.

"But here's the snag. Possibly implicated in this business, if only by association, are David's daughter-in-law and his practice nurse, to say nothing of his son's mother-in-law, Margarethe."

"Me, too, as the doctor," added Whincap.

"Quite. And in cases like this, which I have to investigate, the coroner's officer, who is a serving policeman, starts asking questions. And in cases of

49

mysterious death, policemen have a habit of looking hard at the surviving members of the deceased's family first."

"Oh! You mean ... ?"

"Hear me out, old thing. Not only will our policeman friend be looking at Margarethe, Marian, David, Mimi Hillger and the nurse, but he will be reporting to his senior officer the outcome of his investigations. I don't have to remind you that the senior officer to whom he will have to report is Detective Chief Superintendent Theo Rainford who is the dead woman's son-in-law, husband of one of the women who will come under scrutiny and father of another, to say nothing of the in-law ties he has with David here.

"Sorting that lot out will be bad enough, but the job falls on my shoulders. And who am I, besides being the coroner? I'm David Whincap's brother-in-law and uncle to young Adam and consequently to Marian. So you see, sweetie, what David has been saying—somewhat indirectly perhaps—is that I am faced with a ready-made set-up for collusion in a case of unnatural death. The authorities won't wear it, of course, and the press would have a field day were they to hear of it."

"I see." Flora got to her feet to fetch the coffee percolator from the sideboard. "You know, I don't think I'm going to enjoy the next few days very much."

"Nor any of us," said Whincap.

"Black for both of you?"

"Hold mine for a minute or two, please, Flo." Bennett got to his feet. "If you'll excuse me for a moment or two ... I have a couple of calls to make. I'll be back to have a brandy with you, David."

After her husband had left them, Flora said: "That old trouble-maker, Elke Carlow, seems to be intent on stirring things even after she's dead."

"This time she may be more sinned against than sinning."

She stared at him. "David, what are you suggesting now? So far, as I've understood it, you've been saying that Elke Carlow committed suicide and that any one of a number of women—mostly our friends and relations—can have been guilty of unknowingly providing her with the means to do so despite restrictions, precautions and strictures on your part to prevent it happening. Now you are changing your tune."

"No, Flora, I am not. You have misunderstood me, my dear. I said I didn't believe Elke would ever again attempt to take her own life. That's point one. Point two is that the act of providing somebody with the means to commit suicide is not a criminal act. If I gave you a clothes line and you hanged yourself... or even if one of my patients takes a full bottle of aspirin I have prescribed... not legally criminal." He shrugged. "But I have not attempted to hide from you, nor has Robert, that there may be criminal connotations here."

"Meaning that somebody could have actually given her an overdose."

"At its most euphemistic, yes."

She rose from the table. "I think I'll need a brandy, too. I'll get the glasses, if you'll get the bottle, David."

Robert Bennett returned. "Ah! Coffee and brandy. What a pity we won't be able to linger over them." He looked up. "Patrick Dean, my deputy coroner, and Theo Rainford are both on their way here."

Bennett did the talking. He told the whole story and then turned to Dean. "You will be responsible for the inquest, Patrick, because as you have heard, I am disbarred by personal interest. For the same reason, Theo, you can play no part in any investigation that the deputy coroner may wish to undertake."

Both men nodded their agreement.

"Patrick will take over from me. The question is, who will take over from you, Theo?"

"Obviously I wasn't intending to act as coroner's officer. So I wouldn't be involved at the outset," said Rainford. "But naturally it would become my responsibility if it turned out to be a criminal case. As it is ... well, I, too, have a deputy. D.S. Sandy. You all know him, I expect. I could detail him ..."

"No," said Patrick Dean firmly. "Sorry, Theo, but in handling this case I must take care not only to arrive at a true finding, but also to make sure that the proceedings are completely free from the slightest hint of self-interest. I know and like D.S. Sandy, but he is a great friend of yours, Theo, as well as being your subordinate. He is debarred on both counts, as you must see."

"What then?" asked Rainford. "All the jacks round here are my subordinates."

"Then we must ask the Chief Constable to bring in somebody totally unconnected with you or the case. Somebody from outside. I'm not going to have anybody pointing the finger at you, Theo."

"And whispering," added Whincap. "I can hear the susurration already. Patrick is quite right, Theo. You, Robert and I must not only be off the field of play, we mustn't damn' well be in the stadium during the game, let alone be officiating at it."

"In that case," said Rainford, "I'd better get on to the C.C. I can't see him wanting to call in one of the neighbouring forces. He'll call in the Yard—once he's convinced there'll be need."

"He should know by tomorrow morning," said Dean. "As soon as Robert rang me this evening—before I set out to come here to see him and having some idea of what he wanted me for, I alerted the pathologist. He's prepared to work late tonight once he can get the body and I'm more fully informed."

"I have the key of the bedroom door," said Whincap,

52

handing it over to Dean. "Whoever collects her will need it."

"Thank you."

"The pathologist said he'd have enough information for you by morning, did he?" asked Rainford. "That's quick work."

"He's only agreed to try to let me have it after I had told him we were fairly sure that the deceased had died from an overdose of digitalis. Knowing what you're looking for helps in his line apparently."

"He'll test for it immediately," said Whincap. "He'll do his other tests later."

"That's possible, is it?" asked Dean.

"If he suspects the presence of digitalis, all he will have to do is to take an extract from the stomach contents and the liver and test the extract on a frog's heart. If there is digitalis present it will slow the heart right down."

"And that's the test?" asked Rainford in amazement. "It doesn't sound very scientific to me."

"Testing for the presence of digitalis is usually done biologically, as I've described, as opposed to chemically, which is how his later tests will be done."

"How much is fatal, David?"

"I'm not sure that anybody could give you the absolute figure, but it is very little. We doctors consider two milligrams of the purified drug to be dangerous. That is our rule of thumb. But whether to kill Mrs Carlow would take three or three and a half milligrams I can't say, because we obviously can't test a patient to destruction and every individual reacts differently." He turned directly to address Rainford. "You sounded a bit sceptical about the frog test, Theo. But I should have added that the pathologist will make other visual tests. Severe digitalis poisoning causes the fragmentation of heart muscle fibres, for instance, with areas of necrosis dotted throughout the heart. They'll be found with a microscope..."

"Don't go on, please," said Bennett. "Let's forget it for a bit and have a drink. Patrick? Theo? What's it to be?"

By ten o'clock the next morning they all knew what it was to be. Dr Eric Dampney, the pathologist, had made his preliminary report to Patrick Dean. Mrs Elke Carlow appeared to have died of a massive overdose of a cardiac glycoside. Precise facts and figures would be given later in his written report. Meanwhile, he felt it his duty to advise the deputy coroner to start an investigation into the ways and means by which so great a dosage of dangerous medicine had come to be ingested by the deceased.

Patrick Dean mentally added to this advice a rider to the effect that his inquiry must seek to show whether the toxic material had been administered to Mrs Carlow. If so, it would be up to the police to decide by whom it had been administered. The Chief Constable, already aware that he faced the possibility of calling for outside assistance if the case developed, decided, on hearing the pathologist's report and his advice to Dean, to ask the Yard for the team which he had earlier asked them to earmark in case the need for their help should crystallize.

In the middle of that same morning Detective Chief Superintendent George Masters was detailed to make his way to Croxley in the West Central police area. He was to take with him his usual assistants, D.C.I. Green, D.S. Reed and D.S. Berger. On arrival D.C.I. Green would combine the temporary post of coroner's officer to Patrick Dean with his usual job in Masters' team. Theo Rainford and all his subordinates were thus excluded from playing any part in a business which Dean intended should not only be legally correct, but should be seen to be so. The Chief Constable had assured him that, judging by reputation, nobody could be more impartial than Masters was likely to be, nor more likely to clear the business up quietly and efficiently.

Patrick Dean pronounced himself satisfied with these arrangements.

— 3 —

"Digitalis," said Green. "That's fox-gloves, isn't it?"

He and Masters were walking to the car after lunch. Reed and Berger had already packed the bags in the boot of the Rover and had taken the two front seats. Reed was to drive.

"That's the source," agreed Masters. "At least it was originally. Now they produce it chemically."

Green took his usual nearside back seat. "All I know, George, is that some old bird died last night with too much of the stuff inside her."

"I can't tell you much more myself, because they haven't yet decided whether it was suicide, accident or murder."

Reed pulled away.

"Then why the hell are we being called in?"

"Because there's a dog's dinner of personalities down there. She was related—either directly or by marriage—to just about everybody immediately involved. The D.C.S. is married to her daughter, the son of the doctor who attended her is married to her grand-daughter, the coroner is the doctor's brother-in-law and so on and so on. Very properly the coroner handed over immediately to his deputy who is, by pure chance, not related to any of the others. The deputy barred the D.C.S. and any of his merry men from the inquiry."

"Why any of his men, Chief?" asked Berger. "Because he might influence them?"

"To treat him and his relatives with kid gloves, you mean?"

"Yes, Chief."

"There's that. But you've also got to remember that the opposite could be true. A detective on his staff who didn't like him might decide that this was an opportunity to make it hot for his governor."

"Only if he could prove it, surely, Chief."

"Not so, lad," said Green. "In a case like this you don't have to prove anything. You've just got to sling enough mud surreptitiously to finish a bloke in such a situation. A whisper to the press, a hint to somebody else. All cleverly done and untraceable. The D.C.S. could later be proved as pure and innocent as driven snow, but he'd never escape from the memory of the gossip. And others would remember years later. 'Wasn't he the chap who was mixed-up in the murder of his mother-in-law?' 'So he was. I'm surprised they kept him on after all the talk there was.' You see, lad, the word mixed-up can mean anything you want it to and a lot of people like it to mean the worst."

"I hadn't looked at it like that," admitted Berger.

"So that's why we are going to Croxley," said Masters. "The D.C.I. will be responsible for the deputy coroner's preliminary enquiries and dependent upon what he finds we shall or shall not institute a full-blooded murder enquiry."

The car sped north-westwards through the heart of England. The spring sunshine, now that May was in, gave the whole of nature that new look which promises so much.

"It doesn't always ride when it puts on its spurs," grumbled Green, referring to the weather. "Just look at some of that green. It's so tender you could eat it with chips. Come back this way next week and as like as not it will all be blighted by late frosts, browned-off at the edges and dripping with non-stop rain."

"What's biting you?" demanded Masters, filling his pipe with hand-rubbed Warlock Flake.

"I know," said Reed.

"Do you, clever clogs? Well, you just keep out of this and keep your eyes on the road. And on the speedometer."

"Which is it to be?" asked Reed. "Road or speedo?"

"Both."

"Okay. But just because you don't like the idea of being appointed temporary coroner's officer to a deputy..."

"Can it!" growled Green.

"Is that really it?" asked Masters. "I know that for a man of your experience, length of service and reputation it does seem to be a bit of a comedown. Like making a colonel a platoon commander. But it is a rather special..."

"It's not that at all," grumbled Green. "It's just that I've no experience of the bureaucratic side of things and I don't know how to arrange an inquest—apart from asking for one to take place. You know me, George. I've never been behind any form of desk. If I'd not been at the Yard I would have become an office wallah—with my rank. But as it is, I'm part of a field team and always have been."

Masters looked at Green, with no hint of amusement on his face at the idea of the D.C.I. being afraid of failure. "Do you know, Bill, I've never done any staff work myself, now you come to mention it. Apart from ordinary duty roster turns, of course."

"A fat lot of help you're going to be then," said Green, mollified by the knowledge that Masters, too, would be at a loss.

"I'll tell you what we'll do," said Masters. "We'll

just quietly—and conveniently—forget that particular bit of our assignment."

"Quite right, too," murmured Green. "And if there is anything that actually needs doing, the sergeants can sort it between them."

"I like that!" complained Berger.

"You'd have got it to do in any case, lad. The only difference is that now you're not in the dark. You know the score. It's better that way."

The Chief Constable was waiting for them. As soon as they arrived at the HQ building and made themselves known to the sergeant-clerk on duty, a constable was instructed to guide them upstairs to the C.C.'s office.

"Some building, this," said Green. "Not like any cop-shop I've ever seen before. Standing in its own grounds, too."

"Ronald Harrington," said the C.C., getting up from behind his old-fashioned desk and coming forward to greet them as soon as the constable ushered them in. He shook hands with them one by one. Masters got the feeling that here was a man who wanted to be liked, who hoped that everybody would think him a good chap as opposed to being an autocratic, stand-offish disciplinarian.

"I've got tea laid on," said Harrington, waving them into a circle of low, armless easy chairs congregated round a large low table at one end of the room. "We might as well be comfortable."

"Some place, this," said Green, still harping on the same theme. He sank down on to one of the orange-coloured chairs. "Different from most."

"We've only had it a year or two," said Harrington.

"It's not purpose built, sir," said Masters.

"No, no. It used to be a teacher training college. You may remember a few years ago quite a number of them were closed down because the supply of teachers was outstripping the needs of the pupils. This one stood empty for a while and then we moved in. We were scheduled to start a new HQ building, but the money was proving hard to come by, so the Authority bought this—for a lot less than it would have taken for the new building—and I must say everybody is delighted with it." He looked round. "This used to be the principal's office-cum-study. I can use half as an office and this half as a conference room."

"In comfort. An excellent idea."

"It's not only that. Apart from all the lecture rooms and so on, we got more than a hundred and sixty bedrooms. We kept some of those as bedrooms for recruits, trainees and unmarrieds, so we've been able to do away with the HQ police houses. And then we've got the gymnasium and playing fields. Excellent for our athletics side and for our mounted training, dog-handling and the like."

"Sounds good," said Green. "Large kitchens and dining rooms..."

"All that. And their common rooms for recreation rooms. We're really in clover. I can afford to let you have a good, big temporary office and if you'd prefer to stay with us, well, we have a number of hospitality rooms. They don't come up to five star standard, of course, but at one time, during the college vacations, they were used for all sorts of symposia and holidays."

"We'll do very well in your residential wing, sir," said Masters. "I know you'll want to cut down on expenses as much as possible."

Harrington smiled. "I hadn't budgeted for your visit. And in these days of protests and marches I'm faced with finding large sums at the drop of a hat just to contain the possible trouble they cause."

"We understand, sir. Every C.C. must be pleading poverty—like the rest of us nowadays."

"You're very understanding, Mr Masters. I hope you'll be as understanding over this little problem you've come to sort out for us."

There was a knock at the door, and the messenger constable came in, rattling a laden metal tea trolley as he eased it on to and across the carpet.

"Thank you, Gibson. We'll manage for ourselves."

As Reed and Berger placed the tea things on the table, Masters asked: "All those who appear to figure in this death you have called us in to investigate are either related by marriage or are great friends. Do you, yourself, know any of them intimately, sir?"

"Intimately? By that, do you mean socially? Because you must realize I've had a great deal to do with Robert Bennett professionally. He is the local coroner. Furthermore, I like him very much, but we are not bosom pals. Then there's my D.C.S., Theo Rainford. I know him well, obviously. And in the nature of things I know his wife, Margarethe, and their daughter, Marian. I think I should say they are friends of mine because several times a year I find myself holding a glass and chatting to them at the same social functions. In fact, Theo and Margarethe come to dinner with my missus and me occasionally. They started as duty invitations at first, of course, but now . . . well, they come because we like their company."

"That sounds reasonable enough, sir. Do you know the dead woman?"

"By repute only."

"Meaning she has a bad name in the area? Or has she interested the police officially before now?"

Harrington shrugged. "I'm not from these parts so I can't recount anything but hearsay. However, she has apparently been a thorn in the flesh of many of the locals for many years. You know the sort of thing— haughty and arrogant with shop people and tradesmen and rather given to writing letters to the local paper about the decadence of youth, the filthy state of the streets and the desirability of sacking a few public servants in order to encourage the others to greater efforts."

"That sounds," said Green, "as though she had the guts to put into words what half the population thinks but is too scared to say."

Harrington nodded. "There's a grain of something in most things she says and does. She has always been fiercely proud of being German, but as she arrived in the middle thirties, you can imagine that the local populace has not always regarded her with the greatest admiration."

Masters put his empty cup down and leant back, "That's very helpful, sir."

"Helpful? What I've just said?"

"Yes."

"How on earth ... ?"

"Don't mind the D.C.S., sir," said Green, taking out a—for once—respectable-looking pack of Kensitas. He gestured with it towards Harrington. "Mind if I smoke?" Having been given a nod of consent, he continued: "George here has to be lived with to be understood."

"Meaning that you know why he finds what I've just said helpful to solving a mysterious death which we are almost certain is murder?"

Green blew out his match. "Yes, sir."

"I'd be interested to know what mileage he got out of my gossip."

Masters let Green continue without making any effort to stop him. "George will assume, sir, that since this Carlow bird has been around here for about forty-five years and has been hated by the locals ever since she got here, anybody wanting to bump her off for some incident in the dim and distant past would have had the opportunity to do so long before now. And, he will say to himself, all emotions such as dislike, mistrust, hatred and what-have-you tend to lessen with the years.

So, in George's book, this German bird was, in reality, getting safer from retribution for long-term misdeeds with every day that passed. So, he will argue, the odds are long in favour of her having committed some fairly recent nastiness which caused her to be seen off if, in fact, she was murdered."

"I see." Harrington turned to Masters. "Is that really what you were thinking?"

"More or less. We've got to start somewhere. It makes it easier if we have some acceptable reason for breaking into the time scale and concentrating on the more recent part of it. We may have to go further back, of course. But I don't like murder inquiries that depend on dim memories and fading recollections. They are usually so dim and faded as to be totally unreliable."

"Quite."

"So now, sir," said Masters, "what we have to determine is what we are actually investigating. As I understand it, you are, if not actually treating this death as murder, prepared to do so unless and until the deputy coroner decides otherwise."

"That's about the strength of it. And the deputy coroner will make his decision on the strength of Mr Green's recommendations. So I am totally in your hands one way or another."

"In that case, I think we should settle in here and then report to the deputy coroner. He is a solicitor, I take it?"

"Patrick Dean? Yes. Not in Croxley, though. His home and practice are in Downhampton, about twenty miles away. I've had a list of addresses and phone numbers put in your office, together with a local map and so on. You'll be able to phone Dean either at his office or his home."

Masters got to his feet. "In that case, sir, we'll start to sort ourselves out."

* * *

The residents' rooms were the old academic staff quarters. Not the cubicle-like rooms of the former students, but good solid sitting, bed and study rooms in which former tutors had made their homes. Masters was laying out and hanging up the comparatively few belongings he habitually took with him on these occasions when Green knocked and was invited to enter.

"I'm next door. The bathroom's between us."

"Good. Not too far to paddle in slippers, then."

"No, but don't prance around in the nude. There are some women officers down at the far end. I heard the lads reading out the name cards on the doors as they went down the corridor to their rooms."

"I'll remember to observe the proprieties." Masters shut the wardrobe door and put his empty case beside the dressing table. "By the way, Bill, you rather curbed our activities by your explanation to the Chief Constable."

"I wasn't wrong, was I?"

"Well..."

"I didn't hear you contradicting me?"

"In front of the C.C.? Not likely. We put on a united front at such moments."

"Yeah, well. It doesn't do any harm to let people like Harrington think we're a bit clairvoyant."

Masters laughed. "E.S.P.'s more like it. And I'm not saying you were wrong, Bill, as long as it's understood that if we have to go back a bit with our inquiries, I don't have to feel embarrassed."

"Go back to the year spit, if it'll help," said Green airily. "Nobody except us need know."

"Good. Do they have a mess and a bar here?"

"From six o'clock. Snack meals all day, but set supper or dinner or what-have-you in the refectory from seven to half-eight."

"You've had your spies out."

"No need to send out a light-armoured recce. Young

P.C. Gibson who acted as guide is doing it most of his time. He's more like a hotel receptionist than a copper. All the patter. I asked him if he provided papers in the morning."

"What was his reply?"

"I think he thought I was pulling his leg. That's the trouble with the force these days. The young cops have no idea what is and what isn't important in life."

Masters smiled to indicate that he appreciated Green's chatter but that the talk was now over. "I'm going along to the office they've allotted to us to make a phone call."

"Give Wanda my love, and young Michael William."

"I was going to call Mr Patrick Dean. I expect even deputy coroners will have reached home by now so I'll call him there."

"Want me with you?"

"I think so, Bill. Just in case he gets sniffy about my approaching him direct instead of through you. If he wants to play everything by the book..."

It was Dean himself who answered the phone.

"My name is Masters, sir. I am a Detective Chief Superintendent from Scotland Yard. I have rung to make my number with you and to say that Mr Green, who is to act as your temporary officer, is here with me."

"That's nice of you. We must meet very soon."

"Whenever you say, Mr Dean."

"Well...look, Mr Masters, don't think I'm rushing things, but I would like it to be this evening. That's if you're not otherwise engaged, of course."

"We, too, would like to push ahead. What time, Mr Dean?"

"I shall be at home all evening. Shall we say after dinner sometime?"

Masters did a rapid calculation. "That would mean somewhere round about nine."

"Splendid."

"Right, we'll be there. Just one thing, Mr Dean. Do you propose to let me see your pathologist's report?"

Dean laughed. "Most certainly, Mr Masters. As my officer, Mr Green would have to see it, and I can hardly expect him not to tell his boss, can I? Besides, there is no reason why the wretched thing should be kept secret from you or for you to institute a forensic examination of your own if you don't want to. Apart from everything else, they cost time and money."

Masters thanked him and put the phone down. He said to Green: "Everybody here seems obsessed with the need for economy. So we'd better get on with the job and save their pockets."

The two sergeants joined them in the bar. There were a few others present, but nobody paid any attention to them. Berger commented on it. "Matey lot, aren't they?"

"They're probably all as much strangers here as we are. *You* haven't approached any of *them*."

"They're mostly young coppers, Chief."

"So you avoid them because of their youth and inexperience. They probably are avoiding us because of our age and obvious experience. Besides, though we don't realize it, the reputation of the Yard still sets us apart from local people, and I have no doubt the grapevine has been working and they know who we are."

Masters was right. Nobody spoke to them though it was obvious from the glances that they were the subject of more than one conversation.

"Can you eat this, Chief?" asked Reed when they were reading the menu posted up in the dining room. "It looks like a lot of old stodge from your point of view."

Masters, back at the Yard for only a few days after an attack of hepatitis which had laid him low for almost the first four months of the year, considered the typewritten sheet. "I'll manage the salad and soused herring. Probably they'll give me a bit of brown bread instead of the chips which seem to be a concomitant part of every choice."

"We've sucked a dry one here," grumbled Green. "As my old dad used to say, he wouldn't eat shepherd's pie at home because he did know what was in it, and he wouldn't eat it away from home because he didn't know what was in it. And by the way, is lamb boulangère that white wishy-washy stuff with lumps of chine-knuckle standing up meatless in what looks like onion gruel?"

"That's it," said Reed. "And they never take out those slimy yellow tendons..."

"Do you mind?" Green continued to peer at the menu. Finally, he said: "I'll have rabbit-food, too. With bully and chips."

"The trouble is," he said later, when half-way through his meal, "you can't get a bottle of vino to wash it down with. If we stay here long, George, we'll have to eat out, even if it's only at the Chinese chippy."

They didn't linger at table, and left with no delay for Downhampton, and although they were early for their appointment, Patrick Dean was ready and waiting for them.

He showed them into his sitting room.

"I have here," he said as soon as they were all seated, "a statement from the deceased's family practitioner. He refused to sign a death certificate and personally informed the coroner that he did not feel in a position to do so."

"Are you saying," asked Green, "that he suspected digitalis poisoning the moment he was called in?"

"Yes."

"Why should he immediately jump to that conclusion?"

"Because she had previously taken overdoses of her own medicine—which was digitalis—and the signs were the same, according to Dr. Whincap."

"Attempted suicide in other words?"

"Not according to Whincap. Just plain arrogance and stupidity, thinking she could ignore his orders and take her medicine just as and when she pleased and in any amounts she fancied. It was not attempted suicide but sheer bloody-mindedness."

"In that case," said Green, "why should Dr Whincap assume that this last case was any different from previous occasions on which she had so stupidly overdosed herself?"

"Because he knew she hadn't got any digitalis in the house."

"Ah!" said Green, who had been left by Masters to conduct this part of the interview out of deference to his temporary appointment as coroner's officer. "Now we are getting somewhere. How did he know she had no digitalis?"

"Because on Christmas Day he searched the house and removed what there was. Since then he had arranged for her to be supplied with one tablet daily— the tablet to be taken there and then in the presence of the practice nurse, her daughter or her granddaughter." Dean then explained Whincap's arrangements for Elke Carlow's daily medication.

"Understood," said Green. "And for the moment we'll accept that those arrangements were foolproof and also that the doctor's search of the house on Christmas Day really did ensure that there was no cache of digitalis left hidden on the premises. But, as I understand it—and Dr Whincap must have been aware of this, too—digitalis is only available on prescription."

"True."

"So he must have been aware that his patient could not possibly have got hold of an extra supply of her heart drug."

"Right."

"So why did he immediately diagnose digitalis poisoning?"

"He is a doctor. He recognized the signs and symptoms."

"Did he? How often has he encountered digitalis poisoning, I wonder?"

"Several times with that particular patient alone."

"So you told me. Does Whincap say what symptoms caused him to diagnose digitalis poisoning?"

Dean looked down at the sheet of paper in front of him, and then read: "I based my diagnosis on various symptoms. The first of these was vomiting..."

"Which occurs in virtually every form of poisoning," said Green.

"Slow pulse..."

"Same again. Most poisons play havoc with the pulse. And with the heart."

"He said that his differential diagnosis was helped by noting a circulatory change, tachycardia, cardiac irregularities, reported visual disturbances, delirium, and anal incontinence."

"All of which occur with scores of poisons other than digitalis."

"Are you sure? I'm a lawyer, not a medical man, so I'm more than a little hazy..."

Green appealed to Masters. "I'm right, aren't I, George?"

"In fact, most certainly. But I think you must pay some attention to the fact that this woman had suffered from digitalis poisoning before. Dr Whincap was bound to connect the occasions, and don't forget he would immediately recognize this type of poisoning in this woman. He must have associated her, mentally, with digitalis poisoning. Hence his subsequent actions."

"No," countered Green emphatically. "Whincap is apparently an able and experienced doctor who knows—is certain, in fact—that this patient cannot have possessed nor obtained the digitalis necessary to poison herself with. Why, then, should he even entertain the idea that she was poisoned by digitalis, particularly as every symptom he mentioned could indicate an overdose of any one of maybe a hundred irritant and poisonous substances?"

"I get your point, Mr Green," said Dean slowly. "Whincap knew that it could not be digitalis poisoning and yet he diagnosed it as such with no single positive reason for doing so."

"Right," said Green. "Why not put her death down to a poison of unknown origin or source and leave it to the pathologist to identify? That would be the usual course."

"What are you suggesting, Mr Green? That Dr Whincap knows more than he should? Because if so, he could have signed the death certificate without raising a hue and cry."

"How do you make that out? He was treating her for heart trouble. Had she died of that there would have been no vomiting, purging, coloured lights and so on. She'd just have died from cardiac failure."

"Which in fact is what she did die of according to the pathologist."

"Ah, yes. I know that one. We all die from a cessation of breathing in the long run. It's what causes the cardiac failure or our breathing to stop that matters."

"Quite."

"And Mrs Carlow died in the presence of her sister who had been a witness to two hours of these symptoms. Whincap could not, on any account, have signed a certificate recording cardiac failure."

"That is true. Are you saying he was in some way trying to ... to obfuscate the cause of death?"

"Not the immediate cause. The reasons for the cause. The causes of the cause, if you like. Look at it this way. Whincap had made sure that this woman could not overdose herself with digitalis. But she did have an overdose. So how good were his precautions? That's question one. Question two is why, when he knew she couldn't possess any extra digitalis, did he diagnose digitalis poisoning in a very short visit and without any signs and symptoms specific to digitalis poisoning? My assertion is that digitalis should have been the last poisonous substance he thought of, because he knew it to be impossible."

Dean stroked his chin in thought. Masters, smoking quietly, took the pipe from his mouth and gave, with it, a tiny gesture of approval and support for Green's contentions.

Dean, noticing this tacit support, said: "Mr Green, what you have said to me provides me with cause enough to question Dr David Whincap very closely at the inquest."

"Right."

"But so far you have carried out no investigation into the possibility of others being implicated in this death—if anybody else was implicated, that is."

Green ground out his cigarette. "Mr Dean, I'm not an experienced coroner's officer, but as I understand the job, it is only necessary for me to raise some doubt in your mind—give you some cause to hold a full inquest—for you to act in whatever way you see fit. I don't have to investigate the crime, I only have to suggest that there appears to be reason to suspect one— or not—as the case may be."

"True," said Dean, "but you have pointed a finger at one man, only. Dr David Whincap. It is enough to warrant a full investigation. I agree with that. But I would rather not pillory one man, who may be innocent..."

"Pillory?"

"If I were to ask Whincap to answer—in open court— the questions you have posed, without asking equally searching questions of other people, that fact alone would give the impression that I consider the doctor to have something to hide. And having something to hide is, in the public view, equivalent to being guilty." He looked round the four policemen. "Am I right?"

"Quite right, sir," said Reed. "But do you have to put those questions to Dr Whincap in open court? What I mean is, need you hold the inquest straight away?"

"I would prefer to."

"In that case, sir, why not just open and then postpone for a definite time or even an indefinite time, to allow the police to make their inquiries?"

"Thank you, Sergeant. But that would indicate that there is positively a criminal background to the affair. I would rather avoid giving that impression if it is not justified."

"Fair enough," said Green. "And it's my job, as your officer, to give you enough cause to treat the inquiry as a preliminary to a criminal investigation. I have given you some cause which you believe would give a lopsided impression to the public at large. Perhaps—as Sergeant Reed suggested—you could delay the inquest for a few days..."

"I've already said I would prefer not to."

"Right. Then open as has been suggested, and call me immediately—after evidence of identification. Ask me why I am here. I will say that as the dead woman is related to the senior CID man in the area it was felt that a third party should be called in to make your inquiries. Not because there has been any hint of hanky-panky, but because the law demands that disinterested and, therefore, impartial officers should be employed to help you clear the matter up."

"I think I follow. I then ask you if, so far, you have found any reason to suppose that the death is anything other than suicide..."

"Not reasons, facts," said Green. "I'll tell the truth.

I have no facts. And that gives me the opportunity to add that as I have only just arrived, I should like a bit of time to poke around—not because I suspect anything or anybody—but just to make doubly sure. And I'll add, for the benefit of anybody who's interested, that as I've come all this way to act as your temporary officer I'd appreciate enough time to do the job properly."

"Got it. I then ask you how long you think you would need before you could truly assure the court one way or the other...?"

"Right. I ask for a few days and you grant them. Nobody can complain or get the wrong impression."

"Excellent," said Dean. "There's just one thing. If, subsequently, there is a case to answer, won't your first evidence make you look a bit of a Charlie?"

"No way. I'll have told you the truth first off and if, subsequently, we do uncover something nasty, people will say how right I was to ask for an adjournment. I'll come out of it smelling of roses."

"If that's the way you look at it..."

"It is. As long as you open the inquest very soon. If you delay, circumstances will change. I may not be able to say I've no facts, and then what you want to avoid will happen."

Dean nodded. "Two o'clock tomorrow afternoon soon enough? I could sit without a jury to save complications."

"Just the job."

"So we are agreed. That's a weight off my mind. I don't mind telling you that I was a little apprehensive."

"What about?"

"The degree of co-operation I could expect from senior Yard officers. You see, in spite of my being a disinterested party, I do know a lot of the people involved in this business, and one can't help but hope that the innocent should come through unscathed by

73

gossip. Areas like this are not like London, you know. Malicious chat can spread like wildfire."

Masters intervened. "Mr Dean, though an unnatural death is a serious and depressing business, you must know that there are thousands of similar cases each year, up and down the country. The coroners' reports we receive are various and sometimes bizarre, but few members of the general public pay much attention to them, no matter how sad and inexplicable they are. We shut our eyes to the spectacle of ourselves, the human race, sweeping up its own debris. So why should the death of Mrs Carlow cause much interest? Another old woman dies of an overdose, just as scores of elderly people die of hypothermia, neglect and any number of other regrettable causes."

"That sounds extremely cynical, Mr Masters."

"It is not meant to be. As a policeman, I'm supposed to be case-hardened—in both senses of the word. But I would ask you to believe that all four of us here are more affected by these tragedies than the average citizen. You see, we deal with them. The average citizen doesn't know about them, at least not intimately, and even if he does, he finds it less disturbing to forget—after shaking his head sadly to indicate that he is not entirely unmoved."

"That's right," said Green. "What his nibs is really asking, Mr Dean, is why this case, important as it is to those intimately concerned, should rouse even a ripple of interest or concern among the general public?"

Dean scratched one ear. "The press..." he began.

"Will be looking for a story," admitted Green, "but if you give them nothing to get their teeth into at the inquest, they'll not bother."

"Your presence will interest them. Because of your rank and because you're from Scotland Yard."

Masters grinned. He could sense what was coming next. He wasn't wrong.

"In that case," said Green, "Sergeant Reed or Berger could appear before you to say what I would have said. That gets rid of the rank bit. As for Scotland Yard, need it be mentioned? Can he not describe himself as belonging to a neighbouring force? Your local reporters are not likely to know the names of CID sergeants at the Yard, so they won't jump to any conclusions there."

Green was obviously attempting to wriggle out of the job of temporary coroner's officer. Not that Masters blamed him. A detective of Green's standing and reputation could hardly welcome the appointment, however impermanent.

Dean turned to Masters as if seeking his approval of the suggested course.

"If those of us not directly involved did not attend the court, Mr Dean, the idea could work. Everything would be open and aboveboard. You would not be deceiving the press or the public, but neither would you be presenting them with a stick with which to lambast the people you wish to protect. If Sergeant Reed were to act for you, I personally guarantee that before your court sits, he will be given no facts concerning our investigation. He could, however, work directly for you should there be any inquiries you wish him to make between now and two o'clock tomorrow afternoon."

Dean made up his mind on the spot. "I'll go along with Mr Green's suggestion. And there is something I want Sergeant Reed to do for me."

"What's that, sir?" asked Reed.

"To check the bottle of digoxin tablets held by Mrs Rainford, and to establish whether the number that should be there is there and generally to check that there has been no jiggery-pokery with prescriptions."

"Right, sir. I'll attend to that tomorrow morning."

"That is the most obvious move to make," agreed Masters. "If the bottle is short, the source of the poison becomes obvious."

"Would the case then fall flat on its face, Chief?" asked Berger.

"Be your age, lad," grunted Green. "We'd then have to discover who gave the old dame the excess dosage or whether she'd managed to trick one of them and had saved up the means to commit suicide."

"But at least we'd know where the stuff came from."

"Which fact," said Masters, "could be more of a hindrance than a help."

"How come, Chief?"

"If the toxic material came from some other source, then simply by discovering the other source we ought to get a pointer to the person who administered it."

Dean got to his feet. "Can I get you gentlemen another drink?"

Masters shook his head. "It's getting late. Tomorrow will be a busy day for us. I'd like an early start."

"Of course. I'm indebted to you for coming, and for your help. If you dispose of the rest of this business as easily as you seem to have disposed of my little fears, the full inquest should not be long delayed."

"I hope not," said Green. "If it were to hang over the people involved for too long it could become a bit of a strain."

"Now," said Dean, with a laugh, "you're knocking the sensitivities of those of us who live out in the sticks."

"Never let it be said," retorted Green. "I was talking about the effect it would have on us living in that police HQ building. It's like being back in barracks again."

As they drove home, Masters said: "You're a humbug, Bill."

"Who? Me? Here, young Berger, I'll have one of those fags you're not handing round."

Berger turned to offer the packet to Green who was sitting in his accustomed rear, nearside seat. "I notice you haven't contradicted the Chief," he said.

"Unsubstantiated accusations," said Green airily, "need no denial. One can only refute them when they are given in detail. Nice fags, these. Somebody give you them for your birthday?"

"Give him chapter and verse, Chief," pleaded Berger. "He's dying to argue the toss."

"Very well. Bill, you swore you knew nothing about the functions of a coroner's office, yet you managed to give Dean—and us—the impression that you know everything there is to know about it."

"Well," said Green, sounding highly pleased. "I'd be a mug if I let a deputy coroner get hold of the idea that he was dealing with a rookie, wouldn't I? I mean, he might try to manipulate me."

"So you boned up on the subject before we set out?"

"Shall we say I took a couple of minutes' advice? I hadn't time for more."

"In that case you're a quick learner."

"A moment ago I was a humbug."

"So you are. You were determined to get rid of that job and you did so, very nicely, by offloading it on to Reed."

"Hark who's talking. Who was it came up with all that drivel about the general public not caring about tragedies half as much as case-hardened but sensitive coppers? Dean doesn't know you, George, but I do. You trotted out that load of bilge just to prepare the ground for me to do exactly what I did. And now you say I'm a humbug because I took advantage of it."

"Ah! I hadn't realized I was being quite so obvious."

"You weren't to me, Chief," said Berger.

"You?" snorted Green. "You're like a kitten, lad. Not old enough yet to have your eyes open."

"Maybe not. But I know all about big mouths. As a kitten, I'm carried about in one."

— 4 —

At breakfast the next morning, Green asked: "Where do we start, George?"

Masters viewed his plate. "The baked beans are, I think, a mistake. I definitely shall not start with them. The sausage and egg...?"

"It's going to be one of those days, is it?"

Masters looked up. "Sorry. But then this is a sorry mess."

"Look, Chief," said Reed, "forget that food. You know your appetite hasn't recovered from the hepatitis, so why sit playing with what's there? Put it aside and eat some toast. Then the rest of us won't feel we're eating pigswill."

Masters, surprised, looked straight and hard at Reed as though about to blast him for impertinence. But the outburst didn't come. After a moment, he said: "I apologize. I had no intention of putting you off by belittling the fare, but..." He shrugged.

"It's not too bad," said Green. "Not the right combination of course. And they haven't basted the eggs, so they're like leather underneath and not cooked on top. The beans are a bit watery, too, with all this jizzer-rizzer running about the plate, but I happen to like sausages that are baked so hard you can't get the fork in, so that's all right." He turned to Reed. "You were a bit outspoken, lad. Didn't make proper allowances."

"I did," replied Reed hotly. "I said the Chief hadn't recovered from his hepatitis."

Green shook his head. "That's not it, son. His wife gives his nibs a nice white linen napkin, a Royal Doulton plate and cutlery from Mappin and Webb. You could lob up a dog's dinner with that lot and it would look appetizing. But when you see what his missus does give him...well, when I remind you that his ma-in-law lives in Wiltshire and keeps his household supplied with locally home-cured ham and the like, you'll realize that it all boils down to the old business of comparisons being nauseous."

"Odious," said Reed.

"Not in this case, chum. If you eat this stuff you're liable to get nausea or a pain—somewhere about the lower region of the bowels."

"Now you've put me off completely."

"Remember what Gandhi said."

"What?"

"When he felt nausea—which he often did, apparently—it was usually overcome by sipping water."

"Thanks."

"Don't thank me, try this tea, it's a good substitute for water. What my old dad used to call clover tea."

"Oh, yes?"

"Usually made with only three leaves. Four leaves and you were lucky."

Reed put his knife and fork down in disgust. Green, watching him over the rim of the cup, took a noisy slurp of the despised liquid. Masters, still smiling at Green's humour, said: "All this babbling gossip of the air brings me to the business of the day."

"Shakespeare always had a word for it," said Green, "but I'd like to have heard what he would have had to say about baked beans."

"We shall never know," replied Masters. "But to gossip. You asked where we were to start, Bill. This is the hardest part—breaking in, as it were. There are obvious characters we must interview, but it struck me that in a case where we have so many interwoven family branches, their is bound to be gossip. Not necessarily malicious, but just talk about each other. Titbits that could help us."

"Get a pattern of relationships that way," agreed Green. "Could be useful. Pass the marmalade, young Berger."

"Reed," continued Masters, "I want you to take Berger along with you this morning. And wherever you go, keep your ears open. The D.C.I. and I will not see you until after the inquest—for obvious reasons. For equally obvious reasons we shall not attend the inquest."

"Where shall we see you, Chief?"

"We'll leave a message here nearer the time. Ring in to the desk after the coroner adjourns."

"Right. You'll be driving the Rover?"

"You take it. I've asked for a local car."

Reed got to his feet. "In that case, Chief..."

"Sit down, lad," said Green. "You can't go round asking questions before half-past eight in the morning."

"I'm not intending to. I'm going to try and get breakfast somewhere."

Theo Rainford was at his desk in the HQ building when Masters and Green called on him. The newcomers introduced themselves.

"Come to grill me?" grinned Rainford.

"Not so's you'd notice," said Green. "But then, we never do."

"What then?"

"Background, mainly," replied Masters, taking the

chair he had been offered. "Who would want to kill Mrs Carlow?"

"Just about everybody who ever met her."

"She was that unpopular?"

"All her time here as far as I can make out."

"Yet you married her daughter."

"What's that got to do with it?"

"You tell me."

Rainford's cheerfulness had already gone. "If you insist."

"I think I do."

"Margarethe is a good woman. I met her when I was a young copper. I married her, not her mother."

"But you must have come in contact with Mrs Carlow."

"No more than I had to."

"Why was that? Because of her reputation as an unpleasant woman, or because she gave you cause to dislike her?"

Rainford paused before replying. "That's a loaded question."

"Give me a loaded answer."

"Both."

"Thank you. As a young man, presumably in love with her daughter, you steered clear of Mrs Carlow because of hearsay evidence that she wasn't nice to know. I find that a strange attitude in any young suitor, let alone a policeman taught to mistrust hearsay evidence and—as we all are at such a time—anxious to make a good impression on the parents of the girl we wish to marry. So though your reply was loaded, I shall put less weight on that part of the answer than on the other which means that I incline towards the view that she gave you cause to dislike her."

"Do you honestly mean to say you're sitting there trying to dredge up some sort of motive for me having seen the old woman off?"

"Why not?" asked Green. "You said that just about everybody she ever met would want to kill her. You've been a copper long enough to know that in cases like this the first place we look is among the family. Who's in the family? You, your wife, your daughter and the elderly sister. All prime suspects at this stage in the game, chum. So, among you lot, who has the biggest motive? Your wife? Your daughter?"

"Neither of them has any motive at all," growled Rainford.

"The sister?"

"She's a frail, little old woman, as sweet-natured as her sister was nasty."

"So that leaves you."

"And you said you didn't grill people."

"Has anybody threatened you, leaned over you, raised his voice to you?" asked Masters quietly.

"No, and they'd better not."

"Much better not, I agree. But I wonder how many times your subordinates—or even you, yourself—have used just those tactics with a suspect?"

Rainford was on his feet. "What are you accusing me of?" he grated.

"Avoiding giving me direct answers. I find that reprehensible in a senior police officer. And please sit down, Mr Rainford. You're being guilty of using one of the tactics you claim never to have used."

"I'm not putting up with this. You people come here from the Yard and think you're God Almighty..."

"Please sit down, and tell me what cause Mrs Carlow gave you to earn your dislike."

Rainford sat down slowly. He stared hotely at Masters for a moment and then gradually the anger seemed to drain from him. The choleric reply did not come. Masters waited, realizing that this was a watershed in the emotions of a man striving to overcome wrath and to

82

replace it with moderation and sanity. At last—

"I'm sorry," mumbled Rainford.

"Please don't apologize."

"It's just...well you don't know what it's like to have your wife and daughter as suspects in what is being treated as a murder case."

"He does, you know," replied Green quietly. "His wife...she was more than just a suspect, she was damn' near taken in for murder."

Rainford opened his eyes, wide. "Mrs Masters was?"

"Shortly before I married her," corrected Masters. "And it was Bill Green who saw us through. So, if you would please tell us..."

"The old trout tried to stop Margarethe from marrying me. She reckoned a lowly copper wasn't good enough for her daughter. You can imagine how I felt at the time."

"And how you have felt ever since?"

"If you mean did I feel murderous then, the answer is yes. But not since. I've never really liked her, but we've got by for twenty-five years."

Masters grinned. Green said: "That's about par for the course with mothers-in-law. And for my money, if you didn't see her off in the old days, you're hardly likely to have had a go at her now."

"Thanks. Is that how you decide?"

"Decide?"

"Solve your cases?"

"Very often," admitted Masters, seriously.

Rainford, for a moment looked astounded and then he, too, grinned. "You hadn't the slightest interest in me," he accused. "You came in here to get a cop's personal view of the deceased's character."

"And we got one, didn't we? Not a considered one. A gut-feeling exposure of a rather unpleasant old woman."

Rainford shrugged. "You could have asked."

"I did. I asked you who would want to kill her. If you'd said you didn't know..."

"You're clever, Mr Masters. You got me to talk."

Masters nodded. "Silence sometimes speak, but words usually tell me more." He got to his feet. "I shall want to speak to Mrs Rainford and Mrs Adam Whincap."

"And get them to talk, too?"

"I hope so. But you can be present at both interviews if you wish."

"You're not bringing them in here, I hope?"

"I'd prefer to see them in their own homes."

"In that case...yes, I'd like to be there."

"Right. They will obviously be expecting us to call on them, but when you ring to confirm that we shall be coming, please don't counsel them to avoid some things and to stress others."

"You think I'd do that?"

"It'd be natural, chum," said Green. "And if you don't offer, they'll ask. All his nibs is saying is for you to stop short after telling them what we're like—or what you think we're like. Instructing them about what to tell us will only make them nervous and won't achieve much else."

"By God, you're sure of yourselves."

"No," said Masters, firmly. "We are so unsure of ourselves that we don't know for certain exactly what we are investigating. But it has been postulated that nothing in this world can be said to be certain, except death and taxes. I know I pay my taxes. And we have a death on our hands. Nothing more. So...and I think this applies to everybody who falls under the slightest suspicion in any sort of criminal case...I always have doubts about people I am about to interview."

"Doubts about what?"

"Everybody and everything to begin with. It's the way we play it. The philosophy is not a new one, because again it has been said that if a man will begin with certainties, he shall end in doubts; but if he will be content to begin with doubts, he shall end in certainties." He smiled again. "And so I regard even Mrs Rainford and Mrs Adam Whincap as doubts."

"And if we have doubts," said Green, airily, "how can you say we are sure of ourselves?"

Rainford laughed aloud. "You two are an eye-opener to me. You're a couple of..."

"Con men?" suggested Green.

The receptionist was businesslike but kind and helpful.

"I'm terribly sorry, but Dr Whincap's surgery list is full for this morning. But I could fit you in this evening."

"No, thank you."

"But if it's urgent..."

"We're not sick," said Green.

"Are you with this other gentleman?"

"We're together, love."

"Are you patients of Dr Whincap?"

"No, love. Nor are we reps or insurance salesmen."

Masters took out his warrant card and showed it to the receptionist. After reading it, she looked up and gathered from the gentle shake of his head that she shouldn't disclose their identities to the patients waiting within earshot.

"I...I see. Perhaps...yes, I think you should see the practice manager."

"He or she?"

"Er...Mrs Pine. She's doing the Next Appointments this morning." She leaned forward through her hatch and pointed to her left. "If you go through that door which says Surgeries on it, and turn right, not left, you'll see the exit sign. Mrs Pine is in the little office near the door."

"Thank you. You have been very helpful."

The receptionist blushed with pleasure at this courtesy. Green paused to whisper to her: "Let me know if anybody ever calls you a dragon. I'll come in and breathe fire over him."

She smiled. "They're only rude because they're poorly. You have to ignore it."

"You're as good as a bottle of medicine yourself," said Green, and followed Masters who had already passed out of sight.

"Mrs Pine?" asked Masters.

"Which doctor?" asked the bespectacled woman without looking up.

"Here we go," breathed Green.

"Dr Whincap."

"How many weeks' time?"

"Now, please."

The woman looked up from her juggling with future appointment sheets. "See the receptionist in the waiting room for appointments today. But I don't think Dr Whincap can see you. One of the other doctors may have a blank time."

"Mrs Pine, I am a policeman."

"It doesn't matter who you are, we take patients in strict order."

"A very senior policeman, Mrs Pine. From Scotland Yard." As yet his voice had been quiet. Now it took on added timbre. "Please tell Dr Whincap I am here."

"He's engaged."

"Please tell him, now, or I shall go to his consulting room myself."

The woman hesitated. Green said: "Look, love, you're having to pay for us on the rates. Every second you keep us here is going to cost you another penny in the pound."

At that moment a woman patient came out of one of the consulting rooms down the corridor and approached the practice manager. Masters and Green stood back for her. The woman opened her mouth to announce her business, but Mrs Pine snapped: "I'll attend to you in a minute," and then picked up the internal phone.

David Whincap came out of his room to greet them. After they had introduced themselves, he said: "Excuse me for a moment, gentlemen. I still have two patients on my list for this morning. I'll arrange for Dr Mosser to see them."

"No need for that, Doctor. If they are only going to take a short time..."

"Five minutes or so apiece."

"In that case, is there somewhere we could wait?"

"There's a staff room at the end of the corridor. The door is marked Private. There should be some coffee in there by now. Go in and help yourselves. I'll join you as soon as I can."

"Thank you."

"Hello! Can I help you?" The occupant of the staff room was in the blue overall and cap of a nurse ready for domiciliary calls. She looked wholesome—sturdily built, with strong legs in heavy gauge stockings, sensible shoes, short hair just showing below the cap, little or no make-up and above all, a smile.

"Can I help you? This is a private room. If you're looking for somebody..."

"We are policemen," said Masters. "Dr Whincap asked us to wait in here."

She blushed. "Oh, I am sorry."

"Not to worry, love," said Green. "The doc also told us to help ourselves to coffee."

She handed the cup she was holding to Green. "Have this. I haven't touched it. I'll get another."

"Ta. Can I help myself to sugar?"

"You can, but you shouldn't." She smiled. "You know how we describe it?"

87

"Tell me," said Green, spooning the stuff into his cup.

"Sugar—pure, white and deadly."

"Now you're trying to frighten me."

She had been filling another cup for Masters, who thanked her and then asked: "Are you the practice nurse?"

"I'm afraid I am."

"Afraid?" asked Green.

"Very, because if you two are policemen, you must be here because of Mrs Carlow, and I used to help with the daily visits to give her the digoxin."

"Please believe me, Nurse ... ?" began Masters.

"Scramsie. Audrey Scramsie."

"Nurse Scramsie, thank you. I was about to ask you to believe me when I say that to the best of our knowledge you have nothing to be afraid of. We shall want to talk to you about Mrs Carlow, of course. But we shall leave even that until after we've spoken to Dr Whincap. We shall tell him we intend to have a few words with you—out of courtesy. We have no wish to approach his staff behind his back."

She smiled and shook her head, almost in disbelief. "You've no idea what a relief it is to hear you talk like that after hearing how gruff the police can be."

"Oh, we're gruff," said Green. "Sometimes, that is. When we have to be. We don't like people who hurt kids, for instance."

"Neither do I. My blood boils when ... but it's always so difficult to be sure or to prove."

"Baby battering?" asked Masters.

"Yes. When I see a poor little mite covered in bruises and its mother says it has fallen downstairs, I always feel like ..."

"Murder?" asked Masters quietly.

"Don't answer that, Audrey," said Whincap sharply, coming in at the door.

Masters turned. Whincap said: "I didn't hear much of that conversation, but what I did hear makes me think you are trying to trap Nurse Scramsie into some unworthy admission."

"No, doctor," said the nurse. "It wasn't like that at all. We were talking about parents who maltreat children."

"I see. In that case, I apologize."

"They haven't mentioned Mrs Carlow. In fact they said they wouldn't talk to me about it until they'd got your permission."

"Not quite that, love," said Green. "We can talk to anybody we like at any time. But Chief Superintendent Masters has old-fashioned ideas of courtesy. He said he'd mention it to your boss before we discussed Mrs Carlow with you."

"Whichever it was," said Whincap, "I'm grateful. Now, Mr Masters, I have my rounds to do and I have been summoned to attend the inquest at two o'clock."

"In that case, I can come to see you at a later time."

"My room is free. If ten minutes will do...?"

"Excellent. Help yourself to your own coffee and we'll chat while you have it."

Whincap sat at his desk, with Masters in the patient's chair and Green occupying the spare.

"You reported Mrs Carlow's death to the coroner, Dr Whincap. As I understand it, she was a long-term patient of yours with a cardiac complaint for which you prescribed, repeatedly, and thus, continuously, a daily maintenance dose of digoxin."

"Quite correct."

"So it could be claimed that the deceased was under treatment by you right up to the moment of death."

"I hadn't seen her for more than a month."

"Look at it another way, doctor. If Mrs Carlow had died from what we usually describe as natural causes, would you have issued a death certificate?"

"Yes."

"Even though this usually means that the doctor has attended within fourteen days of death?"

Whincap paused for a moment before replying.

"It is accepted practice that where a doctor has provided active and continuous care for the deceased over a long period of time—even if he doesn't see the body until after death—the certificate can be accepted even though the last visit was not within the usual fourteen days."

"So had your suspicions not been aroused, you would have issued a certificate which stated what?"

"The precise cause of death. It might have been infarction or thrombosis, but I would have stated that whatever the terminal event, it was likely to have been the result of the cardiac disease for which I had been treating her."

"Good. May I remind you of one other point? At present, a doctor can issue a certificate without seeing the body after death."

"True."

"Had Mrs Carlow died before you reached her would you have issued a certificate without seeing her?"

"It is not my practice to do so, but I would have felt perfectly at liberty to do so—an elderly woman with chronic heart disease? Her death at any time would have been no surprise."

"Forgive me for taking you through this catechism, but I am trying to get the feel of events. You state that Mrs Carlow's death at any moment would not have surprised you. I understand you were taking great care to ensure that she hadn't the means to commit suicide; and yet..."

"Yet what?"

"I get the impression from both written and verbal reports that from the moment you were told Mrs Carlow was ill, you acted as though you expected tragedy."

"What are you asking me, precisely?"

"If Mrs Carlow would have died naturally at any time without causing you any surprise, why—before ever you got to her bedside—did you act as though an unnatural death was occurring?"

Whincap scratched one ear. "I really have no answer to that except to say that my background knowledge of the patient and my past experience in treating her caused me to be fully prepared for tragedy and to act accordingly. My fears were justified."

"Were you expecting tragedy, after taking such stringent precautions to prevent it?"

"No. I thought I had successfully circumvented what appears to have happened."

"Yet you still thought, from the moment you were called out to Mrs Carlow, that you would find tragedy."

"Could. Not would."

"So you did not have complete faith in your arrangements for seeing Mrs Carlow got her correct dose each day?"

"Funnily enough, I did."

"A bit of a paradox, then?"

"If you like, Mr Masters. But I assure you I had not—as you appear to be suggesting—any prior knowledge of what I would find at the Carlow house."

"You must forgive me if I have given the impression of suggesting you had prior knowledge of the death or the means used to bring it about. In fact the reverse is true. I was trying to satisfy myself that you truly did not have such prior knowledge, and that your response to the call for help was in all respects consistent with good medical practice."

Whincap looked somewhat relieved. "You could have fooled me."

"Maybe, doc," said Green. "But we have to be a bit like you and not take things at their face value. If some chap comes to you with a bellyache you don't just assume he's eaten too much and give him some minty tablets."

"With some I do—knowing the patient and the rotundity of his figure."

"Yes, but if, like us, you don't know the bloke you're talking to, you prod and test for ulcers or what's the word . . . oesophagitis? Is that it?"

Whincap grinned. "You wouldn't like to stand in as locum for a few days would you, Mr Green?"

Green looked pleased at the compliment on his medical knowledge. Masters got to his feet. "We've kept you too long already, doctor. Just before you go, however . . ."

"What?"

"Our two sergeants will be calling here to establish—as a must—that the amounts of digoxin prescribed by you, those given to your patient and those remaining in the bottle all add up to what they should do. I take it you keep a drug record for each individual patient?"

Whincap nodded.

"Would you be prepared to instruct your staff to let our sergeants see that belonging to Mrs Carlow?"

"Willingly. I'll warn Mrs Pine."

"And warn her from me, too, doc," added Green. "She's not the greatest PR asset in the business."

"I realize that, but she is a good administrator. Which would you prefer? Drug records kept up to date or a languid charm?"

"Both," said Green.

"You want jam on it."

Nurse Scramsie was waiting in the corridor.

"Any urgent cases for me, Dr Whincap?"

Whincap lifted one knee to act as a table on which to rest his bag. He snapped back the fasteners and handed the nurse two sheets of instructions. "Mrs

Lomax and old Mr Fowler. Both the same as before, but I think Fowler's daughter is getting a little tired."

"Has he been keeping her awake at nights?"

"No. It's just that she needs a rest and a change. See what you think. We could get him into the Cottage Hospital for a couple of weeks if she could get right away for a holiday. I don't want to do it if she's going to spend all her time visiting him. Oh, yes. And he is developing a bed sore on his posterior. Show her how to treat it."

"Right, doctor. Nothing special for Mrs Lomax?"

"She's going along nicely. But she never opens a window. Try to get that helpful neighbor to put a chair in the garden so that the old dear can get a couple of hours of fresh air. It's warm enough for her now."

Nurse Scramsie picked up her own heavy bag and left.

"My idea of what a practice nurse should be," said Green. "I reckon people must look forward to her dropping in to help."

"She's a gem. Now, if you'll excuse me..."

"Don't forget to warn Mrs Pride; otherwise she'll certainly prejudice our lads against her," said Green.

"Mrs Pine," corrected Whincap.

"Same difference, doc. If you know your Hiawatha you'll remember he called them black and gloomy pines."

"Ah, yes," said Whincap. "I remember that. By the shore of Gitche Gumee..."

"I think you'd better be going, doctor," interrupted Masters.

"Oh, yes, of course."

Whincap hurried towards the exit door.

"He's forgotten to warn Mrs P after all."

"Not to worry, Bill. You tell her."

"Why me?"

"In theory you're still the coroner's officer."

When they reached the HQ building, Masters and Green went direct to the room allotted to them. On the desk was a note from Reed addressed to Masters.

"Lucky so far, Chief. The pharmacist hasn't sent off last months's prescriptions yet. We saw Mrs C's script and got the details."

Masters passed it to Green who read it without comment.

"The sergeants will have to do their sums," murmured Masters. "There could still have been a few left from the previous supply."

"Back to Christmas I'd say. They should be able to work it out."

"I imagine so, because the pharmacist will be asked to supply a definite number of tablets—as opposed to small packs, I mean. Digoxin can't be sold over the counter, so it will be kept in bulk packs for prescription."

"What amounts would Whincap prescribe each time?"

"I should think fifty. He can't ask the chemist to do up thirty-one in January, twenty-eight in February and so on. It'll have to be a nice round number each time."

"The lads will manage that even though nobody leaves school as a numerate member of society these days—except for chalking up at darts matches."

"Mrs Rainford?"

"Might as well. I'll ring her old man on the internal to let him know we're going to his place."

Rainford led the way in his car. The first part of the journey from the old college building was through countryside, then a mile or so of town, and then out again to a pleasant suburb, past the small, elderly railway station and down a pleasant avenue of as good a mixture of houses, old and new, big and small, as any environmentalist could hope for. There was little moving traffic here and plenty of room to park outside the house. Of thirties' vintage, it stood alone. A four-bedroomed villa with a lot of whitened pebble-dash and applied wooden plates. Masters classified it as a mood house—in some moods he would feel comfortable living in it, but in others he would yearn for something less capable of being pigeon-holed as a classic representation of its time.

"The missus is in," said Rainford as they gathered on the pavement. "I did phone her, but only to warn that we might be coming." He grinned at Green. "I didn't even answer her question when she asked what you were like."

Green grunted his approval of this news and followed Rainford up the drive to the door.

"D.C.S. Masters and D.C.I. Green. Margarethe."

The introduction was simple in a house accustomed to welcoming policemen. Margarethe Rainford, fully composed despite the prospect of the interview, led them into her sitting room.

"It's nearly lunchtime," she said, "so I've brought the drinks tray in. Will it be in order to ask Theo to pour for us?"

Masters smiled. "In weather like this a cold beer would help matters along splendidly."

"Mr Green?"

"Me, too, love, please. If you're drinking yourself, that is?"

Margarethe laughed. "I shall have to keep my wits about me, but I'll hold a small sherry."

Rainford got the drinks. Masters, in an armchair alongside the fireplace, took out his pipe. He held it up towards his hostess. "May I?"

She seemed pleased to find it was to be so informal. Her husband, as if sensing that Margarethe had relaxed said: "They're clever-dicks, sweetheart. They claim they never grill anybody, but by heavens they can give you a roasting. I know. I've had some."

"Oh! Have they sorted you out?"

"And I'm not even implicated in this business except by association." He handed Margarethe her sherry.

Masters put a match to his pipe. There was a short silence while he watched the initial glow grow into an even burn. Green accepted his beer and broke the silence.

"Have you had our two sergeants round, ma'am?"

"They came for the pill bottle and the little duty roster I've kept. They asked a few questions about numbers, but all the information was on the list, because I'd put down when I got mother's new prescriptions."

"That's good." He took a large mouthful of beer. "So's this. Nicely cellared, Theo."

Rainford sat down. Masters turned to Margarethe. "The easiest answer to the problem confronting us, Mrs Rainford, would be if we could truly establish that your mother had fooled one or all of you three ladies who gave her a pill each day."

"By not swallowing them, you mean?"

"And saving them up until she had a lethal dose."

"I can't claim that, Mr Masters. I wish I could. But the whole object of the exercise was to prevent that very thing happening."

"So you are unable to confess to failure?"

"I—we—were at great pains not to fail. For my part I watched mother like a hawk when I gave her the pill. I had the tablet in one hand and a glass of water in the other. I handed them to her in turn and never took my eyes off her. And I'm sure Marian and Nurse Scramsie did the same because we agreed on the drill when we first started."

"Then, like Dr Whincap, you reject the easy answer?"

"The easy-to-come-by answer."

"Meaning what exactly, love?" asked Green.

Margarethe turned to him. "I've no doubt that the answer will be an obvious one, once you and Mr Masters have found it. It is probably staring us all in the face at this moment. But I cannot believe that mother was clever enough to fool all three of us or any one of us, because we were on the lookout for any tricks. And she wasn't a practised prestidigitator, I promise you."

Masters said, slowly, "Mrs Carlow overdosed herself on several occasions. The last time—previous to her death—was on Christmas Day, I think?"

"Yes."

"Your vigilance and that of your daughter and Nurse Scramsie prevented it happening again."

"Until..."

"Quite. But did she, at any time, to your knowledge, attempt to hold back her pill or even to mention the fact that she would again overdose herself if the means were available?"

"Never."

"Did she at any time refer—no matter how obliquely—to the previous occasions when she had overdosed herself?"

"No. Certainly not to me."

"Never? Not even when she was depressed?"

"She was never depressed."

"Between Christmas and May Day, you mean?"

"I mean ever."

"What state of mind, then, would you say your mother had been in on those occasions when she did overdose herself?"

"I know that sort of thing is supposed to be a cry for help from depressed people, but I can never recall my mother being depressed."

"So what state of mind would she have been in?" repeated Masters.

Margarethe considered this for a moment and then turned to her husband, as if for help. "I saw her on

Christmas Eve. She was busy with Mimi, preparing their food and cakes. I told you, didn't I, that not coming to Marian's party the next day didn't seem to be affecting her at all? It was Mimi who was the more upset at not joining us all for Christmas lunch."

Rainford nodded. Masters said: "The more upset? That sounds as if Mrs Carlow was showing some signs..."

"I put it badly. Mimi had wanted to come to the party. Mother had refused, and so Mimi couldn't come either."

"Ah," said Green. "Your mother had refused the invite?"

"Yes."

"Didn't feel like joining in the fun and games, eh? Not feeling too jolly, perhaps? Sort of depressed?"

"Honestly," said Margarethe, slightly exasperated, "you take a lot of convincing. Mother wasn't depressed."

Rainford said: "It's okay, Maggie. Don't let them needle you. I said you'd have to watch these two jokers."

"Oh, come now," said Masters. "I thought the D.C.I.'s line of reasoning was completely logical. Unless Mrs Carlow had a prior engagement for Christmas Day, one would expect her—under normal circumstances—to accept an invitation to a family party, particularly as her sister appears to have been keen to go."

Neither Rainford nor his wife replied to this statement. Masters looked from one to the other, but still neither volunteered a comment. After a moment or two of noticeable silence, Green said: "You're not helping us. Now why's that, I wonder?"

It was as if Margarethe Rainford tried deliberately to avoid replying to Masters' last point. Instead she harked back to the earlier part of the conversation. "Mother was not depressed on Christmas Eve nor, come to think of it, was she on Christmas morning."

"You saw her then?" asked Masters.

"I rang to wish her a happy Christmas."

"Early?"

"Quite early. Shortly after breakfast. I had quite a lot to do that morning before we went to my daughter's house, and I thought it best to get the call in early before I forgot it in all the welter of making the bed and gathering up the presents we were to take with us and so on."

"I understand. Your mother was cheerful at that time?"

"She was her usual mischief-making self," said Theo Rainford before his wife could reply.

"Oh?"

"Margarethe had bought her some very nice underclothes for Christmas. She'd really spoiled her and bought an expensive, dainty set that in my opinion would have pleased a young lass about to get married. Maggie had delivered it on Christmas Eve. On Christmas morning the old trout had opened it. When Maggie rang, there was nothing but complaints. First it was the wrong size. After she was told she was mistaken about that, she said it was the wrong colour. I've no doubt she'd have said it was the wrong material, too, if Maggie hadn't said she would collect it next day and change it as soon as the shops re-opened for business."

"That calmed her down a bit?"

"Not at all. She said she didn't want it changed. If Margarethe couldn't take the trouble to get the right thing the first time, she wasn't going to put her to all the bother of changing it. And so on. I had to step in. I took the phone and asked for Mimi, wished her a happy Christmas and then rang off."

"Could she have regarded your action as some form of rejection which, in turn, led to a sense of emotional deprivation sufficient to cause her to take an immature—but nevertheless dangerous—revenge on the rest of you?"

"Oh, no," breathed Margarethe. "Not that."

"Yes," said Theo emphatically. "Yes. That could be it."

Masters regarded him steadily.

"But I wasn't to know it would happen, was I?" asked Rainford, uncomfortable under scrutiny.

"No," agreed Masters reflectively. "But if I accept that your act of rejection had so explosive an effect on Mrs Carlow, I must enquire what similar act of rejection caused her to take a fatal overdose two days ago."

Rainford seemed pleased, even relieved, at the turn the conversation had taken. "I think that's an easy one to answer," he replied.

"Please tell me."

"An even bigger rejection. Elke was always saying how, when she was a girl in Prussia, the family was all-important and how the young took care of their elderly relatives by housing them, feeding them, etcetera."

"Theo!" complained his wife.

"It's true, love."

"I know. But must you tell all this to Mr Masters and Mr Green?"

"The best plan is to tell them everything, Maggie, because if you don't they'll find out for themselves. You've just had a taste of how they can interpret words and actions, and if we hold anything back they'll interpret that in some way we won't like."

"Don't frighten your missus, chum," said Green. "We're very gentle and we soon forget anything that isn't relevant." He turned to Margarethe. "Somebody you want to protect, love? Your daughter, perhaps?"

"Well, yes. You see, Marian and her husband have

bought a big old barn and are converting it into a house. They've got quite a long way with it. It is very habitable, in fact, but their money has run out and they can't do any more until they've saved up for materials. My mother heard from all of us—and Dr Whincap—what a nice house it is and how big. As soon as we'd told her all this, she decided she'd move in."

"With the youngsters?"

"Yes."

"What happened?"

"As luck would have it, the children have only built one bedroom—their own. So Adam thought he had the perfect excuse for not having Marian's grandmother. He told her—no bedroom and not likely to be until he had saved a lot more money."

"Rejection, in other words?" asked Masters.

She nodded. "But there was worse to come. Mother interpreted Adam's refusal to have her in entirely the wrong way."

"Ah! What did she think it meant?"

"If they regret they can't have me because there is no second bedroom, then they will be happy to have me when there is a second bedroom."

"Please go on."

"If the only obstacle in the way of building the necessary bedroom is lack of money, then if the money is provided, I shall be taken in."

"She offered to pay for the room?"

"Worse. Adam is doing the work himself. He said he was too busy trying to earn money to devote time to more home building, so mother sent a carpenter round to the house to measure up and start the job."

"Unbeknown to the young Whincaps?"

"Completely. It happened two or three weeks ago. On Good Friday actually. Adam, of course, sent the man away."

"I see. So it was now patently clear to Mrs Carlow that she wasn't wanted."

"Yes."

"There you are," said Rainford. "Total rejection. It fits in with your theory. Her day-to-day behaviour follows a pattern. Completely understandable. She repeated the trick she pulled at Christmas, but this time she went too far or Mimi didn't send for David Whincap quickly enough or..." He shrugged. "You seem to have got hold of the gist of your problem."

"Maybe. I'd be slightly happier, however, if I knew how Mrs Carlow got hold of the lethal substance she used for killing herself." Masters got to his feet. "Thank you, very much, Mrs Rainford. We'll be on our way now and let you feed your husband. No doubt we shall meet again before we return to London."

"Won't you stay to lunch? Just a salad and biscuits and cheese...?"

"No, ta, love," said Green. "We've this and that to do."

"Of course. But Theo must bring you in one evening for supper."

"We'll hold him to that. If we've time, that is."

Rainford ushered them out. "I expect you'll want to talk to Marian?"

"This afternoon perhaps. We'll give you a ring if you'd like to be there?"

"I would."

"In that case you can act as guide again. We'll be in touch."

"You were pretty anxious to get out of there," said Masters as he drove in the direction of the town.

"So were you," accused Green. "After having had no breakfast you weren't all that happy at the prospect of a lettuce leaf and a cream cracker for lunch. Any more than I was. And as we came through the town I lamped a healthy-looking pub with a food sign outside. Meat and spud pie at the bar! That's more like it for me."

"Actually," said Masters, slowing gently for a crossing, "I agree about lunch, but I was even more anxious to get away so that we could talk."

"I know," grumbled Green.

"Was it so very obvious?"

"To me. Not to them."

"Good." He pulled away. "Now, where's this pub?"

"Follow your nose. It'll be on your side going this way, but I reckon you'll have to risk a parking fine because it's bang on the main road."

Masters grimaced in reply as he slowed to pass a cyclist going in the same direction. Then he asked, "Did you guess what I wanted to talk about?"

"Something to do with Theo Rainford, not his missus."

"Right."

"He seemed to change his tune in the middle of that little conversation. First off they hadn't given the old girl cause to feel rejected at Christmas. His missus got quite hot under the collar at the very idea. Then Theo himself steps in and says yes, that's what it must have been. A feeling of rejection at Christmas and again at Easter."

"That's how I saw it, too," agreed Masters. "But didn't you think his willingness to accept that explanation was a little too ready?"

"Stuck out a mile."

"So there's some other explanation." He was by now negotiating the busy main street. "Where's the pub, Bill?"

"Up ahead. I can see it. About forty yards. On your right."

"Double yellow line, dammit. I'll have to turn left somewhere . . . ah! Parking sign ahead."

"Arrow pointing the way. Down the alleyway, George."

When they entered the bar it was Reed who called: "Over here, Chief."

"What are you two doing?" demanded Green.

"The same as you, I expect."

"Good. Make mine a pint and shove over one of those menus."

"We were just going round the corner of the bar. It's all laid out there and you can choose from the dishes."

"Tables?" asked Masters.

"Yes, Chief."

"Go and get one. I'll bring the drinks. Bill, I'll have a helping of anything that looks decent."

When they were sitting round the small table, Masters asked Reed how they were getting on.

"Not too badly, Chief. We've definitely established that the old lady only had enough pills to average out to one a day since Christmas."

"Assuming she had no initial stock and taking into account the number remaining on the present prescription?"

"Yes, Chief."

"So you're happy you can appear in front of the deputy coroner and tell him that there is cause for further inquiries to discover the source of the extra digitalis and then to decide how it found its way into the body of the deceased?"

"Just that, Chief. Then he'll adjourn, leaving you free to tackle the job in any way you like."

Green sighed and put his empty plate on the table. "Just the job that. Real tasty. Stopped my belly thinking my throat was cut. I'm tempted to have another helping."

"What's stopping you?"

"I don't want to appear greedy."

Berger spluttered with laughter as he drank.

"You? Greedy?" said Reed in mock surprise. "Who could possibly think such a thing?"

"In that case," said Green, "you can go and get it for me. And make sure there are some of the crispy scallops of spud on top. I like them."

"Sorry, I've got to go and see a coroner about an inquest."

Green grunted, whether in approval or disapproval was not clear. As the sergeants prepared to leave, Masters reminded them that Patrick Dean had promised him a copy of the pathologist's report. They were to collect it from the court and take it to the office in police HQ.

"Now," said Green when he and Masters were alone. "The Rainfords."

"Ah, yes. To my way of thinking, Theo accepted the rejection theory too easily. Why?"

"Tell me."

"If it were true, it would substantiate suicide. But the question would still remain, where did the toxic substance come from?"

"True. But the theory could still be right."

"I tend to think not, Bill. Compare the timings of Mrs Carlow's reactions. The Christmas Day overdose was taken at the time she was rejected—that is, when the party was due to begin. The May Day episode was two or three weeks after her rejection at Easter time. I don't think that a long gap like that would be typical of a would-be suicide who previously had reacted immediately."

"I see what you mean, George, but that raises another point. At Christmas she had the means to overdose herself, so she could react immediately. But what if she hadn't the means at Easter? She could have wanted to overdose at the moment of rejection, but had to wait until she could get hold of the poison. It could have taken her those intervening weeks to lay hands on it. Only after that could she take it."

"Not quite, Bill. Granted she hadn't the means at Easter, but if we accept that once she had the poison she would take immediate action, she could only have got the poison on May Day itself or—possibly—the day before."

"Fair enough. So now we check on her movements for those two days. It'll be a good job for the lads."

Masters nodded. "But we mustn't forget Rainford. I refuse to believe that he worked all this out for himself in the comparatively short time we were in his house."

Green agreed. "He isn't thick, our Theo, but he had some more down-to-earth reason for falling in with the rejection theory. Is that what you're saying?"

"I'd bet on it."

"So would I. So he's protecting somebody. Wife? Daughter? Son-in-law?"

"Somebody, certainly."

"How the hell are we going to find out which?"

"I'll get us another drink," said Masters rising and collecting the glasses.

"Which means you've got a bright idea," grumbled Green. "Okay, I'll wait. Do you reckon you could bring me a couple of those sausages while you're on your feet? The big ones with sticks in?"

"I'll sprout another pair of hands to carry them with."

"One hand will do for a couple of fried dogs."

When Masters returned, Green accepted his beer and sausages and immediately demanded to be told what Masters was thinking.

"We were told that Mrs Carlow refused to go to the family party on Christmas Day."

"Which means she wasn't rejected."

"No, no. Hold on to the rejection bit. Ask yourself why she should refuse to go to the party."

"Any number of reasons," said Green, taking a bite from the end of a sausage held in mid-air. "She probably didn't like turkey for Christmas dinner. I think I've heard it's not traditional in central Europe. The Prussians probably eat pork and wurst with pine cone stuffing or some such. When young Mrs Whincap refused to alter her menu her gran got uppity and refused to attend."

"Could be," agreed Masters. "There must certainly have been something about that party which she didn't like, and because the host and hostess wouldn't change things to suit her, she felt rejected."

"Ah! That's how. I get you, George."

"The result was she refused the invitation and took an overdose with the intention of ruining the day for everybody else."

"Which would have happened if old Whincap hadn't been sensible enough to contain it and didn't mention the incident till the danger was past."

"Quite. So, we've got Mrs Carlow wanting to ruin the party for the people attending it, and Theo Rainford wanting to protect some person. My belief is that the old woman refused to go to the party because she resented one of the people who was to be there and I think that Rainford is trying to shield that person from us."

Green explored his teeth with his tongue to dislodge a strand of meat. "An enemy," he said at last. "Somebody the old girl couldn't stand and, I reckon, who couldn't stand her in return."

"Does it fit?" asked Masters.

"Like a glove. You damn-well know it does. What we've got to do now is to identify the guest and look into his or her comings and goings for May Day and the day before…"

"I reckon that's the size of it. It's a working hypothesis at any rate. The big thing now is to get hold of that guest list."

"Rainford?"

"I think not. If he is trying to shield one of them, well, I'd prefer he didn't know exactly what we're after. If we asked him or his wife for the list he'd begin to divine our line of thought."

Green shrugged. "That cuts out his daughter and her husband, too."

"We'll ask Dr Whincap."

"He's the girl's pa-in-law. Why not try the coroner. Not Dean. The real one. Bennett."

"Fine. But they're all family."

"As coroner he should be able to keep his counsel and he's not immediate family. Only an uncle."

"Right. Are you fit, or would you like more sausages?"

"Enough is enough," said Green, getting to his feet. "Mustn't overdo it."

— 5 —

Bennett's office was in a wide road which ran parallel
to the main street. It had obviously been laid out and
built as a residential area from the Georgian period
onwards. The houses were of every style from those
with pillared porticoes, up to and including Edwardian.

"This," said Green, "reminds me a bit of George
Street, Edinburgh. I haven't been up there for years,
so it may not still be the same as I remember it, but it
always seemed quiet and residentially businesslike."

"I recall seeing a tackle shop with a full-sized stuffed
pony in the window."

"That's right. I liked it, that street. The big chains
had started taking over Princess Street and it wasn't
the same place any more. But that's by the way. Where
does Bennett hang out?"

"Eighty-three. Odd numbers this side, so it's about
a dozen houses further on."

The plate told them that Bennett, Chantler and
Hutcheson were housed on the first floor. Masters led
the way. The typist in the inquiries office didn't like
the idea of disturbing the senior partner for a couple
of strangers without an appointment. She suggested
that the managing clerk or even one of the young ar-
ticled gentlemen might help them, but Green put her

right. "This," he said, "is not business. It's an anti-social visit."

"Oh? You're friends of Mr Bennett, then?"

"I said anti-social, love. That means we're his enemies."

"I'll see what he says."

"Please tell him we're policemen," said Masters. "From London."

The girl disappeared. A moment or two later, Bennett himself appeared to escort them to his office.

"You bewildered young Sandra," he said with a grin. "She came in here and told me there were two police enemies of mine on an anti-social visit from London."

"My colleague likes to pull shapely legs," said Masters, not displeased by Bennett's apparent sense of humour.

"Don't we all." He picked up the copy of *The Times* spread on his desk. "I always try the crossword after lunch. I think I must be one of those afternoon people we heard so much about a few years ago."

"Interesting theory, that," said Masters. "But my wife was telling me recently that one of the women's programmes on TV was postulating that it all depends on whether one eats a hearty breakfast or not."

"How so?" He gestured to them to be seated.

"Some survey among schoolchildren. Those whose mothers gave them a decent breakfast performed normally in the classroom in the mornings. Those who didn't get a reasonable meal performed badly. After they'd all had a school lunch they all performed equally well."

"Sounds reasonable. I must get my missus to start giving me bacon and eggs of a morning. Then perhaps I could do this thing a bit quicker."

"Stuck?"

"And how! There's a twelve letter word here with a g six from the end. The ardent suitor and the runner on whom all eyes are focused have this in common."

"Carrying a torch," said Masters.

"I'd got that far. Never mind, I'll have another bash later. Now, what can I do for you, gentlemen? Something to do with Elke Carlow's death?"

"If you would, Mr Bennett. I'd like you to give me a full list of the guests at the Christmas party which I believe you attended at…what's the name of the house?"

"Helewou. Means end wall in old English or some such. But why come to me? Why not our hostess?"

"Because we don't want to upset the young lady," said Green. "Not nice for a young lass to find a couple of Scotland Yard men enquiring about her party if we can get the information from elsewhere."

"I admire the nicety of feeling," murmured Bennett.

"Flammigerous," said Masters. "Flame-bearing."

"What the hell?" demanded Green.

Bennett stared at Masters for a moment or two, switching his mind from the current discussion to the previous conversation.

"Right," he said at last and reached for his newspaper. "Two m's."

"Do you two mind?" said Green.

"Sorry." Bennett finished printing the word and laid down his pen. "You were asking about the people at the party."

"If we could get back to it," said Green heavily, notebook and pencil poised to make notes.

"Adam Whincap and his wife, Marian."

"What does he do?"

"He's a carpenter."

"A what?"

"Cabinet maker. Makes individual items of furniture. Damn' good they are, too. Destined to be highly prized antiques in about a hundred years from now."

Green nodded.

"Dr David Whincap and his wife, Janet, who is also my sister-in-law." He waited a moment till Green looked up.

"Marian's parents, D.C.S. Theo Rainford and his wife, Margarethe."

"We've met them already."

"Adam's sister, Gwen, and her husband, Tony Kisiel."

"Who is what?"

"A horticulturalist. He works with his father, Josef Kisiel, who was also present with his wife, Alice."

"He's a gardener, too?"

"If that's how you wish to describe a man with a large and flourishing business."

Masters interrupted. "Kisiel? How is it spelt?"

Bennett spelt it. "It's a Polish name. The Josef is e f, not e p h."

"What's a Pole doing in this neck of the woods?" asked Green.

"He came over here after the collapse of Poland and flew with the RAF. He got here in October thirty-nine, served right through the war. He met Alice here, married her and stayed on."

"Fine. Then there was you and Mrs Bennett?"

"Right. That's the lot. Elke Carlow and her sister, Frau Mimi Hillger had, I understand, been invited for lunch, but had refused the invitation."

"Why?" Masters shot the question out so suddenly that Bennett was momentarily taken aback.

"Why?" he repeated.

"Why did the two German ladies refuse Mrs Marian Whincap's invitation?"

"I realy don't know. I was just told they weren't coming, and like everybody else there, I suppose I heaved a sigh of relief. Old Elke was a damn nuisance to have around."

"I see. Please venture a guess as to why she and her sister stayed at home."

"I know why Mimi stayed. She couldn't come without Elke."

"Couldn't or wouldn't?"

"Couldn't. She was under Elke's thumb. She lives— or lived—in that house virtually as unpaid housekeeper."

"Mrs Carlow kept her? Gave her free food and lodging?"

Bennett seemed surprised by the question. "Do you know, I've never thought about that. But if I had to hazard a guess I'd have said that Elke was too mean-minded to do that."

"Mean-minded or mean?"

"I mean small-minded as opposed to stingy. It would be an effort for her to think of doing the generous thing, but, I suspect, once she'd thought of it, she would produce the wherewithal."

"A complicated woman, apparently."

"I'm talking off the record. I have no proof, merely an impression gained of acquaintance."

"Actually, I think we have a little proof to substantiate what you've said. But to return to my main point. Please give me your opinion as to why Mrs Carlow refused to attend the Christmas party."

"My opinion—guesses if you like—can have no place in your investigation."

"You shouldn't have said that," murmured Green. "His nibs here will now assume that you've retreated for safety on to the invalidity of guesswork because you do have an opinion—one you don't want to give us."

Bennett had the grace to laugh. "You're a couple of cross-talk twisters," he said. "The likes of poor solicitors like me need a court and the rules of evidence to protect us from the likes of you."

"Maybe," agreed Green, "but you're doing a good job of ducking the question, just the same. And the more you do it, the more we think you've got something you'd rather not tell us."

Bennett opened his mouth to reply when, after the tiniest of knocks on the door, Sandra entered. "There's Dr Whincap to see you, Mr Bennett."

"Show him in," said Bennett, jovially. He got to his feet to move round the desk to greet his brother-in-law.

"David! Come in, my dear chap. I think you've already met these gentlemen."

Whincap nodded. "This morning. But I'll go, Bob. I didn't know you were busy. Your girl didn't say."

"Join us," said Bennett, drawing up another chair.

"I've just come from the inquest," said Whincap."

"Dean opened and then adjourned immediately, I take it?"

"He heard a brief request from Mr Masters' detective sergeant for time to pursue inquiries. He said— luckily for me—that as the tablets prescribed seemed to be in order numerically,the question of where the lethal dose came from would have to be decided. Only then could the means by which it found its way into the body of the deceased be investigated. And that was that."

Bennett turned to Masters. "So now it's up to you officially."

Masters inclined his head. But to Bennett's surprise, he did not pursue the question as to why Elke Carlow had refused to join the Christmas party. Instead he turned to Whincap. "Are you anything of a psychiatrist, Dr Whincap?"

"I have never specialized in it."

"That sounds as though you are not entirely ignorant of psychiatry as a branch of medicine, however."

"Many years in general practice, allied to a bit of common sense, teach one quite a lot—building on the little one learned as a student. I must confess I read papers in the medical journals from time to time—if they are not too esoteric and appear likely to be of value to a family doctor."

"Good."

"But if we are going to discuss Mrs Carlow who was, remember, one of my patients..."

"You are reluctant to break confidentiality even in a case such as this?"

"Confidence is confidence. Oh, I know that I can be required to testify in the courts but, yes, I am reluctant."

"If I promise to keep the conversation general and recognize that you have your brother-in-law, who is a solicitor after all, present throughout...?"

Whincap thought for a moment. "I never treated Mrs Carlow for a mental problem, so if you really mean to stick to psychiatry, then I'll answer your questions if I can while reserving the right to refuse at any time."

"Just the jobbo, doc," said Green. "But keep it simple. George, here, took a degree in biological studies before he saw sense and joined the force. Me, I'm an elementary school product and don't know the difference between psychiatry and psychology."

"Psychiatry is the treatment of diseases of the mind. Psychology is the science of the nature and functions of the mind. They overlap of course."

"Ta."

"I promised to keep this general," said Masters. "And so I will."

"Thank you."

"Am I right in thinking that mental illness has many causes about which we know comparatively little?"

"It takes such a variety of forms that getting to grips with it is extremely difficult."

"There is a distinct possibility then that there are many cases of mental illness which are not treated."

Whincap grimaced. "Scores of thousands," he said.

"We—that is society—do not interfere so long as the peccadilloes caused by the mental illness don't cause us too much trouble or the patient himself harm, pain or inconvenience."

"Meaning there are lots of mental disorders not recognized as such?"

"There are all grades—from slight personal aberrations to the stage where the sufferer can become legally certifiable."

"So, we can assume that there are many people who do not reach a serious grade of abnormality but whom we regard as eccentric or slightly peculiar in some way who are, in fact, suffering from mental illness?"

"Wait a moment, Mr Masters. I'm not saying that Elke Carlow..."

"Please, doctor! We agreed to keep the conversation general. I was to try to avoid mentioning Mrs Carlow. But you have brought her name up."

Whincap apologized. "Your last assumption is correct," he said.

"Thank you. Now about the causes of mental disorder. Could you—if it is possible to do so—tell us what they are, doctor?"

"That is fairly well documented. There are two broad groups of causes. Causes which might not cause most of us any trouble at all, but which in those with a tendency to become disordered, can be devastating."

"Or relatively harmless?"

"Quite. It is a matter of degree."

"And the two broad groups of causes?"

"They are called predisposing causes and exciting causes."

"They sound almost self-explanatory. Are they?"

"Judge for yourself. In the first category you must appreciate that a mental weakness may be either inherited or acquired. You'll have heard the arguments concerning heredity and environmental factors. For myself I am of the opinion—based on experience—that the major predisposing cause is an abnormal temperament and that alone can be either inherited or acquired."

"Am I right in believing that the abnormal temperament is shown by what I would call bad or criminal behaviour?"

"Oh, yes. Not necessarily criminal, but irritating to society at large. Irritability, pessimism, disobedience, waywardness, jealousy. People who evince these traits to any great degree are the ones most likely to suffer a mental breakdown."

"Thank you." Masters looked across at Green. "Are you with us so far, Bill?"

"Just."

Masters turned back to Whincap. "I think you said the second category was called exciting causes. Does that mean actual physical stimuli contribute to mental disorder?"

"Most assuredly. Disease, exhaustion and so on are important causes—in those already predisposed to mental illness."

"Such causes produce stress, in fact?"

"Yes."

"Would poison produce stress?"

Whincap looked slightly taken aback. "Well, yes, as a matter of fact it would. These causes are divided by some authorities on the subject into toxic and exhausting causes."

Masters inclined his head to acknowledge this nugget of information. "Disease was mentioned. Influenza, typhoid, pneumonia? Things like that?"

"Yes."

"Only the acute ailments?"

"No. Chronic ones too. Anaemia, myxoedema, thyrotoxicosis, arteriosclerosis, kidney disease. Virtually anything."

"In that case would heart disease be an exciting cause of mental disorder in a predisposed patient?"

"It could," said Whincap heavily. "And now I'm going to mention Elke Carlow. She had very pronounced individual peculiarities and she had chronic heart trouble and she had, in effect, posioned herself on previous occasions. You are supposing that she was a mental case and, therefore, that I should have treated her as such."

"Not at all. I would not presume to question your treatment of any patient. Particularly as I know from my own experience that mental illness tends to disguise itself."

"How do you mean?" asked Bennett.

"It doesn't usually develop suddenly. It creeps up insidiously for the most part. And though sometimes there are indications of approaching breakdown which a doctor might notice, so often these symptoms are so slight as to be missed by even the keenest observer. Particularly when the patient is getting on a bit in years and it comes as no surprise if they do act a bit oddly."

"I'm pleased you appreciate that point," said Whincap. "I've known Mrs Carlow for so long as a cantankerous old woman that none of her foibles would ever come as any surprise to me. What I mean by that is that I would not notice an alteration in a disposition which I already knew to be characteristic unless that alteration were to be so exaggerated as to rouse my suspicions."

"Well said." Masters smiled at Whincap. "That is my point. A person could be mentally ill without showing specific symptoms, unless and until they became acute to the point of —shall we say—driving that person to suicide. And unless he were actually present at the time, the doctor would know nothing of the onset of such symptoms."

"Right."

"So, if I ask you if I am right to say that people who do suffer in this way fall into one or both of two categories..."

"Insane beliefs and or insane acts?"

"Precisely."

"You'd be right."

"A person of a naturally suspicious nature may begin to think that other people are slandering him, threatening him?"

"Yes."

"Rejecting him?"

Whincap nodded. Green gave a grunt as if to indicate that he was appreciating Masters' aim.

"That would be the insane belief. Could the insane act be to plan to take some form of revenge?"

"Undoubtedly. If the delusion was strong enough."

"Sometimes in the form of childlike petulance?"

"Meaning?"

"A refusal to go to a party in the hope that it would upset other people?"

"Ah! Other people? In the mass?"

Masters smiled again. "Your question suggests that in such delusions the sufferer attributes the causes to specific known persons."

"Just so. Their annoyance is not caused by something or someone they can't put a name to. They know the ones they think they can blame."

"Thank you. That's all I wanted to know, doctor. You have been most helpful and I am more than grateful."

"I can't see what I've done for you except to suggest that Elke Carlow was suffering from a mental illness which I didn't diagnose or treat."

"You don't know half of it, doc," said Green.

"Oh? Would you care to enlighten me?"

"Keep on listening."

Masters turned to Bennett. "Now, sir, before Dr Whincap joined us I asked you to give me your opinion as to why Mrs Carlow refused to join the family party at Christmas. You avoided giving me an answer though it was apparent from what you did say that you had a fair idea what the reason was. Now, after hearing that I have established cause to believe that Mrs Carlow was probably suffering from a mental illness which would drive her to imagine some personal slight or inimical action on the part of a specific person, which would in turn cause her to contemplate revenge, would you please answer my question?"

"You mentioned rejection."

"I believe I did."

Masters waited for Bennett to continue. The solicitor seemed at a loss. Eventually he said: "I spoke to Theo Rainford at lunchtime."

"Please go on."

"You mentioned rejection to him."

"I did indeed. I was considering it at the time. He seemed anxious to accept imagined rejection as a reason for suicide."

"Elke wanted to live with Adam and Marian. They turned her down, decisively."

"True. But that rejection had not occurred by Christmas. And I can hardly suppose that Mrs Carlow felt rejected by a granddaughter who invited her to a party and whom she held in such high regard that she wanted to live with her."

"She adored Marian," said Whincap.

"Your son, too, apparently, if she wished to make her home with him."

"And she liked her daughter, Margarethe, didn't she?" asked Green.

"Yes."

"And yourself? She relied on you, doc?"

"I suppose so."

"That leaves us with seven centres of fear, suspicion, hatred or what you will," said Masters. "Her son-in-law, Mrs Whincap senior, the four Kisiels and you, Mr Bennett, and Mrs Bennett."

The solicitor turned to his brother-in-law. Whincap replied to the mute appeal for help. "There's no point in keeping our counsel, Bob. In fact, I think it would be for the best were we to say what we know."

Green said: "A bit of enmity around and about, was there?"

"Yes," said Bennett sadly. "Elke Carlow and Josef Kisiel were lifelong enemies and neither would appear in the presence of the other."

"Thank you," said Masters. "I shall not ask you to tell me what the bone of contention was. My only question is why, if she knew of this ill-feeling, did Mrs. Marian Whincap invite both to her party?"

Bennett shrugged. "You'll have to ask Marian that. All I can say, and I'm sure David will support me in it, is that Josef Kisiel is as gentle a man as one could wish to find and would not harm anybody."

"Even a lifelong enemy?"

"I think..." began Whincap.

"Yes, doctor?"

"Josef Kisiel is a garrulous foreigner. As is the way with Poles, his language is sometimes a little extravagant. At times he says more than he means."

"Been uttering threats, has he?" asked Green in a matter of fact voice.

"No. Not threats. He has sometimes expressed the wish that...that some miracle would rid the world of Elke Carlow. But that is as far as it went. Intemperate language, but never translated into action. Like Bob, I'm sure of that."

"We'll remember your remarks," said Masters. "But there must be another side to the coin. The dead woman hated Kisiel. What had she to say about him?"

"Ah! Now she was, in my opinion, the more venomous of the two. Wouldn't you have said so, Bob?"

"Without a doubt," said the solicitor. "Her hatred was based on Prussian arrogance. She considered the Poles a lesser breed."

"One of the old school," said Green. "Did she spit when she heard his name?"

"Almost. It was ludicrous—or would have been if it hadn't been so meant. But there, you three say she was mentally ill. Not clinically, perhaps..."

Masters got to his feet. "Thank you, gentlemen."

Bennett also rose. "Am I allowed to ask if you are definitely treating the case as one of murder?"

"I am not unwilling to give you a direct answer, Mr Bennett. But I'm not prepared to be specific. I mean, were I to say yes and we eventually discovered a suicide, I should emerge with egg on my face. Perhaps the best way to describe our investigation is that it will be all-embracing. In other words, we want to get to the bottom of it, whatever happened."

"It leaves those of us connected with the case in an uncomfortable position," said Whincap.

"Not you, David," protested Bennett. "You were at pains to protect the old bird from herself and it was you who set this inquiry in motion. You could have signed the death certificate and said nothing of your suspicions."

"Then the doctor really would have felt uncomfortable," said Masters. "And I suspect that you, as coroner, might then have instituted an inquiry."

"Not if I hadn't known what David had to say about it. After all, I knew Mrs Carlow had had a dicky heart for years."

"But you also knew she had overdosed herself on several occasions previously. It would have been incumbent upon you to call for a pathologist's report even had she died—apparently—of natural causes."

Green looked at Bennett. "You see, chum, when

George talks about an all-embracing investigation, he means he has to consider whether you and the doc, here, aren't in collusion to appear as pure as pure, having pulled a very clever fast one on us."

"Wait a minute!" exploded Whincap.

"Don't get your hair off, doc. We're not accusing you or Mr Bennett..."

"I should hope not."

"But stand aside from your real selves for a moment. Think of two other chaps in your situation who decide to get rid of somebody. The doc does his bit of hanky panky and the coroner says to him. 'You're in the clear because nobody will think you would report this if you weren't. Now I'm going to put myself in the clear by handing it over to my deputy. Everybody will agree that if I'd been guilty I'd have kept the job in my own hands where I could do a cover-up job.'"

"And you mean to say you really think along those lines?"

"Not exclusively," said Green. "But we consider the possibility. You see, we look for means, motive and opportunity. Judge for yourselves how many of those three categories you two could fill quite easily were you to put your minds to it." He grinned suddenly. "Oh, I know it sounds fantastic to you two gents, but we're outsiders, remember. We don't know you as pillars of society. And here's a thought for you. If this is murder, and we find the person responsible, given the present cast list, it seems highly probable that the person whose collar we feel will be just that—one of your own highly respected group."

There was a short silence. Then—

"You're right, of course," said Whincap. "And that doesn't make me feel any the less uncomfortable."

"Nor me," admitted Bennett. "That damned woman was a pain in the neck alive and a hell of a sight worse now she's dead. And quite frankly I don't like the prospect of one of my friends having to spend the rest of his life behind bars on her account."

Masters said: "Sorry to have upset your afternoon, gentlemen. But I don't suppose I need comfort you with the thought that clear consciences will make for a swift recovery."

"You put it across them, Bill," said Masters as they walked to the car.

"Funny thing is," said Green, "that I didn't intend to. I liked both of them."

"You don't see either of them as our man?"

"No. And I'm experienced enough to realize that I can't judge by outward appearances. But I was just a little irritated by a coroner and a doctor trying to shield a name from us. They should know better and both should have a sense of public duty."

"I'm sure they have. But it is conflicting with private loyalty in this case."

"Right. But when they appeared to think we should assume their innocence—on their own sayso—then I thought I'd look for a mental pin with which to burst their balloons. No harm in that, was there?"

"None whatever. Right, in you get."

"Where are we off to now?" asked Green fastening his seat belt.

"HQ first. The sergeants could be there. Then we'll tell Theo Rainford we're going to see his daughter."

"He'll love that."

"We're doing him a courtesy," said Masters, starting up and drawing away. "But he's like the two we've just left. Rank and station cut no ice when outside investigators like us are brought in, and so he's unsure."

"About what? His own position?"

"His own if he is implicated. But he can't be sure about his missus and daughter. He'll be at our side whenever we give him permission. And he'll try to pump us."

"Us?"

"The sergeants are part of us. If he doesn't go for you and me he could have a bash at Reed and Berger, in the hope that they will stand in awe of his rank and that they will be privy to our thoughts."

"They won't trot it out for him," said Green with conviction. "We sometimes forget how bright those lads can be, even though they act as soft as Joe Soap at times. They've enough sense to know when they're being got at."

"I don't underestimate them."

"No?"

"You obviously think I do."

"As often as not you operate in a rarified atmosphere. They can't get up there. Sometimes you don't make allowances."

"That's not it," said Masters petulantly. "My mind ticks over in private. I can't be expected to explain its processes."

Green lit a Kensitas. "I know. Like that crossword clue. Flammigerous. It just came into your head and you didn't know how."

"Right. I've got that sort of mind."

Green grunted. "That's all right then. The sergeants won't have anything to tell Rainford even if they wanted to—except where we've been and the people we've talked to."

Masters glanced at him. "Is this a rocket, Bill?"

"If you like. But nobody's ever going to get you to keep your feet on the ground."

"I see. Now, what's the trouble? Something's worrying you about this case."

"Not the case," confessed Green. "Personal."

"Ah! You've got the hump, is that it?"

"You could put it that way."

"And you need my help—even if only as a listener—but you think my feet are too far off the ground for me to be of use."

Green grunted. It was impossible to say whether it conveyed agreement or the opposite. Masters, used to such equivocal replies, waited a moment in case his subordinate wished to expand the reply and then said: "If you care to tell me, Bill, I'll try to remain anchored."

"Retirement," said Green laconically.

"Ah yes! The A.C. Crime called you in a couple of days ago. I think I guessed why."

"So you know what he said?"

"No. It was a private and personal matter—or so I assumed. Had it not been, Anderson would have mentioned it to me."

"I'm living on borrowed time. Anderson's words."

"Then our revered lord and master was talking through the top of his hat. For two very good reasons, the Yard has kept you on after the normal retiring age. The first reason—you're a valuable asset, the second—there's a shortage of coppers."

"A year at a time," replied Green, not displeased by Masters' remark about his value to the Yard. "It's time for the annual review—well, in six weeks' time at any rate."

"And?"

"The money-saving boys have said nobody is any longer to be kept on after retiring age."

"Did Anderson say definitely that you had to go?"

"Ninety-nine percent certain. He said you'd recommended I should be kept on, but he didn't think he could swing it."

"Did he say he had endorsed my recommendation?"

"Yes. And thanks for what you said."

"I put the truth as I see it in those reports. There's no need to thank me for doing that. It's my job."

Green grunted again. Masters waited.

"So, George, this could well be the last time I'll be around with you and the lads."

Masters pulled the car up in the space allotted to him at the HQ building. He stayed in his seat.

"Bill, I know it's easy for me to say, but you're not done yet. If you really want to stay..."

"Would I have stayed on this last year, otherwise?"

"True, but attitudes can change."

"Not mine. I'm as set in my ways as the sphinx."

Masters turned to him. "In that case, have I your permission to see what I can do? Obviously I can promise nothing, but please believe that I have thought of this problem for some time, and I'm prepared to go in to bat for you."

Green unfastened his seat belt. "Doris would be grateful," he said.

Masters smiled. Even at such a time Green found it hard to say thank you on his own behalf. His wife would be grateful, indeed! Masters decided to keep it on the distaff side. "Wanda would want me to do what I can."

Reed and Berger were waiting in the office.

"Everything went as planned, Chief," said Reed, "and I've got you a copy of the pathologist's report."

"Thank you. Have you read it?"

"Yes, Chief."

"And?"

"I don't think there's anything in it we didn't know."

"Let me see."

Masters studied the report for a few moments.

"Cardiac glycosides," he murmured. "A large overdose."

"Now what?" asked Green.

"Thinking aloud," said Masters. "These technical

127

bods! He doesn't refer to digitalis or digoxin—he calls them cardiac glycosides. He estimates she had more than ten times the normal dose."

"So?"

"He says it must have been a single overdose as opposed to medicinal doses which were too large, taken over a long period."

"No build-up, you mean? That's dandy for Whincap."

"Quite. He says she would have been extremely ill long before the day of her death if it had been a build-up to that amount. So he estimates the overdose was taken about two hours before she became seriously ill. There are no punctures on the body, so the overdose was not injected."

"Taken by mouth. That's what we thought, isn't it?"

"He had to mention it."

"These glycosides, Chief..." began Berger. "She was on digoxin. Is that a glycoside?"

"Somewhere here," said Masters, running his finger over the text, "... where is it now? Hold your ears back. Digoxin is a crystalline glycoside obtained from *Digitalis lanata*. It is used for the same purpose as digitalis."

"Then what is digitalis?"

"Foxglove," said Green. "It means fingers or thimbles or some such."

"What colour is it?" asked Masters.

"Purple."

"Thanks. Then that explains the difference. The latin for purple is purpurea. So, I suspect straight digitalis comes from *Digitalis purpurea*, while digoxin comes from *Digitalis lanata*. And before you ask, lanata means woolly or hairy. In other words, they are both species of foxglove and... ah, he does refer to digitaloid drugs."

"Like mild and bitter," said Green. "Both have the same effect but taste different. Now, if that's the lot, how about telling Rainford we're about to call on his daughter for a cup of tea?"

"I've told Marian you're going out to Helewou," said Rainford. "Just to make sure she's at home when we get there."

"Thank you. Would you mind leading the way?"

"All four of you going out there?"

"Yes. For your information, since Mr Dean adjourned the inquest to allow further police inquiries, none of my team is now acting as coroner's officer, and I propose to treat the case just as one of unnatural death and not necessarily one of murder."

"That's something at any rate."

"They are not mutually exclusive."

"Maybe. But we all know the death was unnatural, so we accept that. We can still believe it was suicide or an accident. But murder in one's family takes some swallowing."

"I appreciate your point. We'll try not to distress Mrs Whincap. So if you'll lead the way..."

After motoring a few miles the cars pulled on to the concrete apron on the front side of Helewou.

"Cooee."

Masters, getting out of the car, saw Rainford waving to a young woman standing at the top of the flight of steps that led up to the bank at the end of Adam Whincap's workshop. She had a scarf round her head, a washed-out cotton dress, bare legs and sandals, was wearing red rubber gloves and had a trowel in one hand.

"Doing a bit of gardening," said Rainford.

"So I see."

"Sorry. What I meant was that their garden is up there on the bluff—higher than the house, actually."

"Interesting and different. I can see why the house

is called Helewou, too. I like the idea of it being end-on to the road. Far better than facing it."

"Hello."

Marian had removed her headscarf and gloves. Rainford kissed her cheek. "These are the big bad wolves from Scotland Yard." He introduced them in turn to his daughter.

"Mummy rang me after you'd visited her this morning."

"To say we were ogres, love?" asked Green.

"Actually, she said you weren't too bad."

Reed and Berger exchanged grins. Masters would love hearing himself described as not too bad. But he seemed to be taking it fairly well. "In that case, Mrs Whincap, our third degree will hold no terrors for you."

"Don't you believe it, Mr Masters. I'm shaking like a jelly."

"If you are nervous, love," said Green, "how about making a dirty great pot of tea to settle your nerves before we begin the conversazione? That'll give you a chance to get your legs back and we can have a look at the inside of this nice house of yours."

"Make yourselves at home," she said, leading the way through the stable door. "Daddy will act as guide if you need one."

"I like it," said Masters a few minutes later after Rainford had given him a brief conducted tour. "I admire the way youngsters are prepared to take on a property like this these days and literally build a home."

"Most people are of the same opinion," said Rainford. "Of course, the likes of us couldn't have done it. But young men like Adam..."

"What about Adam?" asked Marian coming in with a tray of tea cups.

"We haven't seen him yet," said her father. "Is he about?"

"If he's putting a finish on something you won't see him until he reaches a stage where he reckons he can stop." She put the tray down. "If he's waxing or polishing it would take an earthquake to get him to leave it in the middle."

"Understandable," said Masters. "If one is putting the top coat of paint on a door one is loath to break off before it's finished."

"I won't be a moment. I'll just fetch the teapot and milk jug."

"Let me help," offered Berger, following her out of the sitting room.

"Nice lass," said Green to Rainford. "Nice and nice looking."

"Not bad," agreed Rainford, striving hard to prevent the parental pride from breaking through. "She's a hard worker, too."

"She goes out to work?"

"No. She runs the house and garden and does Adam's accounts, to leave him free to work. But it's not just ledgers and journals, you know. There's cost accounting comes into it and VAT and so on."

"Quite a job," agreed Masters.

"But now she's started up a part of the job on her own. She's actually earning money in the workshop."

"Helping her old man stain and grain?" asked Green.

"No. Entirely her own show."

"Good for her." Masters got to his feet to clear some magazines off the low table Marian was approaching with the teapot. Berger was carrying a stand for the pot and a cork mat for the milk jug as well as the jug itself.

"Was daddy telling you about my industrial venture?" she asked after thanking Masters.

"He was. I'm very anxious to hear all about it."

"I've only made a few pounds," she said modestly.

"Dammit, Marian," said her father, "you didn't start

up until well after Christmas."

"Tell me," requested Masters, accepting the first cup of tea poured.

"It's very simple really," she began. "Adam keeps very carefully all his offcuts of wood. But even so, there are hundreds of little pieces of all shapes. Bits about as big as a matchbox or smaller—cubes, rectangles, circles, comma-shaped, every shape in fact. Of all sorts of wood—oak, mahogany, walnut, pine..."

"Marian collects them all," said Rainford.

"And all the old bits of glass paper," continued Marian. "I tear that up into quite small pieces and I put it, with my little bits of wood, into a rotating drum. Adam fixed one up for me. He made it out of an oil drum and the electric motor from a washing machine."

"Belt driven?" asked Berger.

"Yes. All the bits came from a washer. I switch it on for an hour or so, and the little pieces of wood come out as smooth as smooth. It really is amazing."

"Like those pebble polishers," said Berger.

"Much quicker than those," said Rainford. "And I think it might be quicker if we could find some really fine sand. We could throw a handful in."

So you get highly polished little bricks?" asked Masters.

"I don't stop there," said Marian. "I've got a net made of fine chicken wire. I bundle all my bits into it and then dip it in a bath of linseed oil. I only leave it there for a few minutes then I lift it on to a hook above the bath so that the bricks can drain and dry."

"Boiled linseed oil?" asked Berger.

"Oh yes! That leaves a sort of polish on the wood like a varnish. But it isn't varnish and it's not dangerous if children put them in their mouths."

"You sell them as bricks?" asked Masters.

"Yes. Children, it seems, like all the odd shapes. Prefer them to regular bricks, in fact. They can build

132

such different things with them. I've only sold to infant schools and play schools so far. I just weigh them up and put them in plastic bags."

"Sold by weight, eh?" said Green. "And no fancy packing. I reckon the teachers will go for those in a big way."

"They appear to," said Marian.

"A very good idea," said Masters. "I hope you are successful with it."

"But the idea isn't new," admitted Marian. "There's at least one firm been producing them for years. I'm having to break into the market. But it doesn't matter, because they cost me next to nothing. The oil has been the only real expense so far."

"I still congratulate you," said Masters.

"She's going to buy a press with the money she earns," said Rainford.

"What sort of press? Welsh dresser or...?"

"Mechanical," said Marian. "To press and bale all the wood shavings and sawdust into bricks for burning. We think we'll be at least able to beat the workshop with it. I sweep it up every day. I've got sacks of it to start on when I can afford the press."

"I'm impressed," said Masters, putting his empty cup on the table.

Marian blushed with pleasure. "It seems such a pity to throw it all away."

"Too true, lass," said Green. "And talking of presses, do you mind if I squeeze that pot to see if there's a drop left in it? Better belly bust than good tea be lost, as my old mother used to say."

Marian laughed and rose to take his cup. "We seem to think alike, Mr Green."

"I hope so, love, because we've got a question or two to ask you."

"Oh, yes. I'd almost forgotten what you came for."

"Ta." Green took his refilled cup and sat down again.

Masters took out his pipe, looked at it for a moment and then put it away again. Everybody seemed to be waiting for him to speak.

"Mrs Whincap," he said at last, "were you aware of a feeling of mutual enmity between your grandmother and Mr Josef Kisiel?"

Rainford drew in his breath. "What sort of a question is that to ask her?" he demanded.

Masters turned a bland face to the Chief Superintendent. "What was wrong with the question?"

"You're asking for a young girl's impression as to a motive for murder."

"I am asking a mature married woman for a factual reply to a question which was in no way loaded to provide reason for a motive for anything." He turned to Marian. "I'd be glad of an answer, Mrs Whincap."

"I did know they didn't like each other. I've always known."

"You've always known that there was a deep-seated hatred between them?"

"She said dislike," growled Rainford.

Green said, "Don't keep chipping in, chum. You're making everybody nervous."

"Deep-seated hatred, Mrs Whincap?" repeated Masters.

"I suppose so."

"I'll take that as meaning yes. Now, knowing that they were enemies, why did you invite them both to your Christmas party?"

"Why?" She seemed amazed by the question.

"Because they were both family," snapped Rainford.

"Why, please, Mrs Whincap?"

"Well . . . as daddy said . . . though Josef and Alice aren't really family, Adam's sister Gwen is married to their only son, Tony, and I thought that they would like . . . oh! don't you see, it was Christmas and our first party and I wanted everybody to be together and be happy."

"You are saying you hoped for a reconciliation between Mrs Carlow and Mr Kisiel?"

"Yes, I suppose so."

"Did you really think you could bring that about?"

"What's that supposed to mean?" asked Rainford.

"It's plain enough," growled Green.

"No," admitted Marian, "I didn't think that. In fact I knew that one or the other of them wouldn't come if I invited both."

"Then I can only assume that the person you didn't wish to have here was your grandmother."

"How the hell do you make that out?" demanded Rainford.

Masters turned to him. "If Mrs Whincap had wished to have her grandmother here, she would not have invited Mr Kisiel, knowing that the two refused to attend the same functions. By inviting Mr Kisiel, she was as good as saying to her grandmother that the invitation issued to her was nothing more than a duty invitation which she, your daughter, did not expect to be accepted."

"But that...that's monstrous," protested Marian.

Green shook his head sadly. "No it isn't, love. You knew they couldn't be reconciled, yet you invited both. One had to give way. If you'd really wanted your gran here, you wouldn't have run the risk of having her refuse for the sake of a distant relative by marriage of your husband's. But by putting her in the position of having to make a choice—a choice of which you already knew what the outcome was bound to be—you virtually said to the old girl that she wasn't wanted."

"No. No. It wasn't like that."

"Then how was it, love?"

Marian didn't answer. She looked unhappily at her father, who shrugged his shoulders as if to say that he had at last realized the logic of the Yard men's claim.

"I wish Adam was here," said Marian.

Masters looked across at Reed. "See if you can find Mr Whincap, please, Sergeant. He's probably in the workshop building behind the house. Tell him Mrs Whincap would like him to join her."

Reed rose to go on the errand. Marian said: "Daddy, do you really think gran was clever enough to work all that out?"

"More cunning than clever," replied Rainford. "She'd probably sense it by instinct rather than by thinking it through."

Masters addressed Rainford. "At the end of our talk this morning, you accepted the rejection theory that I put forward."

"Aye! You conned me into that."

"Did I? I thought you accepted it with relief and a good deal of alacrity."

"Well I don't accept it now if by proving that Marian rejected her grandmother at Christmas you're somehow going to pin the blame on her."

"On whom?" asked a voice from the door.

"Adam!" Marian ran to him. He held her close. "What are they blaming you for?"

"Gran's death."

Adam Whincap looked across as the other men sitting in the easy chairs and sofa near the empty fireplace. "Who is?" The tone held the beginnings of belligerence.

Masters stood up. Compared with Whincap, who was himself a very tall young man, Masters appeared huge, almost intimidating when the atmosphere grew tense. "Please tell your husband which of us has accused you, of what, and in what words." It was a command rather than a request.

Marian was near to tears. It was her father who answered for her. "Nobody has actually accused Marian of anything, Adam. It was me, shooting my mouth off, who mentioned blame. I said it was not to be attached to her."

Whincap looked down at his wife. "Is that right, darling?"

"Their questions were... they were horrible and accusing. They twist everything so."

"Not true, love," said Green, going across to her. "We've twisted nothing. All we've asked you for is exact meanings of what you've said and what you did. Because that's what we have to do. Don't forget, either, that we came out here to see you. We didn't ask you to come and see us. And we let your dad sit in to give you moral support."

"I still think you were trying to trap me."

"Into what, love?"

"Into saying something that would make me seem guilty of something."

"No," said Masters sternly. "I won't have that. The last thing I want is for an innocent person to appear guilty. For one thing it offends my sense of justice, and for another, false ideas like that are a nuisance. They get in the way. So can we please get on? My last question to you, Mrs Whincap, was whether Mrs Carlow could have come to the conclusion that your action in inviting Mr Josef Kisiel here on Christmas Day was as good as saying that you did not wish her to come despite her invitation."

Marian looked at her husband, who answered for her. "We felt in duty bound to ask both, knowing that one or the other would not come."

"Thank you. So I am right in my belief that you really preferred the presence of Mr Kisiel to that of Mrs Carlow."

"I don't know how you make that out."

"Mrs Carlow was more a member of the family than Josef Kisiel. Therefore she had a prior claim on your hospitality at an avowedly family party. Yet you jeopardized her acceptance by inviting a man whom you knew she would refuse to countenance. That indicates that you were not completely enthusiastic about her acceptance, while the fact that you invited an unacceptable man outside the family circle argues that you had hopes he would accept."

Whincap wiped floury sawdust from his chin. "You may be right, but I can assure you Marian and I did not think like that."

"Thank you. Your thoughts at the time do not concern me, so I will take your word that the outcome of your actions did not occur to you. But I am concerned with the interpretation Mrs Carlow put on them. Mrs Whincap mistakenly believes that I am accusing her of something. I repeat, I am not. But I should like to know if Mrs Carlow interpreted her action—probably mistakenly—as I have done."

Whincap, dressed in dusty, soiled old slacks and sweat shirt, released his wife before attempting his reply.

"My answer to that is that I believe she would not interpret it at all. She would just be bloody angry that Josef Kisiel had been invited. Reason would not enter into it."

"So you don't think she would feel rejected?"

"No."

"Thank you. That's all I wished to establish."

"That's it?"

"I think so."

"So I'm wrong in your eyes, am I?" asked Rainford.

Masters smiled. "Not at all. I think you're both right—you and Mr Whincap."

"How do you make that out?"

"Mrs Carlow couldn't have felt immediately rejected by your daughter because she sought on several occasions to come and live with her. That supports Mr Whincap's belief. But—and before I continue, let me stress I am not laying blame at anybody's door—these young people quite rightly did all they could in as nice a way as possible to stop her descending on them, bag and baggage. Eventually she must have realized she wasn't wanted in this house." Masters turned to Whincap. "It was probably when that particular penny dropped that Mrs Carlow harked back over past grievances and came to the conclusion that she hadn't been really wanted at the Christmas party either."

"A question of timing then?" asked Rainford.

"Just so. But to set Mrs Whincap's mind at rest I should add that I think she would have been wrong to have brought her grandmother here."

"You can say that again," said Whincap. "She really was the most objectionable old bird..."

"Adam!"

"Sorry, darling. But she was."

Green said: "You know, love, I think you've got this room just right. And I like those little pots of lily of the valley about the place."

Marian opened her eyes wide at this sudden and unexpected switch. "Do you like lily of the valley?"

"Well, now, I have to confess that it's my missus who's really gone on them. She uses the scent, you see. When I was courting—and it stil happens occasionally—I used to buy her little bottles called Muguet de Bois for presents. The packs always had lilies of the valley on them."

"That sounds nice. I grow them in the garden."

"Up on top of the hill?"

"That's right. Where I was when you arrived."

"I'd like to see your garden."

"Would you really? It's not in very good order yet. We've not had it a full year you see."

Whincap said: "Marian's proud of the garden as she's every right to be. She's done it all herself."

"Except the heavy digging," complained Rainford. "She roped me in for that."

"And mummy helped," confessed Marian. "The bulbs are over, but she put them all in." She moved towards the door. "But if you'd like to look..."

Masters went along, too. He chatted to Whincap as they fetched up the rear of the procession.

"Do you design your own pieces, or do you copy?"

"I design, but I lean heavily on traditional examples."

"Not modern stuff?"

"No."

"You don't like it?"

"It doesn't happen to be my market. I've found there's a definite return to the traditional after the flurry of modern stuff in the sixties. Youngsters—or some of them—like the newer stuff, but even the best of that is on traditional lines. All this very popular pine furniture—round tables, Welsh dressers and rush-bottomed chairs—all old stuff newly presented."

"Kitchens?"

"Ah, yes. Very modern. That's where the new caught on and has stayed. Quite right, too. It makes for easier work."

"George!" Green's voice from the upper level caused Masters to look upwards as he climbed the steps slightly ahead of Whincap.

"George, come and look at this."

As he reached the top, Masters imagined Green was referring to the general layout of the garden which certainly looked impressive though obviously, as yet, new and undergrown. The shrubs were not bushed-up, the perennials not yet massed into the cushions which declared a year or two of comfortable occupation of their beds, nor were the fruit trees more than spindly.

But the grass—obviously old turf—had been mown so often—last year and this—that it was fast turning into a lawn with well trimmed edges and an interesting rolling unevenness to declare that it had not been laid for formality.

"Very nice, indeed," said Masters. "Your wife must have worked hard to turn this from paddock into garden in about one year."

"She's determined to get everything just so. And fast."

"George, just look at this." Green was becoming a little peremptory. Masters moved over towards one of the flower borders where Green was standing with Marian. They were looking down at lily of the valley plants, each one covered by a jam jar.

"You use the jars as cloches, Mrs Whincap?"

"They act as cloches, but the jars are better. Mr Kisiel taught me. This is how he brings on his lily of the valley for May Day. You know he has a big garden centre and grows thousands of plants?"

"I had heard."

"He gave me these plants. In Poland and Russia and places like that, lilies of the valley are important flowers. Long before there was communism and labour days May Day was celebrated just as it was in England. Only where we had maypoles to go with the fairs and feasting, they gave each other little posies of lily of the valley for good luck. To make sure the blooms were ready in time and not knocked about by the weather, they always put jam jars over them. I suppose they were cheaper than cloches would have been for the peasants, but Mr Kisiel says they are better, too, because they are narrower and you can hold the leaves up straight inside."

"They do get rather floppy," agreed Masters. "They're so wide and heavy."

"Yes. And the plants come up all higgeldy-piggeldy

and so close together that you need a narrow thing like a jam jar for each one, rather than those wide bell-cloches."

"I'll remember this wheeze," said Green. "When I see how nicely yours are flowering... well, when I left home there was just a hint of a flower or two on mine. But yours... lovely, and such fat flowers."

Marian turned to him shyly. "If you would like some to take to Mrs Green just before you go home, please ask me. There'll be plenty left. Look, the stolons are still coming up all over the place."

"Thanks, love. I'll remember that."

"And for Mrs Masters," said Marian, as if suddenly remembering the presence of the man who had questioned her so closely a short time before.

"Thank you. Wanda would like them. She always lived with a garden until we married. Now we have to make do with large pots dotted about a very small paved yard. The D.C.I. had to give me a sack of soil with which to fill them."

"What a pity. You can buy bags of peat and potting composts, you know."

"Don't be fooled by him, love," said Green. "His little missus has got it lovely."

Before Marian could reply, her husband joined them. "I've got a deadline to meet on an order, gentlemen, so if you'll excuse me, I'll get back to my bench. If you have time and are interested, I'd be happy to show you over the shop before you return to London."

"Thank you, Mr Whincap. I'd like that. And we must be going, too, otherwise, we shall be eating into your evening leisure time."

— 6 —

"Talking of eating," said Green as soon as they were in the car, "I hope you're not thinking of patronizing the HQ cafeteria again. There must be somewhere round here where we can get a decent meal."

Rainford was not guiding them. He had stayed behind with his daughter, so he was not likely to be available to recommend a good place for dinner.

"We saw a couple of reasonable-looking places," said Berger.

"Pubs?" queried Green.

"Restaurants. One Greek and the other British."

"Greek," said Green in disgust. "Everybody wrapped in vine leaves or cut to bits and stuck on a skewer. And the wine's got cat-gut polish in it."

"Meaning you would prefer the British one?"

"Too right. You've heard of Montezuma's revenge," Malta Dog and Gippy Tummy?"

"Go on."

"The equivalent on the other side of the Adriatic from Italy is called Agamemnon's Agony. It catches you in the middle of the third hour after you've eaten..."

"What the devil are you talking about, Bill? If it caught you in the middle of anything, it wouldn't be the third hour after you'd eaten."

"No?"

"No, such things are never specific as to time, only to place. It might catch you in the middle of nowhere, which might not be too bad, but generally it strikes when you are three miles from what are coyly referred to as mod cons."

"Chief," said Reed, puzzled at what was going on, "have you solved this case?"

"No."

"You're acting as if you had."

"In that case I apologize for misleading you."

Green lit a Kensitas from a battered packet. "As long," he said, "as any misleading there is doesn't result in us missing the first proper sit-down meal we'll have had since we got here, I don't mind."

"I'd prefer to have a bath before we eat," said Masters. "The day has been long and sticky."

"Sticky, Chief? I thought we were going to have a few hysterics from that girl. Fortunately she calmed down a bit."

"They're all strung up to top doh," said Green. "You've got a group of nice, hard-working people, getting on with living their ordinary lives, coping with a damn' nuisance like this old Carlow bird and then wham! Sudden death and cops all over the place. Any young lass could be forgiven for feeling herself entangled when his nibs here starts his questions."

"You put in your pennorth."

"That's what I'm paid for, lad."

"Then why blame the Chief exclusively?"

"Because he's more sinister than I am."

"He's what?"

"You heard. Upmarket voice churning out remorseless logic. Deadly. When I chip in—usually—I talk the sort of stuff that people can answer in the same sort of way. Like you do. Colloquially, I suppose you'd call it. And they're more comfortable because it's like conversations they have every day."

"I see what you mean," said Reed. "I could never tell the Chief he was talking rubbish, like I can you."

"Now you're getting sassy, lad."

"For agreeing with you?"

"There you are. That proves my point."

"Which is what?" demanded Berger.

"If I told you you wouldn't understand."

"Try me."

"Well..."

"Come on."

Masters grinned. "Do you know, Bill, I reckon they've caught you out."

"Will you put a fiver on it?"

"On what?"

"That I've forgotten the quotation I was going to spout?"

"Never. Not on your forgetting."

"'In things that are tender and unpleasing, it is good to break the ice by some whose words are of less weight, and to reserve the more weighty voice to come in as by chance.' There, then! How's that?"

"Full marks. Mr. Bacon, I presume?"

"That's him. I learned that bit because I thought it was a good description of the way to run an interrogation. I've been reading bits of Bacon ever since your pal, Sir Frank, used that bit about roast eggs. I like him. The bit I quoted comes from *Of Cunning*."

"I see. Thanks for the lesson. I shall leave our next interview to you at least to start with."

"Who's it going to be, Chief?"

"I think we must make a point of talking to Mr Josef Kisiel first thing tomorrow morning."

"Why not tonight, Chief?"

"I think tomorrow would be better." The car turned into the grounds of the HQ buildings. "By the way, when you took the suitcases in, did you take in my personal briefcase, Reed?"

"Yes, Chief. Everything except the two murder bags. I put your briefcase in your room and the case file in the office."

"Thanks."

"A bit of light reading tonight?" asked Green.

"I didn't have time to read up before we set out, so I brought Martindale and one or two other bits and pieces along, just for laughs."

"I'll bet. That nice toxology book of yours. The one you call the recipe book."

Masters laughed. "I like reading in bed."

"Now this restaurant..." began Green.

"Actually it's a bistro called Punters."

"You're joking. I thought you said it was British?"

"When you see who's waiting at table you'll not care," retorted Reed.

Green didn't reply. Masters asked: "Can we get a reasonable meal there? Something more than a hamburger or pasta?"

"There's a full menu, Chief. And it's pretty good. We had a quick look in at lunchtime..."

Green snorted. "I'll bet you did. And got your eyes on a bit of capurtle, too, from the sound of it."

"What was it he said just now?" asked Berger airily. "In things that are tender..."

"We don't want to hear about young women in maudlin tones."

"I wasn't talking about women, I was talking about the minute steak."

The car drew up at Punters. It had obviously been a shop at one time. Now it had been opened out by the simple expedient of knocking a back room into the sales area to make space for perhaps a dozen tables of varying sizes.

The front door of the shop had been permanently fastened. Painted across it was the name, and below

146

that a cartoon of a man clinging to a punt pole while his vessel drifted away on blue wavy lines of water to leave him stranded. The large plate glass window had been decorated with a more decorous punting party who seemed to be managing their affairs more skilfully. A large red blind, with white binding to its scalloped edges, lent a touch of gaiety to the little establishment.

"The door's down the side," said Berger, leading the way along a wide passage.

Green entered and looked about him. The fact that he made no comment seemed to indicate that he liked what he saw. It was a bit of a quart-in-a-pint-pot set-up. The bar, built of bricks topped with a polished wooden plank was at the back and obviously not meant for standing at. Barely six feet long, it was backed by a goodly array of bottles with in-and-out doors for the kitchen at the ends. Presiding over it was a young man whom Masters mentally categorized as a recent student.

"A table for four, please?"

There was a short conversation between the young man and an equally young and very personable girl. It seemed there was a question as to which table could be used before the arrival of those who had booked for later. Eventually the matter was decided and they were seated and given menus.

"Italian job?" demanded Green of another girl who came to take the order. "What's that?"

"It's a steak with a special tomato and mushroom sauce."

"And Punter's job?"

"The same with cheese and onion."

"Good, are they?"

"We think so."

"Right. I'll have the Punter's. But first I'm going to have some French onion soup."

The others decided to follow his lead. The girl

brought a newly sliced bloomer and pot of butter to the table, followed by two half-litre carafes of the house wine.

"Not bad at all," said Green, eating bread and butter and looking around. "They've used plenty of scarlet paint."

The chairs and tables were all brilliant red, the walls cream. Low above each table was a hanging light in a dark brown, loosely woven shade made of stiffened hessian in the shape of a large, upturned bowl. On the walls were enlarged pictures of punting parties, interspersed with regatta notices from Edwardian days. The table-cloths were chocolate coloured, and the napkins scarlet. Suspended from the ceiling was a punt with poles alongside it.

The soup, when it came, found immediate favour with Green. The bowls were deep, and the *croûton* laden with cheese seemed just to fit the narrowed tops.

"Not stingy with it, are they? You can't get at the jizzer-rizzer without cutting through...ah! Lovely." A strand of brown onion hung on Green's chin. He wiped it off and bent low to take another spoonful. "Strong cheese, too. That's what I like."

"It's what the people on television call 'talking us through' an event," said Reed. "Rather boring and self-evident, really."

"Just showing appreciation," said Green. He was having a little difficulty with a thin thread of molten cheese which had somehow escaped his mouth and was causing him a certain amount of irritation. He turned to Masters. "Have you noticed how these days the young have no proper sense of gratitude?"

"I have, indeed," said Masters, remembering that not so long before Green himself had found difficulty in saying a direct thank you.

Green showed his appreciation of this support by

noisily finishing the soup. Reed said to Berger: "And I thought you told me they didn't have music in here."

"Some spread," said Green, soon after nine o'clock the next morning.

He was referring to the Kisiel Garden Centre and allied plant growing area.

The Centre itself was a modern building surrounded by plants ready boxed or potted for the amateur gardener to come in and buy. Small plants, like alpines and heathers, were on long tables. Taller plants were displayed in rectangles, each four or five metres square, delineated by concrete curbs and separated by paved paths. The front end of the building had two sliding panels up to which customers could draw trolleys for assistants to add up the charges and take the money. Inside, the building was a gardeners' supermarket with every type of tool, implement, spray, compost, packeted seed and flower pot—clay and china—imaginable. Garden gnomes stood assembled in tiered ranks. Plastic pool shells were neighboured by electric pumps and fountains. Garden rope, garden twine, garden wire, garden ties, canes, rustic arches, benches, tables, sun umbrellas...they were all there. A door from the side of the shop led into a greenhouse reserved for exotic plants, water lilies and cacti. A central pillar was surrounded by a wide collar of cut blooms, bunched ready for sale. Behind the building the sheds, the greenhouses, paving blocks, sundials, epergnes...

"Some spread."

Masters, having made a leisurely tour of the building, went outside to survey the surrounding fields. Row upon row of marshalled plants, some already in bloom, others waiting for later to show their true colours. Two or three workers, armed with hoes, moved about the fields. One area was covered in vast greenhouses, the top lights open to let in the air. As he moved round to the side of the building opposite the exotic planthouse, Masters saw the more practical aids to gardening— heaps of paving slabs, grey, yellow and red; piles of broken stone for crazy paving; bags of sand, of gravel, bone meal, lime and giant sacks of compressed peat.

"A thriving business, apparently," he said to Green who joined him.

"He's got a raft of retail customers even this early in the morning. And I see he has a mail-order section. I reckon he must supply seedsmen for miles around."

Masters nodded. "He obviously does the thing properly. Grows new strains and propagates. I get the feeling that it is a self-satisfied business. One that gives as much pleasure as profit."

Green grunted his agreement. "I'd even work Sundays if this was mine," he added.

Reed came up to them.

"We've found a Mr Tony Kisiel, Chief. He's the old boy's son. He's marketing director of this set-up."

"Where is he?"

"Talking to Sergeant Berger in the office."

"That glassed-off bit in the main building?"

"That's only the shop office. The main office is the whole of that house beside the entrance gate. The one with the hanging baskets outside."

"Is Josef Kisiel there?"

"No, Chief."

"We'll go across and have a word with the son."

"He'll know all about us," said Green. "He's married to Whincap's daughter. I bet the phones were ringing last night. In every direction."

"They'll not know whatever it was the Chief was thinking about, though. What we said and did yesterday may now be common knowledge, but they can't creep into minds."

"Trot along, lad," said Green. "If they've got a set

of offices as big as that, they'll have somewhere where you can scrounge us a good cup of coffee. I could have read the paper through that tea I had at breakfast. Lot of old wash, it was. So I'm ready for something better."

Reed grinned. "I know when I'm not wanted. Coffee for you as well, Chief?"

"Yes, please."

As soon as there was some distance between Reed and themselves, Green said to Masters: "Any joy last night?"

"I was hoping you wouldn't ask quite so soon."

"Meaning you got nothing to help."

Masters grinned. "Bill, do you really want to know what I did after we got back to HQ last night?"

"I know you went into the office to phone Wanda. Then I reckon you went to your room to do some reading."

"I did phone Wanda. But then I phoned Anderson."

"At home?"

"It was pretty late."

"Ten o'clockish."

"Are you going to tell me what it was about or was that what I wasn't supposed to ask you yet?"

Masters stopped on the pathway that led to the house and took out his pipe. As he started to fill it with War-lock Flake, he said: "It was about you, Bill. A proposition. I'm to ring him later for the answer. I'd rather have waited to have given you his reply. That's all. No mystery."

"I see."

"But seeing that you are now aware of what I did, I can see no reason for not discussing it with you. First off, naturally, I asked for a normal extension of service for you."

"That sounds as if he turned you down."

"He stated categorically that he didn't want you to go." Masters took out a box of Swan and, striking a match, applied it between cupped hands to the bowl of the pipe.

"Nice of him," growled Green. "But?"

"He told you himself the pressure he is under, so he held out little hope of keeping you on as you are."

"As I am? What in heaven's name does that mean?"

"My proposition..."

"Yes?"

"I know that our lords and masters are extremely keen to build up a really first class team of Scene-of-Crime Officers to back up the CID."

"Oh no, George, thank you," said Green. "I'm not becoming an S.C.O."

"Listen, Bill, please. I know you wouldn't want that. Not after what you've been and done. But I suggested to Anderson that you should be given a special appointment as Senior S.C.O...."

"There isn't such a thing in..."

"Listen. S.S.C.O. permanently seconded to this team."

"No good, George. Five would be too many and I don't know much about the technical side of testing for dust transfer and all that sort of thing."

"I realize that. To begin with, there wouldn't be five of us. Anderson said he could envisage our team with only one sergeant and a young D.I., besides the two of us. He'd want the D.I.—your replacement, as it were—to be trained."

"So I'd take the place of one of the sergeants?"

"Hardly that. We're counting heads, not arranging pecking orders. My proposition was that you and I would continue as we are, but your appointment would be different. That's all. Anderson wants to bring along a young D.I., so a sergeant goes to make room for him."

"If he's out to save money, how's that going to help? It'll cost more."

"No, it will save money. You'll get your pension and

your S.S.C.O.'s pay to top it up. But the S.S.C.O.'s pay is not likely to be more—or even as big as—that of a senior D.S. They'd have to pay your pension anyway. And they'd have to give me a D.I. So, in fact, they would be saving a few quid a year."

"And you thought all this up?"

"In essence. But we hammered out the details between us. How does it strike you?"

"We continue as we are?"

"Absolutely. You know we rarely need the services of an S.C.O. You would be sailing under slightly false colours, but you'd be no worse off financially and the Yard would reap the benefit of your experience."

Green grinned. "You old bastard, George. It's this little plan you've been cooking up which caused the lads to think you were coming up with the answer to this case."

"I suspect so."

"I reckon it'll work. Anyhow, I'm ready to give it a whirl."

"Whoa!" cautioned Masters. "I haven't got Anderson's agreement yet. He's got to get approval from on high."

"He'll swing it," said Green confidently. "If it's your idea he'll be able to say it has your backing and being the jammy bastard you are, you usually get your own way."

"Thanks."

"What? Oh, yes, well…" Green seemed at a loss for words.

"Will Doris approve?"

"Need you ask?"

Masters turned towards the door of the house. "I forgot to tell you, Doris dropped in on Wanda for a cup of tea yesterday."

"And to see young Michael William," said Green drily. "She's nuts about the choker."

Reed met them. "Upstairs, Chief. The back bedroom. And the coffee's coming up."

Berger was chatting to Tony Kisiel. The subject was cricket in general, but specifically the merits and demerits of the limited-overs game as opposed to the three-day county matches.

"Mr Anthony Kisiel, Chief."

"How d'you do, Mr Kisiel. I don't suppose you are unaware of our presence in the area?"

"I've heard of little else since you arrived, Mr Masters. Gwen—my wife—is always in close touch with her parents and brother. And she's friendly with Marian Whincap, so that brings in Theo and Margarethe. They've been playing an animated version of Marjory Move-all, both by personal visits and phoned conversations, for the past forty-eight hours. But I must say I wasn't expecting to be honoured by a visit from you."

"Come to see your dad," said Green.

"I thought that must be it, though why he should interest you ...?"

"His name's cropped up from time to time."

"In connection with Elke Carlow?"

"That's it."

"But he and she ... they were never in each other's presence. He'll be able to tell you nothing about her."

"You've said it all, Mr Kisiel. Why were they never in each other's presence though their families were closely connected by marriage?"

"Quite frankly, because they couldn't stand the sight of each other."

"Enemies, in fact?"

"Yes," said Tony, without trying to qualify the reply. "They were enemies. But it doesn't mean he killed her."

Green shook his head sadly. "We're not saying he did. But somebody did her a bit of no-good..."

"Herself, probably."

"Perhaps. But she was somebody. Somebody who was her own worst enemy, maybe. And we'll be investigating all her enemies, herself included. So your dad, also an enemy like you said, will have to be interviewed."

"That's specious," said Kisiel. "How the hell can you interview a dead woman?"

"Ah!" said Green. "You'd be surprised how loud the dead can speak and how much they can tell us. Oh, yes, we'll be talking to her all right."

Kisiel turned to Masters. He was a thick-set, powerful and, one would guess, pleasant-natured young man. He was dressed in grey slacks and a short-sleeved white shirt with a breast pocket, open at the neck. He looked as if he would be as much or more at home in the open air than in this office.

"Do you subscribe to this nonsense, Mr Masters?"

"Without reservation. My colleague may have put it slightly differently from the way I'd have put it to you, myself, but I can't see where he went wrong or could have given you a false impression."

"My father is the gentlest of men."

"You may know that, Mr Kisiel, but I don't. To me, as yet, he is just the name of a man known to have been inimical to a woman whose death I am investigating. If you were in my shoes, what view would you take?"

"I'd try not to upset everybody I met. Some of us must be innocent, you know."

"True."

"Well?"

"Well what, Mr Kisiel?"

"Why upset everybody you meet?"

"The beauty of conversations like this, Mr Kisiel, is that one invariably learns something. For example, I was unaware I had upset anybody, but no doubt you can put me right on that score."

"My father-in-law and Mr Bennett to begin with. You upset them."

"But I didn't, Mr Kisiel. They upset themselves."

"Come off it."

"They grew very upset because they felt obliged to reveal to me your father's name when they would have preferred to suppress it. Men in the positions of Dr Whincap and Mr Bennett know full well they should co-operate with the police. When, against that knowledge, they attempt to withhold information, it is their own natures which cause them distress, both because they feel disloyalty to somebody who is a friend and also because they realize they are failing in their duty as responsible citizens. And before you add Mrs Marian Whincap to the list of those I am supposed to have upset, let me assure you that she jumped to the erroneous conclusion that I was accusing her of some crime. Nothing could be further from the truth. I was questioning her closely, but in the presence of her father who is a senior police officer, and asking that she should face an unpalatable truth. Facing that truth upset her far more than I did."

Kisiel was not to be mollified by this speech. He countered: "They also said you have a knack of twisting words to mean what you want them to mean. After what I've just heard I understand their reasons for saying so."

"In that case, Mr Kisiel, it is as well that I did not come to interview you."

"What's this if it isn't an interview?"

"Conversation, Mr Kisiel. Not too friendly a conversation perhaps, but nevertheless nothing more than that. Now, could I ask you to tell me where I will find your father?"

Kisiel relaxed a little. "My father is a Pole. He speaks English, of course—with an accent—but he will not be up to your weight in polemics."

Masters smiled. "I'm sure no pun was intended there, Mr Kisiel, and I can assure you that we shall not seek to take advantage of your father's more limited knowledge of English. But perhaps you would like to be present when we talk to him?"

"You will allow that?"

"Why not?"

"He's out taking his morning walk."

"Where?"

"Among the plants." Tony picked up a pair of binoculars from the desk and moved to the window. For a moment or two he scanned the distant fields. "There he is. It's the roses this morning."

He handed the binonculars to Masters and pointed out the direction.

"The one in the trilby, carrying the bag?"

"He has twine and ties in one pocket, with a knife and secateurs in the other. He walks slowly round a different area each day, inspecting the plants. He likes to see if they need feeding or watering, or if there are any pests. He cuts out dead and damaged bits, too, and ties back when it's needed. He drops his cuttings into the bag to bring back to the dump because bits left lying about attract pests. After his inspection he tells the gardeners what he wants them to do in that area, if anything."

"When will he be back?"

"I'll call him in."

"From here?"

Tony picked up a phone. "I can call the glass house office. One of the lads will take him a message."

While the telephone conversation was going on, the office door opened and a girl pushed in a metal trolley laden with coffee jugs, crockery and a plate of biscuits wrapped in plastic clingfoil. Tony put the phone down. "Thank you, Jenny, we'll serve ourselves. But bring another cup for Mister Josef, would you, please."

"No need to hurry over it," said Tony as he handed round the biscuits. "It will take the old man at least ten minutes to get here."

Ten minutes was a gross underestimate. Josef Kisiel took his time, as if to indicate by his tardiness that the arrival of the Yard team was of so little consequence to him that he could finish his previous business first.

Masters guessed the Pole's thoughts.

"You were expecting us to call, Mr Kisiel?"

"Police are all alike in every country."

"Like your friend Theo Rainford?"

"He is an exception, maybe."

"To those whom he knows, or to everybody?"

Kisiel sat down in his son's desk chair and removed the trilby. He was dressed in heavy ankle boots with woollen socks turned down over them and holding the bottoms of his trousers in. A navy blue woollen shirt and a disreputable but still serviceable grey jacket clothed the upper portions of the still powerful frame.

"I would not come running for Theo if he came here in an official capacity. As a friend, I would hasten."

"I understand. You mistrust us and prefer to let us know it rather than to hide the fact. That at least is honest, and honesty, however displayed, causes me no concern."

Josef looked up at Masters, blue eyes twinkling. "You are a man,' he said. "You do not let things disturb you."

"Some things do," confided Masters, "but not a disinclination on the part of somebody such as yourself to meet me. But that is by the way. What I am here for is to ask you why you and the late Mrs Elke Carlow were enemies."

"Why?"

"If there is a reason you can put into words."

"You have not come to ask me if I killed her? To ask me what I was doing every minute of the day on which she died?"

"That could come, but we haven't got that far yet."

"You ask me why we were enemies. The answer is because we always were."

Green said: "From the moment Hitler marched into Poland, you mean?"

Kisiel nodded. "The Germans! Even now I cannot speak their name lightly."

Masters sat on the end of the desk. "Mrs Carlow was married to an Englishman before the war. She lived here. A young woman with a child. Did you blame her for the rape of your country?"

"She was still a German. Listen, and I will tell you. I was a flyer. I came here before Christmas that first year. I was stationed just a mile or so beyond the fields I now own. I learned to fly Spitfires. By the next summer we were ready. But the British did not trust us. They thought we could not fight. The battle was fought by British flyers until the Few became too few. Then, because they were obliged to do so, they allowed us to join the battle. Your people had not realized that the hatred the Poles felt for the Germans made us capable and eager in action. We were angry. We fought like tigers."

Masters nodded. "I know the history of those days."

"Then you will know we were coming in for just long enough to refuel before scrambling again. We flyers stayed with our aeroplanes. And that is when they started to send in to us the mobile canteens. The local women—they worked hard. We were grateful. But there was one woman—a woman who had been pressed into service—who had come from Prussia."

"Mrs Carlow?"

"The same. The Polish Corridor, our route to Danzig, split Prussia. The peoples who lived near there and in the Free City could understand each other's tongues. You must imagine my surprise when a conversation with a brother officer—at a canteen truck—

was understood and broken into by the woman serving tea. We had been cursing the Luftwaffe—one of our great friends had not returned that day.

"The comment? It was a tirade against the Poles and full of praise for the Herrenvolk and the Luftwaffe fighters. We were astounded. The words we understood. But the accent was German. A Boche on a British airfield in wartime! A Boche praising the men who had shot down our comrade."

"What did you do?"

"We replied to her."

"I'll bet you did," said Green.

"Hatred had been born," said Kisiel simply. "We were full of hatred before. Now it was running over."

"What action did you take?"

"We had her removed from the airfield."

"At gunpoint?"

"Our commanding officer was not happy that she should have been allowed among us," admitted Kisiel. "He was not an English gentleman. He was an angry Pole."

"And?"

"Shortly after that, you British woke up. Such people were rounded up and confined on the Isle of Man."

"Eighteen B," murmured Green. "That got her out of your hair, at any rate."

Kisiel shook his head. "She blamed me. She believed until her death that it was I who had arranged for your police to take her. She never forgave the lowly Pole who could manage to have a Prussian put behind barbed wire." He looked up at Masters. "You see, they regarded us as dirt. And we knew it. The hatred on both sides was implacable. When I married and decided to stay in England, I vowed that never would I again appear in her presence. From time to time she tried to damage me in other people's eyes and in the business world, to take her revenge on me for having sent her to prison. But she never succeeded. I prayed for her death many times when lying awake at night and for her torture in hell fire. Now she is gone. But I am too drained to rejoice."

There was a short silence.

"Thank you," said Masters at last. "Your son led me to believe that—not unnaturally—your command of the English language was not great. You gave us, however, a description graphic enough to satisfy the most punctilious among us."

"You didn't ask dad a lot of searching questions," said Tony. "If you had done he would have it difficult."

"I'll accept your word for that, Mr Kisiel. But we don't normally harass those whom we interview, despite what you may have heard to the contrary."

"We get a bit narky with anybody who isn't forthcoming or who tries to pull the wool over our eyes," said Green. "We regard that sort of thing much as you would if some joker stopped you getting on with your job by breaking the cultivator or whatever it is you use for turning over those fields of yours."

Tony Kisiel nodded his acceptance of this point and asked: "Does that mean that you accept unreservedly what my father has told you?"

"Why not? We knew he didn't like the old woman and she didn't like him. All we wanted to find out was why. Your dad has told us. If we hear anything from anybody else that doesn't tie in with what he's said, we shall come back and sort it with him. Check and cross-check until everything holds water, as you might say."

Tony Kisiel pondered this for a moment. "So you've finished with him for the moment?"

"P'raps for good."

"I wonder," said Masters tentatively, "if Mr Kisiel

senior hasn't finished his morning inspection of the plants, whether he would mind if I had a look round in his company?"

"What for?" demanded Tony, suspiciously.

"To get a few ideas," replied Masters.

"So you think there's something here that..."

"No, Mr Kisiel. I don't think there's anything here other than flowers. It's just that I have a small garden in London which does not lend itself to normal cultivation. My wife is, however, anxious to make something of it by using the walls for creepers and pots for plants that will provide colour. I've often heard of these small enclosed areas being turned into miniature gardens but until this moment I've never met an expert who might be able to tell me how to go about it. I know there are books on the subject and television programmes, but they don't seem to cater for our needs exactly."

"Come with me," said Josef Kisiel. "We can talk as we walk."

"Are you going alone with him, Chief?" asked Reed.

"If the D.C.I. wishes to come and Mr Kisiel doesn't mind I think the party will be big enough. Too many big feet among the rows could cause havoc."

"In that case, Chief, do you mind if we take the car? I promised Mr Dean I'd try to keep him in the picture. If I went over now and reported, I wouldn't have to bother later."

"Don't be too long about it. We mustn't take up too much of Mr Kisiel's time."

Josef Kisiel was knowledgeable and helpful. He questioned Masters closely as to the size of his garden, the height of the walls and nearby buildings so that he could get some idea of the problems of shade and sun. Then he spoke of the plants which thrived in shade, half-shade and those that loved the heat.

As they went along he told Masters to make a note of their names together with those of plants which preferred north-facing walls and those which did best on warm, south-facing brickwork.

After this he spoke of lime-haters and lime-lovers and how to treat the soil to accommodate each, pointing out that if separate containers were to be used, this would be easier for Masters than for most gardeners.

He stressed the value of humus and peat; of bone meal, dried blood, nitrates, phosphates, potash, lime and other plant foods; and explained their uses and the little-and-often theory of plant chemical dressing. He was more than an expert, he was an enthusiast, too, and so he held the attention of his audience, answering their questions when asked and encouraging more.

As they walked between the areas of plants in bloom, Masters asked him where he had gained his knowledge.

"For one year in Poland at our agricultural school of Warsaw University, I studied at a desk. Then I worked for one year in the State Gardens near Lodz. I was to return to the university in the autumn when war began, so I did not complete. But here, they let me go to Glasgow when the war was over. For one year I attended, then, because I was married, I came back here. My Alice, she had been working, and I had saved and there was a gratuity. We bought a little bit of land. I was sold a Nissen hut from the airfield. I took it down into pieces and brought it back to put up in our field. It had partitions in it. My Alice and I, we lived in half of it. I did my work from the other half. The authorities did not like it, but others were doing the same. The work prospered. For many years there had not been seeds and plants. I grew them, and I grew our food to add to our little meat ration. It was a time to make money—no big bills for electricity and gas like now and only small rates because of none of the amenities in the hut. I could build a greenhouse and cold frames from waste material because there were no bricks—bricks and timber needed licences to use, even old materials, in those days. So we made a profit. And when the time came we could buy more land and more implements." He shrugged. "You see what we now have."

"All very modern and bustling," said Green.

"Except for the jam jars," said Masters, stopping and shading his eyes from the glare of the sun reflected by the rows of jars just ahead of them.

"My lilies of the valley," said Kisiel. "That is how we grow them in Poland. Under jam jars so that they are ready for the May-game."

"May-game? Merrymaking on May Day?"

Kisiel nodded. "In Poland and Russia and even in France the people make more of May Day than the British. At one time it was not so. You had your May Queen, where we had our May Lady and you had your Maypole dance where we had our May-game. But you did not have lilies of the valley for good luck. You had your roses."

"That's right," said Green. "The flowers of Merrie England! 'The May Queen comes, let her path be spread, with roses white and with roses red.' That's a quote," he added for Kisiel's benefit.

"I have heard it," said Kisiel gravely. "The children sing it at their school."

They moved forward to the rows of lilies. "Many of these have gone to market," said Kisiel. "Even in England people like them, but they don't hold them in the same reverence as my people do."

"Reverence?" asked Masters.

"We use many herbs and flowers for medicines. Every housewife used to grow them just as she grew sage and thyme and parsley. Before we had all the modern pills and potions the country folk brewed simples for all their ailments."

"I see. Now, about roses. Am I right in believing that if I buy those that have been brought-on in containers I can plant them at any time—not just in early spring or autumn?"

"Quite right, Mr Masters. Buy a perfumed climber and plant it in a big tub so that you can lead it up the wall of the house to bloom outside the bedroom window of your wife. Each morning when she rises she will have the scent as she sits at her dressing table and in the evening it will come to her as she brushes her hair. It will be romantic for her, and for you..." He grinned widely. "What man does not want his wife to be romantic in the evening, eh?"

"Sounds like good advice," conceded Masters. "I'll try it." He turned to Green.

"I could plant a rose in that small bed sheltered by the house-return at the back, Bill. I could train it on wires so that it would go up to the bedroom window."

"The bed where the winter jasmine is?"

"That's the one."

"Yellow winter jasmine?" asked Kisiel.

"My wife is very fond of it," replied Masters. "She always hopes there'll be some left for picking on Christmas Day for her table centre. So far we've always been lucky."

"How long is the bed?"

"Five or six feet long, but no more than nine inches wide."

"And it carries only the jasmine?"

"I shall put the rose in the end nearer the house."

"Good. But if your wife likes the little yellow flowers particularly..."

"She loves yellow flowers. Daffodils, for instance, are a great delight to her."

"Well, my friend, a plot as large as the one you have described is very big for just a winter jasmine, even with a rose at the end. And if your wife loves yellow

...well, to follow the winter jasmine, why not plant a witch-hazel—a hamamelis to give it a more formal name? Witch-hazel produces little yellow flowers, too, in February and March, and then, you would still have room for a forsythia with *its* little yellow flowers to follow on after that. So Mrs Masters would have her little yellow flowers there for many months when there is not much else in bloom."

"I could put all these in the one bed?"

"Why not? Feed them and they will grow."

"But I always thought forsythia tended to grow quickly and to take over?"

"You would have to prune it, of course. Quite severely, perhaps. But they are good-natured plants. They do not take offence. They come back for more of such treatment."

They turned to head back to the now distant office.

"Does Mrs Masters like reds and pinks?"

"Flowers, you mean? Yes, I think so."

"I did not mean flowers exactly." Joseph spread his hands. "You have a little box of a garden with high walls and a stone floor. All grey and brown. Flowers such as one would grow in a herbaceous border—stocks, aquilegia, petunias—are not possible. You can grow bushes—a few. Three yellow ones in one patch. But what about elsewhere? In two corners at the bottom of the garden? In one corner a tamarisk and in the other a dogwood. The tamarisk is pink, dusky pink, in the late spring before it turns green. The stems and branches and twigs, all bumpy with little buds and all dusky pink. And in the other corner a dogwood with a cluster of long, straight, bright red stems. Shiny red, in winter as well as summer. Colour all the year, Mr Masters. Beautiful to see."

"I don't think I know tamarisk," said Green.

"It is sometimes colours other than pink," conceded

Kisiel. "But the pink is supreme. It is the dusky pink of a lovely Persian rug or whatever they are called nowadays. Nothing is the same as it was. Dutch cheese is now called Edam and I saw in a delicatessen last week they were advertising shoulder-ham. It is a contradiction. There are two hams on an animal, including man. And we sit on them. Shoulder ham! It is taking money by false pretences. But a housewife who would never pay as much for a hand of pork as for a leg will do precisely that if the same animal is smoked or salted and called ham. I do not understand it."

"I don't either," growled Green. "But you're always coming across that sort of thing nowadays. My missus tells me that quite often you can pay more for a pound of something if you buy it in a big amount than you pay by buying it in a smaller one. Just the reverse of how things should be."

The conversation lapsed as they reached the environs of the shop and turned towards the office. Masters was evidently chewing something over in his mind other than flowers for Wanda's garden, as his next observations showed.

"Mrs Carlow has a sister, Frau Hillger."

"Yes," acknowledged Kisiel.

"I've heard she has a character very different from that of her elder sister."

"True."

"Did your dislike of Mrs Carlow include other members of her family, Mr Kisiel?"

"No. I like Margarethe and Marian. They are nice people. And their husbands, too. They are all friends of mine."

"Frau Hillger?"

"She is not a friend of mine. But not because I feel any enmity towards her. It is simply that living in the same house as Mrs Carlow has prevented any sort of intimacy between us other than that of acquaintance-ship."

Masters smothered a smile at the quaint but never-theless descriptive way of making a point. "On the few occasions that you did meet Frau Hillger, what were your feelings concerning her? Were they neutral?"

"Mimi is different from Elke. She is a pleasant woman. An ordinary, pleasant woman. People who abhorred Elke liked her."

"Were they alike in any respect?"

"One had to look hard to find resemblances."

"Of any sort?"

"Even their voices were different. Elke was gut-tural, Mimi is not."

"Thank you."

"You have not seen Frau Mimi?"

"Not yet."

Kisiel stopped and looked up at Masters. "You are not conventional. I understood that policemen always go straight to the nearest relatives when a murder oc-curs."

"Murder, chum?" asked Green. "We do not even know whether this is murder or not."

"In that case, why bother me?"

"Why not? You have a nice garden."

Kisiel gazed at him for a few seconds. "You English are all alike. You and Robert Bennett, David Whincap and Theo. You hide what you mean by saying some-thing different."

Green grinned. "It's safer that way. You chaps from the continent always show your feelings. No English-man would announce he had prayed for somebody to die. When you do that, it makes us think."

"You would prefer me not to say what I think?"

Green shook his head. "It's the same difference, chum. Things always come out in the end."

They moved the last few yards in silence. As they reached the door of the office house, the Yard car drew up.

"Chief!"

Masters and Green turned as Reed hurried up the little path towards them.

"Chief, there's a..." Reed realized that Kisiel was still present, and paused in what he was about to say.

"There's a what?"

"A message for you, Chief. Personal."

"Thank you. I'll be with you in just a moment." Masters turned to Kisiel. "Thank you, sir. I've enjoyed our chat, I've enjoyed seeing your plants and, I hope, I've remembered your advice. But even if I haven't, Mr Green will have done so, and he'll recount it to my wife, word for word."

"I will see you again," said Kisiel.

"Was that a statement or a question?"

"It was a fact. I shall see you again, I think."

"I see. Well...in that case, goodbye for the time being."

As they walked towards the car together, Green asked: "What the devil did the old boy mean by that, George?"

Before Masters could give a considered reply, Reed, who had been waiting outside the car, said: "Dean's received an anonymous phone call, Chief."

"About Mrs Carlow's death?"

Reed nodded. "He'd like to see you about it."

"We can't stand about here. Get in the car and we'll talk as we go."

"What did this mysterious caller say, lad?" asked Green.

"Dean wrote it down—as best as he could remember. Evidently this woman rang up..."

"What woman?"

"This woman...*a* woman then. She rang up and asked to speak to Dean, so the girl on the switchboard put her through."

"Just like that? Without asking her name and business?"

"The caller," interjected Berger, who was driving, "gave her name and business without being asked."

"A bogus name?" demanded Masters.

"Yes, Chief." Reed had again taken over the job of raconteur. "She said her name was Mrs Leafe and she wished to discuss with Dean certain provisions of a will he was preparing for her."

"And?"

"Well as the woman seemed confident and, I suppose, had the right sort of accent, and Dean hadn't got a visitor at the time, the office girl put her through to the boss."

"In other words the girl thought she was a genuine client?"

"That's about the size of it, Chief."

"We know the form," grunted Green. "Impudence and fortitude will get you anywhere, as my old mum used to say."

"That about sums it up, I suppose."

"Did Dean tell you what the unknown woman said?"

"She alleged that Mrs Carlow had been murdered and that there was a cover-up."

"Nothing more? No names mentioned?"

"Yes, Chief."

"Whose?"

"Josef Kisiel's."

"You mean this Mrs Leafe actually said that Josef Kisiel had murdered Mrs Carlow?"

"Yes, Chief."

"Did the caller say how he had achieved it?"

"No. She just said that Kisiel had always vowed to see her in hell...those were the actual words she used

...see her in hell, and that now he'd done it."

They rode in silence for a few minutes. The weather was so delightful that the car seemed a prison. Masters wound his window down and sat staring out. The new season's green shone brightly, not yet dusty and stained by time. The houses, growing more numerous as they approached the town, seemed bright and cheerful with windows open and net screens just fluttering in the lightest of breezes. Multi-coloured garments hung on washing lines and small children played in gardens, enjoying the new freedom of being out doors without coats. Their mothers were wearing summer dresses and displaying bare arms and legs that needed a few days of such weather to tone down the anaemic whiteness of the skin to the light tan that shouts of health and firmness of flesh.

Green allowed Masters time to take this in and to think for a minute or two before asking: "Do we pay much attention to this, George? Poison tongue? It could be anybody in the district."

"Not quite anybody," replied Masters quietly. "Somebody who knows Kisiel."

"And Mrs Carlow, Chief," said Berger.

"Not necessarily."

"No, Chief?"

"Course not," grunted Green. "Somebody who heard Kisiel shooting his mouth off at some time about the old frau. She needn't have known Elke Carlow, but she remembered the name, and when the news of the death got about, put two and two together and made the usual five."

Berger grimaced. "So an enemy of Kisiel's. He's a decent old boy. He wouldn't have made all that many enemies."

"Don't you believe it, lad," retorted Green. "Those Polish airmen thought they were great lovers in the war. They caused a lot of trouble. Lasses fell for them left, right and centre and were then left stranded. There's still a few who will have a grudge against Polish airmen."

Masters didn't add to the conversation. The car drew up at Dean's office door and they were shown through direct to the deputy coroner.

"An educated voice," said Dean. "Not one I would expect with such a message. Not that I have any experience of such matters, but one always imagines that they will belong to the heavy-breathing brigade."

"And you think all those who indulge in such games are rough and tough?" asked Green.

Dean nodded. "Less than highly articulate, certainly. But, as I say, I have no previous experience, so I suppose I could well be mistaken."

"Too true. They come in all shapes and sizes."

"Is this going to complicate matters, Mr Masters?"

"I think not."

Dean waited for Masters to continue.

"For one thing, the mere fact that somebody has gone to the trouble of ringing you up with such a message means that, in spite of the efforts made to play down Mrs Carlow's death until we are sure of our ground, your caller knows something about the affair. Quite what her knowledge is, we don't know. But however trivial, it reassures us that there is something to learn. For another, she used the word murder which, as far as I know, has not yet been uttered publicly either by you or by us."

"And you take that to mean that the thought that murder has been done is lurking at the back of the caller's mind?"

"Back or front, yes. And finally Josef Kisiel was named. I need hardly tell you that police investigations often rely heavily on information received..."

"Surely you're not saying you are intending to bring in Mr Kisiel on such slender evidence?"

"No. I was about to say that whoever your caller was, she is an acquaintance of Kisiel. She is also very much in the know concerning Mrs Carlow's death because, as we have mentioned, it has not been publicized. For these reasons I was able to say that I don't consider your unknown caller to have complicated matters. If anything, she has eased the situation."

"By helping to crystallize your thoughts?"

"Every little helps," grunted Green.

"I see. What happens now?"

Masters pondered for a moment. Then—

"In cases like this—where one gets an unknown caller ringing in—the person doing it is rarely content with just one call."

"She's liable to repeat her accusations?"

"It would be usual were she to do so, and strictly speaking I should arrange for some sort of listening watch to be kept in the hope that the call could be traced. But I don't propose to do that unless and until your unknown informant becomes a nuisance to you."

"Why's that?"

"First, because it would mean that somebody would have to be here to monitor incoming calls. I don't suppose you would like the inconvenience of having them here, Mr Dean, or, as this is a solicitor's office, of having them listen in to strictly confidential conversations between you and your clients."

"You're damn' right, I wouldn't, and my partners would be equally against it."

Masters nodded. "That's fair enough. The second reason I was going to mention was the fact that the monitoring would have to be done by the local police and as I am under instructions not to involve them in my investigations I would prefer to avoid setting up the mechanics for tracing the calls."

"Quite right," agreed Dean.

"We may have to change our minds, however," counselled Masters. "If your informant were to come up with some startling titbit of information..."

"I understand."

"The local Chief Constable will be happy," grunted Green. "He wouldn't have liked being put to the expense for no very good reason."

Dean smiled. "He's very economy-minded." He turned to Masters. "I'll keep paper and pencil handy to take accurate notes."

"Excellent." Masters got to his feet. "We've taken up more than enough of your time, Mr Dean."

Dean laughed. "Meaning, I suspect," he said shrewdly, "that there's somewhere you'd like to rush away to."

"We have several visits still to make," admitted Masters. As the four policemen moved to the door, however, he turned back to Dean. "By the way, I think we just took it for granted that you didn't recognize the voice. You said it was light, clear and cultivated, but did it remind you of anybody connected with this case?"

"I'm not really familiar with any of them except Mrs Bennett. It was most definitely not her voice."

"Mrs Whincap, perhaps? Senior, that is?"

Dean shook his head.

"Her daughter? Mrs Gwen Kisiel?"

"I've met her on occasions, of course, but...no, that strikes no chord."

"Any of the others? Margarethe Rainford, Marian Whincap, Alice Kisiel, Mimi Hillger?"

"I don't know either Alice Kisiel or Mimi Hillger— apart from seeing her briefly in court yesterday. Of the other two...not Marian, definitely, because I seem to recall her voice is very young, girlish, almost."

"And the voice on the phone was more mature?"

"In my opinion, yes."

"Like Margarethe Rainford's then?"

"Oh, come, Mr. Masters..."

"I was talking of maturity, not timbre."

Dean's brow furrowed in thought for a moment or two. He was the solicitor preparing a considered reply. Finally he looked up. "The tessitura was wrong for Mrs. Rainford's voice."

"I see. Thank you."

"You're familiar with..."

"Quite. I listen to a deal of vocal music, and by that I don't mean pop."

Dean reddened. "Forgive me. I wanted to be sure I had conveyed my meaning correctly."

"There's no need to apologize, Mr. Dean. Had I not understood, your question would have saved me the embarrassment of asking for an explanation. Would you say the tessitura of the caller's voice was higher or lower than that of Mrs. Rainford?"

"Higher."

"You are a singing man?"

Dean blushed. "We have a local choir. A big one. We're very active. I line up with the first basses."

"To bash out the choruses of the *Messiah* every year?" asked Green.

"Among other things. We're quite well known hereabouts."

"And appreciated, I'm sure," said Masters. "What's your next big work?"

"The Bass in Me?" asked Green with a grin.

Dean smiled in reply. "The Mass does come along about once every two years. But actually we're preparing for a concert version of *Faust* next month and after that it'll be *Hiawatha*—in the open air. In the park, actually, near the lake, with canoes on the water and wigwams on the island. All good clean fun."

"I'm sure—if the weather is kind."

Dean shrugged. "In theory I suppose we should get as much enjoyment from the rehearsals as the performance, so the weather ought not to matter."

"Except to those who pay for their seats." Masters held out his hand. "Thank you once again, Mr. Dean. Now we really will be on our way."

When they reached the car, Berger asked: "What does tess something or other mean actually, Chief?"

"Put at its simplest," replied Masters, "it is that area of the range of pitch—or the scale, if you like—where the voice is strongest or most authoritative."

"I still don't get it, Chief."

"Think, lad," said Green. "You speak at your natural best pitch. And everything you say comes into that range. If you go higher or lower you're not as firm or strong. Singers know where they are best, so when they choose songs to sing, they pick the ones that have a general level of pitch at their strongest level. Some notes will be above it and some below and they'll reach them all right. But they wouldn't want the whole song to be written higher or lower because it would be a strain and they'd bust a gut trying to sustain their mastery of the tune."

"Is that right, Chief?"

"Certainly. Literally, tessitura means texture and, as the D.C.I. says, is the compass embraced by the notes most frequently used in a vocal composition. So as Dean said that the tessitura of his informant's voice was somewhat higher than that of Mrs. Rainford, we should look for just that."

"Look for, Chief?"

"Keep your ears open for, lad," grated Green. "It won't be easy, but at any rate you'll know you're wrong if you suspect some dame with a voice in her boots of being the phantom telephone caller."

"I know that. I got the impression the Chief was going to disregard the call as just one of those things and only said what he did in that office out of courtesy to Dean. I didn't think we'd actually be searching for the woman who phoned."

Masters didn't reply to this comment. He had again apparently lapsed into deep thought. The others, sensing this, left him out of the further conversation, which seemed to be solely concerned with the choosing of a suitable hostelry for lunch. At last Reed spoke to him direct. "Chief, is it all right with you if we go to the same pub for lunch as we went to yesterday?"

Masters turned to him. "Have we got the marked map the Chief Constable left in the office for us?"

Reed opened the glove compartment. "It's here, Chief."

"Good. I'd like to go out to the Carlow house."

"Before nosh?" asked Green.

"Yes, please. It isn't very late is it?"

"Midday."

"We'll probably find a country pub after we've had a quick word with Frau Hillger."

Reed was consulting the map. "Turn her at the first opportunity," he said to Berger. "We'll have to go back and turn left about five miles back."

Berger obeyed instructions. He swung the heavy car round a 180-degree turn where a crossroad gave him room. As he swung in his seat with the movement, Green asked: "Something important to ask Aunty Mimi?"

Masters, employed in removing a dark, rectangular flake of tobacco from the brassy Warlock tin, nodded. "I want to ask her who her sister's solicitor was—if she had one."

"You could have asked Rainford that. It 'ud have saved petrol."

"I'd also like to meet Frau Hillger. I should have done so earlier."

"True," agreed Green airily. "Most CID men would

agree that it's a fairly normal thing to visit the scene of the crime when investigating a case of murder. I know there are some of us who can manage without paying attention to such elementary rules. But it is usual, as is meeting the next of kin of the deceased."

"I met her next of kin. Margarethe Rainford. At the first opportunity."

"So you did. But the sister who actually lived with her, at the aforesaid scene of crime, might, in some people's opinion, have been an equally immediate call."

Masters was rubbing the tobacco vigorously in the palm of his hand. "Are you propounding the old saw of first things first, Bill?"

"Something of the sort. It is not without merit as a course of action in our business."

"I would never dispute that, but you and I—all of us here—since we've worked together have never tied ourselves down in routine. Our maxim—had we needed one to account for our order of doing things—would have been Dryden's thought: 'For Tom the Second reigns like Tom the First.'"

"You're making that up, Chief," said Reed.

"No he isn't, smart Alec," said Green.

"So you know it, too?"

"Never heard it before in my life."

"Then how do you know he didn't make it up?"

"Because if somebody like his nibs wanted to make something up to sound authentic he'd have used a different name from King Tom. He'd have used Charles or Edward or somebody we've had at least two of on the throne." He paused a second and then continued. "Where you made a mistake, lad, was in thinking that because Tom's an unlikely moniker for a monarch, the quote was bogus, whereas that's the clue that should have taught you better."

Reed didn't think of questioning this appreciation. Instead, he directed Berger on to the new road he was to take. Within three or four minutes they were drawing up at the gate of the Carlow house.

"Virginia creeper," said Green. "You don't often see that these days. People think it holds the bugs too much."

"Denatures the cement, too," said Reed. "Look at it. Right up to the roof. It'll be forcing some of the slates off if somebody doesn't hack it down soon."

"Lovely in autumn, though," replied Green. "All red and yellow." He turned to Masters. "There's a car nosed into the drive, George. Could be she's got visitors."

Masters nodded and edged past the parked car which took most of the room in the little drive. The others followed him to the door, which opened as they arrived.

"Mr. Masters."

"Hello, Mrs. Rainford. We meet again."

"Have you come to see Aunty Mimi?"

"If Frau Hillger is at home..."

"She's at home and quite all right. What I mean is she's not all depressed and weepy."

"In that case I should like to ask her a few routine questions. We'd like to know the details of your mother's illness."

"Of course. It was very kind of you not to have pestered aunty earlier. Theo said last night that you had shown a delicacy of feeling in not questioning her immediately you arrived. Come in, do. Mimi is in the garden in a deck chair. I had just come in to get her a glass of sherry when I saw you arrive."

It was a very ordinary house. Not too small. Just about right for a family with one child. Masters felt that the hall needed brightening—it was too narrow for the dark paint and almost equally dark paper. To the left was the sitting room—all dark mahogany and leather as far as he could tell at a glance through the open door. He followed Margarethe into the dining room. There was little relief here, either. Dark, heavy furniture relieved only by the colours of a row of steins on the sideboard and a small round bowl of spring flowers as a table-centre.

The French window was open. After the gloom of indoors, the brightness of the day was startling. The sun, almost overhead, shone straight into the garden which, surrounded by trees in full leaf, provided a sun trap. The heat seemed to beat back from the turf, so close-cropped and compact that it provided an almost mirror-like reflective surface.

"It's the police, aunty. This is Mr Masters, the one I was telling you about."

Mimi Hillger was sitting in a deckchair with its own sun shade protruding across her head. Compared with the sunlight, the shade cast across her face was so dark as to cloud the features. Was her hair grey or fair? Was her skin smooth or wrinkled? It was difficult to tell, but the eyes seemed mild enough as they gazed up at Masters.

"How do you do, Mr Masters?"

"How do you do, Frau Hillger?" Masters nodded towards her legs. "Have you got rheumatism?"

"This?" She lifted the edge of the travelling rug that covered her knees and feet. "Oh, no. It is here to stop the sunburn. Did you not know that the sun burns skin through nylon stockings?"

"Aunty got both insteps terribly burned last summer," said Margarethe. "On about the only occasion we had any sun she dozed off out here and the tops of her feet were painful for several days."

"Seeing you've got a modesty screen on, love," said Green, "do you mind if we squat on the grass while we talk? We look untidy standing up."

"I could come indoors."

"Please don't bother to move," said Masters. "Mr. Green and I will do very well on the grass." He turned to Reed and Berger and motioned with his head for them to move away. "Have a look round the garden you two. We don't want to overwhelm Frau Hillger." He moved closer to them and murmured a few words inaudible except to the two sergeants, who then moved away. Masters joined Green on the grass. Margarethe lifted a tray from the little folding stool beside her aunt and say down.

"Please get your aunt her sherry. We shan't mind her having it while we talk."

"Can I get you a drink, too?"

"No thank you, Mrs Rainford. We shall not be here very long."

"Just looking in, really," said Green. "To ask the usual questions."

"What are they?"

"When? Where? That sort of thing."

"Don't be fooled, aunty," warned Margarethe. "Their questions will be Why? What? How? and—most of all—Who?"

Masters took out his pipe and began to fill it without looking up at Frau Hillger.

"When did Mrs Carlow begin to feel sick?"

"About four o'clock."

"But I thought you told Dr Whincap that you had afternoon tea at half-past three—slightly earlier than usual—because she felt a bit off-colour by then and you thought a cup of tea might help her?"

"That is so. But she did not feel sick then."

Margarethe said: "My aunt is getting a bit mixed up between vomiting meaning being sick and feeling unwell meaning being sick."

Masters nodded and struck a match for his pipe. As he drew on it, he said slowly, between draws: "I understand, Mrs Rainford." He turned to Mimi. "So we can safely say that it was nothing she ate at the tea-table that disagreed with your sister."

"Certainly not. We had bread and butter and ginger-bread and..."

"All totally innocuous, I'm sure, Frau Hillger. But at some time during the day Mrs Carlow must have ingested something that made her ill. Did you see her take any pills, for instance?"

"No. She had none."

"Drink a glass of water, perhaps?"

"Meaning to drink after some pills?"

Masters nodded.

"No."

"A glass of sherry, such as you are having now?"

"On that day? I think not. No, I know not, because that is the day when she said to me..."

After a moment, Masters asked, "What did she say, Frau Hillger?"

Mimi hesitated a moment before replying. Then:

"Elke always used chilli wine in her soup. She said I had not filled up the bottle, but there was plenty for her. I had noted that. But when I said she should not take so much she replied that as she had not had sherry before lunch she would take a large sprinkling to make up for that. As you will know, Mr. Masters, chilli wine is made from the very dry sherry, but it is hot, very hot, because it has the long, red chilli beans soaking in it for weeks. And so it is...how would you say?...it is potent."

"Never heard of this stuff," said Green. "What's it for exactly?"

"Putting a bit of zip into soup," said Masters quietly. "You stuff a swag-bellied bottle full of chilli beans and top up with sherry. You need a sprinkler top, of course, so that you just get a few drops in a plate of soup. You can keep the brew going for ages with the same chillies. You just keep topping up the sherry."

"You have one, have you?"

Masters nodded.

Margarethe interrupted. "Aunty! You didn't serve hot soup for lunch in this weather, surely. No wonder mummy felt..."

"It was cold coup. Elke asked for it."

"Vichyssoise?" asked Masters.

"Bortsch."

"Cold beetroot soup?" asked Green, scandalized by the mere thought of the concoction.

"We have always eaten bortsch."

"But not cold," objected Masters.

"Certainly cold. It is the summer soup in my part of the world. Now that there are blenders and one no longer has to sieve, it is even more popular than before."

"It is peculiarly Russian, or at least eastern European," said Margarethe. "In the cold version you cook the beetroot first, dice it and add it to beef tea with some cream or yoghurt and lemon juice. Then you blend it, chill it, and serve with scissored chives." She turned to Green. "I don't care for beetroot myself but cold bortsch is not quite as ghastly as it sounds, particularly with a sprinkling of chilli wine."

"I'll take your word for it," said Green.

"There seems little that could have upset Mrs Carlow in the soup," said Masters. "What else did she have for lunch?"

"Duobrot...crispbread...and cheese. Your simple English Cheddar cheese, though Elke always preferred a German Limburger if we could get it. But the grocers here..." She spread her hands in dismay and derision. "We could not often get it."

"Any sweet?"

"We have the Swiss almond and chocolate biscuits with our coffee. That is all."

"Thank you."

"A pretty cosmopolitan meal, by and large," said Green. "Russian soup, German crispbread, English

183

cheese, Swiss biscuits and, I suppose, Brazilian coffee. That's a bit of a mixture."

"Not enough of a mixture to upset my mother, I would have thought," said Margarethe.

"All very bland," said Masters getting to his feet. "Well, that's it, Frau Hillger. Thank you for your time. Enjoy your sherry." He turned to look down the garden where Reed and Berger were showing an interest in the well-kept beds, squatting to examine some of the plants.

"What are they doing?" asked Mimi querulously.

"Only showing an interest, ma'am," grunted Green, pushing himself off the ground. "They'll not be doing the petunias any lasting harm."

"The petunias are not in that place," retorted Mimi.

"Sorry," said Green. "I wasn't speaking literally." He raised his voice to call the two sergeants. "Come on, lads, get your skates on."

"They're doing no harm," said Margarethe. "Leave them if they want to look."

"We have to be going," said Masters. "Thank you once again, Frau Hillger."

As Margarethe escorted them through the house, Masters asked her: "Did your mother and aunt stick very much to sherry? I mean, could Mrs Carlow have taken a glass of vodka or schnapps perhaps without her sister knowing?"

"She could have done so. They keep all the usual drinks in the house, but mother drank comparatively little. Certainly not enough to…wait a moment, Mr Masters, you're not suggesting she could have drunk enough to make her tipsy to the point where she didn't know what she was doing and then poisoned herself, are you?"

"Something of the sort," agreed Masters. "It is a possibility and I want to consider everything."

"Oh, no," said Margarethe, firmly.

184

"She seemed keen on her chilli wine, according to Frau Hillger."

"But that doesn't mean she was an alcoholic. She would never indulge in more than one small drink before lunch—if she had one at all."

"And another in the evening?"

"Sometimes. Quite often, in fact."

"But she was definitely an abstemious person?"

"Absolutely abstemious."

"Thank you. That clears that point. Goodbye, Mrs Rainford. We shall see you again, no doubt."

"No doubt," repeated Margarethe wryly.

— 7 —

"You finished that a bit quick, George," said Green as they got into the Rover. "What's up? Didn't you take a shine to the old girl's face?"

"We'd asked the obvious questions. Short of getting the sergeants to search the premises there was little more we could do, so I thought I'd give the ladies a chance to have their lunch while we did something about ours."

"Rubbish."

"You think so?"

"I know so. And what about our two pals here? Why send them down the garden path?"

"To see the pretty flowers," said Reed.

"And did you see anything nice?"

Reed turned. "Pansies, petunias—not very far on, some little old-fashioned marigold seedlings, a couple of dozen handsome-looking delphinium plants and... yes...a nice bed of lily of the valley."

Green grunted. "Under jampots, I suppose?"

"Some were. Some weren't. It looked as if there'd been a bit of weeding and pulling going on round there. A couple of jam jars were rolled aside. Sergeant Berger and I put them back."

"That's why the old dear got twitchy, was it? She thought you were pinching her blooms."

"Who? Us?"

Masters had dropped out of the conversation. He seemed content to sit back occupied by his own thoughts. He came back to earth when the car drew up in the forecourt of a little old-fashioned country pub.

"Hot and cold grub at the bar," said Green. "Let's hope they've got something decent to offer."

The bar was almost empty when they entered, but even so, in answer to their inquiry, the landlord told them they were too late for the shepherd's pie. There was plenty of choice, however, when it came to sandwiches.

"Are you sure?" asked Green, suspiciously. "There's a bloody good smell of cooking coming from somewhere." He sniffed the air. "A right good pongeroo it is, too."

The landlord who was, by this time, drawing pints of best bitter at Masters' request, looked behind him. "Sorry," he said. "I left the private door open. The wife's making a bit of soup for my dinner."

"I know we're a bit late," grumbled Green, "but not that late. It's nowhere near closing time yet."

"'Nuther half-hour," admitted the landlord. "I'll get the sandwiches for you now, gents, if you'll tell me what it's to be."

They chose beef, and the landlord left the bar for the kitchen quarters. He was back in no time and said to Green: "The missus says you can have a bowl of the soup if you want it."

Green accepted. In a few moments he had a large plate of the good-smelling liquid before him. He took a sip of the first spoonful. "This," he announced with relish, "is not half bad." He continued to eat it, and was a long way down it when the landlord reappeared with the sandwiches.

"Tell your missus this is just the ticket," said Green.

"You like it?"

"I do, chum. And I know the flavour, but I just can't place it. Got some exotic name, has it?"

"Yes," said the landlord with a grin. "Bubble and squeak."

Green opened and closed his mouth a couple of times, savouring the after-taste. "You're right, chum. No wonder I recognized the flavour, but...bubble and squeak soup!"

"My missus never wastes anything. She had a few tablespoonsful of bubble and squeak left over last night. You know—spud, carrots and brussel sprouts. So she put it into some chicken stock she'd got and blended the whole lot in her mixer. We often have it. Not too bad, is it?"

"Bloody good," said Green appreciatively. "And I tell you what, pal, I bet it beats cold beetroot soup any day."

"What's beetroot got to do with it?"

Green put his spoon into the empty plate. "Nothing, really. It's just that I heard an hour ago about somebody who liked cold beetroot soup which isn't, I'll tell you, something I'd go for."

"Me neither. Beetroot!"

"Called bortsch," said Green. "Russian name."

"That's why you asked if this had a fancy foreign name, I suppose?"

"That's right. Give me bubble and squeak every time."

The landlord retired with the empty plate.

Reed said to Green: "All very interesting. I suppose you'll be telling this story to all and sundry for the next twenty years."

"If I live that long. I'll certainly be telling my missus. He took a long gulp from his tankard. "Not bad beer either. I wonder if he's got a name like bubble and squeak for this, too."

"Yes," said Berger. "Ale and 'earty."

"Clever clogs," retorted Green.

"Where to now, Chief?"

"Back to Police HQ, please."

"Any special reason for going there?" asked Green. Masters nodded. "I'm expecting a phone call."

"Oh?"

"I spoke to you about it earlier."

"Got you. You're expecting a reply so soon?"

"There's a chance."

Green didn't reply. Berger, sitting in the front passenger seat asked: "A call about the case, Chief?"

"Private."

Berger faced front. There was no more conversation until they reached their destination. Green snoozed in his nearside back corner seat, while Masters smoked contemplatively. It was as though the warmth of the early afternoon sun were urging them to take a siesta. Even Reed, who was driving, appeared to be doing so automatically so that the car, though competently handled, seemed to be playing its part soporifically.

Masters paused at the desk to ask if there were any messages for him.

"Just one, sir. Would you ring the Yard or if you haven't got time in working hours would you ring a Mr Anderson at home. He said you would know what it was about."

"Thank you. Would you get me the Yard, please. I'll take the call in our office."

"Right, sir."

Masters turned to the two sergeants. "Make sure the car is filled up, please. And one of you get on to Dr Eric Dampney, the pathologist, and ask him if I can call on him this afternoon—any time after half an hour from now."

"Right, Chief."

"He doesn't want us to hear what he's getting on to the A.C. Crime about," muttered Berger to Reed as Masters and Green went upstairs to the office. "Any idea what's going on?"

"He told you it was private."

"That doesn't stop me from wondering, does it?"

"Maybe not. But does your nosiness go as far as speculating why the Chief wants to see the pathologist?"

"Haven't a clue. But he's gone all thoughtful, which means he's on to something."

"What, for instance?"

"I said I hadn't a clue. Perhaps he's checking up to see if the old girl really did have beetroot soup."

"Nothing toxic about beetroot, is there?"

"How the hell should I know? I never touch the stuff myself. Not since I heard a doctor say it could turn your urine red and I'd no wish to frighten myself by letting that happen to me."

Reed nodded his agreement. "You check the tank. I'll call the pathologist."

"D'you want me with you, George?" asked Green when they reached the office door.

"You're the one most involved, Bill. You might as well get the answer direct."

Green grunted and closed the office door as Masters picked up the phone.

"Hello, George? How's it going out there? Nearly finished? I damn-well hope so. We need you back here."

"I'm hopeful, sir."

"You mean you think you've cracked it?"

"With a bit of luck, yes."

"That's what I like to hear. Now about Bill Green..."

Masters raised his eyebrows in a signal to Green to come closer in an effort to overhear the words coming over the phone.

"...the committee will play, at any rate for the time being. They think you've had a damn fine idea..."

"The D.C.I. is to become an S.S.C.O., sir?"

"Yes. In name only, of course, as we agreed."

"For how long?"

"No definite time. They wouldn't commit themselves. In theory he could go on till sixty-five, but in practice, if we have many more of these damn cuts, the Lord alone knows how long we'll be able to keep him."

"That's good news, sir, but in fairness to Green, he should have a contract of employment."

"Don't push it, George. He'll be safeguarded by the Employment Acts. The committee has gone along with us so far, but they're dead set on what they call their siege programme and that's only another name for cutting us to the bone."

"Right, sir. Now about a young D.I. to replace Green..."

"Nothing doing, George. They won't wear it. They'll only keep Green on as an S.S.C.O. if he'll agree to continue doing the job he's doing now. They won't agree to the money for another D.I. to take his place."

"I see."

"Will he play along?"

Masters looked across at Green who was grinning widely.

"He'll play," said Masters.

"And what about you?"

"I'm more than content, sir. But I would urge that we reconsider bringing along a young..."

"I've told you, George. If you want to train up a young D.I., you'll have to lose Green. It's a case of take it or leave it."

"I'd like to keep Green, sir."

"I thought so. Tell him to make an appointment to see me immediately he gets back."

"That could be tomorrow, sir."

"I'm glad to hear it. So long, George. Love to Wanda when you ring her."

Masters put the phone down.

"Well, Bill?"

"Couldn't be better." He peered at Masters. "Or could it? You don't seem too pleased."

Masters sat down. "I'm obviously delighted that you're still going to be with us, Bill, in whatever capacity."

"But?"

"But I object to them getting a D.C.I. on the cheap merely by rechristening him an S.S.C.O."

"It doesn't make any difference to me. We'll be exactly the same as we have been."

"No, Bill, we won't. For instance, you won't be able to appear in court as a police officer because, officially you won't be one. In the absence of a D.I. it means I'll be doing the lot, and that will seriously cut into our working time. Then again, you took over the bank case when I was ill. You did a great job and we were able to come out of it smelling of roses. But from now on you won't be able to take over in similar circumstances, whereas, in fact you would be able to if we had a young D.I. to front you. That sort of job will have to go elsewhere in future."

Green took out a battered Kensitas packet and selected one of its contents carefully before smoothing it out in his fingers. "Sorry, George. I hadn't foreseen the difficulties."

"It's no fault of yours, Bill. We shall get along famously on cases such as this we're on at the moment. Status quo ante, as the Yanks would say. But we spend a hell of a lot of time not on cases like this, where a young D.I. would, nominally at least, take some of the weight off our shoulders."

"What you're saying is that by keeping me on you've increased your own work load."

"Not quite. By keeping you on on *their* terms we are either increasing my work or weakening the team. Had they consented to our terms there would have been no drawbacks."

"So what do you want me to do? Accept or refuse?"

"Accept, of course. That's what we both want isn't it?"

"If you say so."

"Come off it, Bill." Masters stood up and grinned. "Half a loaf, old timer! We'll still be able to wipe their eyes."

"I'm that valuable?"

"Invaluable. Even if it's only to discover pubs where they sell bubble and squeak soup."

"You should have had some," replied Green, satisfied with the exchanges. "It would have put a new refill in your ballpoint."

Masters was about to reply when there was a knock at the door.

"Come in."

Reed entered. "Sorry to interrupt, Chief, but the pathologist says he will see you if you can get to the hospital before half-past three. After that you've had him till tomorrow night at home."

"Thank you. You know where to take us?"

"All sussed out, Chief."

"Right, we're on our way."

"What's the object of this particular visit?" asked Green. "Or is it asking too much to be let into the little secret?"

"I'll tell you what I hope to do, and that is to throw a stone into a pool and see where the ripples fetch up."

"Thanks very much. Very graphic. I suppose you've been reading up all those toxicology books at night and you've found something you hope will stump this poor pathologist."

"Roughly right."

Green looked across at him. "You're looking smug, George."

"I hope not. But if I am so transparent as to appear self-satisfied at least you cannot accuse me of concealing..."

"Oh, no you don't. It's been said that..."

"Not more quotes from the ragbag of memory. You know, Bill, I read a year or two ago that the captain of the England cricket team, an erstwhile don and accustomed to fielding in the slips, when asked what he and his close colleagues talked about while waiting between the bowlers' deliveries, confessed that they discussed Greek philosophy or whatever his academic subject was. It struck me at the time that those who were obliged to participate in this educational exercise would find it hard going after quite a short time. Now, were somebody to ask me what my team discussed in the intervals between interviews I should be obliged to confess that we were in the habit of dredging up quotations, apposite or otherwise, with which to salt our conversations. I feel my scepticism concerning the entertainment value of philosophy in the slips could well be equalled by that concerning the amusement potential of literary quotations in a CID car."

Green sneered. "Having tried to head me off the subject of concealment because it is an embarrassment to you, I'll say what I had in mind when you started spouting that last load of rubbish."

"If you must."

"The true use of speech," said Green emphatically, "is not so much to express as to conceal. And it could have been written about you. You've not answered any question we've put to you, and here we are at the end of the ride. Yet you've said a hell of a lot. I reckon we could say you've equalled any politician in the land in rabbiting on without saying anything."

Masters didn't reply. As the Rover pulled up in the

area reserved for medical staff he opened the car door.

"Lead on, Reed."

"I was told to go to the separate block on the left, Chief."

"That sounds reasonable, considering there's an arrow pointing that way saying Path Lab," grunted Green.

"Consultant pathologists don't normally have their offices where all the patients go to have samples tested," protested Reed.

"This one does, evidently. He's probably got a morgue close by, too."

The Path Lab was a long building, just two storeys high, very low compared with the rest of the hospital which seemed to be a mixture of an old central building with new wings attached.

"Is this chap a genuine forensic man?" asked Green.

"According to Rainford he is, but he's not called on all that often. The area seems to be comparatively peaceful."

"Rubbish. There's no police area these days that doesn't have at least one death requiring a medico-legal autopsy each week. That's fact. Most have several a week while the city areas don't know how to cope."

"What's your point, Bill?"

"I can't see how this Dampney character can be so underemployed. Not called on all that often, you said, as though there was only about one mysterious death round here every other year."

"I was playing your game of quoting. Rainford's words, not mine. I suppose there could be several pathologists they can call on, which would lighten the load."

They entered the building and were directed to the consultant's office.

"What can I do for you, gentlemen?"

Dampney was dressed in old grey slacks and a sports jacket that had a very obvious darn on the right hand side pocket. Masters suspected that Dampney was a pipe smoker who had, unsuspectingly, pocketed a still-glowing pipe which had burned the material from the inside.

He was a big man, with a fleshy face, a big nose, a crackling but jovial voice and, Masters suspected, an almost total disregard for convention.

"Answer a few questions, I hope, sir," replied Masters.

"Right. Park yourselves and let's hear what it is." He sat back. "I suppose old Paddy Dean knows you're here, does he? My report is legally his property, you know."

"My colleague, D.C.I. Green, is coroner's officer to Mr Dean who has agreed that I can make whatever use I like of the report you sent him."

"Fair enough. There wasn't much to say really. I did the whole bag of tricks, of course, but there was nothing to find except that the old girl died from a massive overdose of cardiac glycosides. I don't think I can usefully expand on that except to say that is was ingested as opposed to being injected."

"All that is very clear, sir."

"What's your trouble, then?"

"Mrs Carlow was receiving digoxin which is, in essence, I believe, digitalis."

"If you like to put it that simply."

"I'm a layman, doctor, but I like to be precise."

"Meaning what exactly?"

"You refer to cardiac glycosides, which intimates that there are a number of such substances other than digitalis."

"Go on."

"It is my understanding that the leaves and seeds of various species of foxglove, strophanthus, oleander, the corm of squill and, indeed, a number of other plants all contain toxic glycosides."

"Quite right. And such knowledge isn't too bad for a mere layman."

"Thank you. As I said, I like to be precise. Would you, therefore, please tell me which of the glycosides you discovered in the body, or rather from which source it came?"

Dampney laughed aloud. "You're joking, of course."

"Not at all."

"Have you any idea...no, of course, you wouldn't have...but to determine the plant source of a toxic glycoside would need a number of very comprehensive tests which could, in the end, prove to be completely non-conclusive. The tests for glycoside poisoning—both biological and chemical—*are* conclusive, and these I have done. The woman died of an overdose of cardiac glycosides."

Masters replied quietly: "I am well aware that in the Bonino Test, for example, the colourimetric reactions of cardiac glycosides support what you say because the same colours are given by sugars as well as by different glycosides. So, admittedly, that test is non-specific. But there are other tests are there not, which might help? The Baljet Test, the Keller-Kiliani, the Richaud and the Sanchez? Wouldn't they, as it were, because of their differing reactions, discover the culprit by a process of elimination?"

Dampney regarded Masters shrewdly. "You did say you were a layman, didn't you?"

"A layman who does his homework."

"Fine. I admire the attitude, even if you are, in essence, virtually accusing me of not doing my job."

"Such was not my intention, sir."

"Maybe not. But it amounted to that. However, that is by the way. There are many glycosides which have an action on the heart similar to digitalis—or what we blithely call digitalis. For instance there are digitonin, digitalin, digitoxin, digitalinum, digitaligenum, digitoxigenin, gitoxin and gitalin to name but a few. All that lot comes from foxgloves. You mentioned strophanthus. That produces strophanthin and ouabain. And so on and so on. Scores of them, all with the same action on the heart. So what? you say. You are a pathologist, a forensic man, tell us which was the culprit. But the deceased had been legitimately medicated on digoxin—which is a form of digitalis—and the action of digitalis can be demonstrated as late as two weeks after the last dose. And that is in a living person. In a person who suddenly dies while still receiving digitalis treatment, there is not even the fortnight of normal excretion to lessen the effects of its presence. So what was I presented with? A cadaver full of digitalis after prolonged treatment. Some substance, closely resembling digitalis in every respect, had been ingested to turn the former therapeutic dose into a fatal toxic dose. And you say to me, what caused the death? My preliminary tests were biological and they told me that a digitaloid drug or drugs had caused death from cardiac failure. Being a scientist and, therefore, not quite so precise as you might wish, I appreciated that the overwhelming digitaloid drug would be digitalis—simply because that is what she had been taking, but because I couldn't be positive it was the only culprit, I blamed cardiac glycosides in general—a fact I could be sure of. I even went so far as to consider doing the tests you mentioned. But because I knew that there was a goodly amount of digitalis present, I realized that I could never separate out another digitaloid. Why? Because all those tests rely on colour and, therefore, every colour I might manage to get would be compromised. I'll explain that. You mentioned the Bonino test. In that, pure digitonin comes out violet. Pure digitalin comes out rose to rose-violet. Pure digitoxin an instant rose colour. If any two of those are present, what colour would I get? In the Richaud test, strophanthin develops a rose colour. In the Sanchez test it gives a violet-blue colour, but digitalis gives blue. Mix digitalis with strophanthin and what colour results?" He spread his hands. "Mr. Masters, had the patient not been on digitalis I could have helped you. But as it is..." He shrugged. "It would take me a year, even if it could be done."

"So you cannot say whether any toxic glycoside other than digitalis was involved?"

"Ah! That's not what you asked me."

"No. That's my second best question."

"You're a clever bastard, aren't you? You led me on to get all hot under the collar and explain why I couldn't tell you exactly what substances were involved just to get me to confess that I should be able to decide if there was a second agent present in the body even if I couldn't identify it."

Masters lowered his head. "Can you?"

"I can test for an adulteration, certainly. But you do realize, I hope, that it will not alter my report. Because I will be unable to name a second peccant substance, should there be one, I shall still have to say death was caused by a toxic dose of cardiac glycosides. So you'll be no further forward."

"Nonetheless, sir, I should be most grateful to know if there was adulteration or addition."

"I'll bet! Give me an hour. I'll do two quick tests at once—different ones. One will confirm the other, I hope. If they tell different stories..." He left the sentence uncompleted and rose to his feet. "Ring through here at four. If I've gone I'll leave a message for you. One of the lab staff will pass it on."

"Thank you. Just one quick point. Had Mrs. Carlow taken beetroot soup shortly before she died?"

"Had she not! Fortunately she'd got rid of a lot of it when she vomited, but the colour was still there, and a lot of the sugar from the beet. That sugar was one of the obstacles in the way of testing."

"I understand. Thank you once again for your help, doctor. I shall await the outcome of your tests with no little impatience."

Dampney laughed aloud once again. "Don't worry. I take the hint. The result is obviously important so I'll take great care."

Masters nodded his thanks.

As they left the building, Green said: "For a time, in there, George, I thought he'd got you. I should have known better."

"He had got me," confessed Masters. "But he was so wary he was peering ahead and by so doing almost gave me the hint as to how to retrieve the situation."

"Maybe. But isn't that what always happens in questioning people, Chief?" asked Reed. "You pick up the hints from what the other bloke says so that you can keep the interview going till it reaches a satisfactory conclusion?"

"With a suspect you do," said Berger.

"With a witness, lad," corrected Green. "And Dampney was a witness. A suspect witness if you like, because his report was not full enough for his nibs."

It was after they had got into the car that Green asked: "You got what you wanted, I expect?"

"I'm going to proceed on the assumption that I have. So far, everybody has said Elke Carlow was killed by an overdose of digitalis—probably an extra lot of her own medicine that she or somebody else procured from somewhere. Dampney did nothing to dispel that belief."

"You, however, decided she'd been killed by some other agent? Something that resembled digitalis so closely in its action that the good Dr Whincap would be fooled and the clever Dr Dampney would see no need to probe further?"

"That's about it."

"What if Dampney doesn't find a second agent, Chief?" asked Berger.

"Be your age, son," said Green. "He knows he will, otherwise he wouldn't be doing those tests."

"Where to, Chief?" asked Reed, sitting in the driving seat. "Or are we going to wait here until four o'clock?"

"I want to see Josef Kisiel."

"To the garden centre, then?"

"Please."

"You've got him in mind, have you?"

"I want to talk to him."

"He said you'd go back."

"Second sight. Premonition perhaps."

Green took out his cigarettes and in an unusual fit of generosity, offered them over the front seat where Berger accepted one. Then he turned again to Masters. "She didn't chew some digitalis leaves herself, did she George?"

"I think not, Bill. Foxgloves are summer flowering as opposed to spring flowering, and so their leaves are very small and their seeds are non-existent by the first of May. But there are recorded deaths from eating the leaves and even one from the inhalation of smoke from a bonfire on which green oleander cuttings were being burnt."

"Is that right, Chief?"

"Absolutely."

"Imagine trying to solve a case where somebody was killed by the smoke from leaves on a garden fire. Apart from the impossibility of solving the problem, it begins to make you think that no human action is ever anything but dangerous."

"That's a good lesson to bear in mind, lad," said Green. "You might repeat it for Sergeant Reed's benefit right now. The speed he's going is the pace that kills."

"Okay," said Reed, slowing slightly. "But if the Chief wants to interview old Kisiel before he rings the path lab at four, there's not much time to waste."

Josef Kisiel was in his own office in the house at the gate of the garden centre. He received them courteously enough, but seemed amused to see them again so soon, as though his powers of foretelling the future had been confirmed as much by the speed of their return as the event itself.

The ensuing conversation took place between Kisiel and Masters alone. The other three stood by listening intently, but not interrupting. It was a tense discussion, with Kisiel doing most of the talking. He emphasized his points with generous hand gestures and within very few minutes had satisfied Masters on all the points the detective had put to him. But the conversation continued with minor matters being cleared up until Masters was able to recapitulate the whole unerringly. Only then did he sit back and thank the Pole for his help.

"What are you going to do now, please?"

Masters looked at his watch.

"Just after four, Chief," said Reed, quietly, as though he disliked having to break the tension.

"Thank you," Masters replied without looking at his colleagues. Still facing Kisiel, he said: "I have a phone call to make."

"You shall use my phone."

"Thank you."

"You wish me to leave?"

"No, no. Can I get straight through?"

"On the white phone, yes."

Reed supplied the number of the path lab. Without delay, Dampney answered.

"You're still there, doctor?"

"I was writing a message to leave for you."

"To tell me that you have isolated convallaria?"

"What the hell are you, Masters? A wizard?"

"Hardly."

"You expected me to find convallaria glycosides?"

"Shall we say I hoped you would."

"But when you were reeling off that list in my office this afternoon you didn't even mention convallaria."

"I was careful not to."

"Why?"

"I think it was because I didn't want to prejudice any finding you might be able to make."

"Bloody sauce! Have you any idea how insulting a chap like me could find a remark like that, coming from a layman?"

"It was not my intention to insult you, Dr Dampney."

"I know, Mr Masters."

"Thank you."

"That's that, then. I'll have to do a bit of measuring to find exact amounts and so on, but you can take it from me that the dose was pretty hefty. By that I mean comparatively speaking. Actually the amount will be minute, but when you consider that three hundred micrograms—that is about a third of a milligram—is virtually toxic on its own..."

"On top of the daily digoxin tablet?"

"Right. You've got it. Enough to work on, anyhow. There'll be a written report for Patrick Dean, of course."

"Of course. Thank you again, Dr Dampney."

They left the office after thanking Kisiel.

"Where to now, Chief?" asked Berger.

"Dean's office, please."

"Will he still be there when we get there? It's a long way," said Reed.

"Stop at the first phone box and ring him, lad," said Green. "Find out where he is and tell him his nibs wants to see him."

"Thanks, Bill. That's a good idea. In fact, after Dean,

203

I'd like to talk to the Chief Constable. We can call him at the same time and get him to hang on until we get to his HQ."

Green nodded.

"I'm not going to ask what it's all about," he said, "but it's obvious things are moving."

Masters smiled. "That's as good a way of asking a question without making it a query as I've heard in a long time, Bill. And I'm going to answer it as soon as we've made those phone calls and we've got an un-interrupted run in the car."

"Fully?"

"In its entirety. I want your opinion on several points."

"Why visit Dean?"

"Courtesy more than anything else. It'll make a dif-ference to the way he conducts his court if we make an arrest before he re-opens. And we mustn't forget that you and or Reed are in theory working as his of-ficer. We are in duty bound to talk to him."

Green was about to reply when Berger said, "Phone box coming up, Chief."

"Let's hope it hasn't been vandalized." Masters felt into his change pocket. "We shall want some ten pence pieces."

"I've got three," said Reed as the car halted. "Shall I make the calls, Chief, or will you?"

"I will."

Green, Reed and Berger listened as Masters spoke on the way to Dean's office. When he'd finished, Green said: "It all fits, George. Means and opportunity are both there, but you haven't mentioned motive. Or if you have, I've missed it."

"Me, too," said Berger.

"Deliberately," said Masters. "It's tricky. What I mean is, it's real enough to me, but I'm going to have to pick my way through it for all those characters at HQ and I'd rather only do it the once if you people will bear with me."

"Fair enough. There's no time now, anyhow. We're at Dean's place."

Dean, too, listened patiently to Masters' story. When it was over, he merely said that he was grateful for the job they had done. He would now be able to reconvene his court and bring in a verdict that would hand over all responsibility to the police.

"That was painless enough," said Green when they were back in the car. "He'll not be allowed to name names in court, but he can bring in person or persons unknown, add that he understands we have somebody in custody and call it a day. And talking of custody, when do we do it?"

Masters paused for a moment before replying.

"That's going to be the most difficult bit, Bill."

Green grimaced. "We'll have to do it. We can't expect Theo Rainford to..."

"Unthinkable."

"We do it, then. *And* the magistrates' court tomorrow."

"I can see no alternative."

"Bail?"

"On no account. The same thing could happen again." Masters glanced at his watch. "Why not now?"

"The C.C. will be waiting."

"Not yet. I said between six and six thirty. He's gathering a few characters—Rainford, Bennett and Whincap."

"Why?"

"I asked him to. I'd like them all to hear and not be in any doubt."

"Okay. Warrant?"

"In for questioning, I think. Arrest later."

"Would you like me to do it? Me and the lads?"

"I said it was the most difficult bit. I don't want to appear to be ducking out."

"You won't be. Besides, we'll need your seat in the car."

"You mean—literally—that you'd rather have my room than my company?"

"Summat of the sort. Look, if we drop you at the gate of the college grounds, can you walk up? Then we can go straight on."

"If you're sure?"

Green grinned. "This," he said, "will likely be the last time I perform this service. I'll do it without you."

"Fair enough. I was forgetting."

Reed asked: "What's going on, Chief? The D.C.I.'s last lift? Is he retiring?"

"The D.C.I. is not leaving the team," said Masters firmly. "He'll be here to plague us for a long time yet."

"That's good hearing, Chief. For a moment I thought we were going to be denied the doubtful pleasure of his quotations."

"You mind your own barrer, young Reed," said Green, not displeased by the sergeant's comment. "And if you can't push it, shove it."

"See what I mean. Chief? Where would we be without such helpful advice so generously and so courteously given?"

"Where, indeed?"

Berger said: "I grew momentarily sad, too. No more buying drinks for senior officers, no more watching fried spud being scoffed for breakfast, no more..."

"That's enough," growled Green. "That's the gate to the college just ahead. Dump his nibs and let's be on our way."

They were gathered round the coffee table at the end of Harrington's office away from his desk. Harrington himself had brought his desk chair, and the two sergeants had the C.C.'s normal visitors' upright chairs. The rest occupied the modern, low, armless pieces that, at a pinch, could be pushed together to form a settee of infinite length. P.C. Gibson, the HQ messenger, had brought in a trolley with bottles of beer and glasses.

"Who are we waiting for?" Harrington sounded slightly querulous. He did not seem best pleased at being kept in his office until after half-past six in the evening. Masters suspected that he would have preferred to be at home with the prospect of a large gin before dinner rather than bottled beer in the company of the mixed bag that now confronted him.

"Dr Whincap," said Rainford. "He's left his surgery so he should be here any minute." Masters eyed the local D.C.S. closely. Rainford had not spoken to him since they had entered the office. The grapevine had probably been working and Rainford was more than likely aware of the presence of the suspect at HQ. The fact would not make him happy. But he was chatting fairly readily with Bennett who, though behaving very quietly, was nevertheless as cheerful as usual.

"The doctor's here, sir." P.C. Gibson showed Whincap into the office.

"Good evening, everybody. Sorry to be the last." Whincap took the chair beside Rainford. "Now, what's going on? Your message, Chief Constable, told me very little except that there were some new developments in the Elke Carlow business."

"I shall leave D.C.S. Masters to tell you what those developments are, gentlemen. I should add that he has given me merely the gist of what he wishes to say, but he particularly asked that I should invite you here to listen to the full report he is now about to make because he feels that you are all—each in his separate way—interested in the outcome of his investigation. I shall not, therefore, hold matters up any longer except to say that I hope you will all help yourselves to beer as and when you want it. There's plenty on the trolley and more where that came from." He turned to Masters. "If you'd like to begin, Mr Masters...?"

"Thank you, sir."

Masters proceeded to speak without notes. On the coffee table in front of him he had one sheet of A_4 size paper lying face downwards and on top if it, as if to hold it in place or to prevent it being inadvertently picked up and examined, were his pipe, matches and brassy tin of Warlock Flake.

"Gentlemen, you are all aware that Mrs Carlow died of a fatal overdose of cardiac glycosides. I use that term because that is how the pathologist's report describes what Dr Whincap, in his on-the-spot diagnosis, described as an overdose of digitalis.

"There was no disagreement between the two doctors as to the cause of death and so, when we arrived to investigate the case, we accepted unreservedly that Mrs Carlow had in fact died as Dr Whincap stated she had.

"The problems facing us were, basically, only two in number. The first, where had the extra dose come from and second, had Mrs Carlow ingested it herself or had it been fed to her without her knowledge.

"As you all know by now, Dr Whincap had on several previous occasions been called to treat his patient for what was undoubtedly overdosage of her medicine. On each occasion he was satisfied that Mrs Carlow had intentionally overdosed herself. She was, in fact, a stubborn old woman who would not stick to the dosage pattern laid down for her. Out of his concern for his patient, the doctor instituted a system of daily rationing which ensured that not only did Mrs Carlow not have the opportunity to overdose herself, but also that she should not miss taking the daily tablet which was so important for her well-being. When a doctor makes provisions such as that, there is every reason to assume that the precautions he took to make sure that there was no cache of spare digoxin left in the house were absolutely foolproof. So we could be satisfied from the outset that the drug used to overdose Mrs Carlow did not come from an obvious source such as a hidden supply of formerly prescribed tablets."

Whincap moved to a more comfortable position on his chair, as though the words just spoken by Masters had relieved some tension that had been holding him fixed on the rack.

"So we had to find another source of the excess drugs or..." Here Masters paused a moment. "...or find another drug: a drug which would mimic the action of digitalis so closely as to deceive Dr Whincap and, indeed, Dr Dampney.

"Please remember that his experience of his patient and the fact that he was maintaining her on digoxin led Dr Whincap to stipulate digitalis poisoning. The pathologist, warned of these circumstances, did not disagree with Dr Whincap. He merely gave a more general name to the toxic substances—cardiac glycosides.

"Now, I said we had to find another drug that mimics the action of digitalis, and this path was not denied us because there are many sources of cardiac glycosides which in themselves are numerous. Digitalis as you probably all know occurs in the leaves and seeds of various species of foxglove. But other plants produce toxic glycosides, too. Strophanthus, oleander, squill and convallaria are some of them.

"We wondered whether any of these plants could have been the culprit. Our investigations did, in fact, point strongly to one of them. Consequently I asked Dr Dampney to try to isolate the peccant substance and to our great satisfaction he was able to do so. The culprit was convallaria."

"But that," said Whincap, "that's the common or garden lily of the valley."

"Convallaria is?" asked Bennett, astounded.

"Gentlemen," chided the Chief Constable.

"Sorry," said Whincap and Bennett together.

"Please don't apologize," said Masters. "Though this is a presentation, it is not a lecture and I shan't mind reasonable interruptions. As I go along, I may invite comment to clarify certain areas and I hope you will help where you can.

"Convallaria is indeed lily of the valley, and wherever we have been during the last two days we have encountered these, all in full flower, and mostly brought on under glass."

"That's old Josef Kisiel's influence," said Rainford. "Lily of the valley has some sort of ritual significance in Eastern Europe. For May Day or some such."

"Quite right. Mr Kisiel grows them on a commercial basis. But Mrs Marian Whincap, for instance, grows them in exactly the same way in her garden. We discussed them when we visited Helewou."

"You're not implicating Marian, I hope?"

Masters shrugged. "Does Mrs Rainford grow them in the same way?"

"Yes."

"So did her mother."

"And my daughter Gwen," said Whincap. "Of course, she's married to young Kisiel."

"Quite. They are a common enough flower and for a number of weeks now the leaves have been through and the stolons have been breaking through the earth in great clumps.

"The leaves, stolons and rhizomes are the dangerous parts of the plant, gentlemen. As I said, all have been available for some weeks now. And that point is important."

"Why?" asked Rainford.

"Simply because those parts of the plants which yield the toxin have to be dried and then powdered before extraction can begin.

"Extraction, itself, is simple to carry out. One simply pours alcohol through the powder and captures the resultant tincture. When prepared as medicine, of course, the amounts are carefully measured. Eight parts of dried leaf to one of alcohol is usual according to my text books."

"Text books?" asked Bennett. "You mean you carry them with you?"

"A small library," said Green. "Toxicology books, Martindale and the like. He calls them his recipe books. He dips into them for light reading in bed at night. They've proved mighty useful in more than one case like this."

Nobody commented on this revelation, so Masters continued.

"We have shown you where the active ingredient of the toxin came from. The alcohol is equally easy to get hold of. You—we—all have it in our houses."

"Vodka or gin," suggested Whincap.

"Quite so. The text books quote the use of sixty per cent alcohol for the percolation. It need only be poured over the powdered vegetable as one does when using a filter paper in a funnel. In a domestic setting where such things may not be available, I am sure suitable alternative utensils can be found."

"Every house has a funnel," said Bennett. "We have an orange plastic one. I use it myself for decanting vinegar from a litre bottle into the bottle we use on the table when we're eating salads."

Masters nodded his acknowledgement of this contribution and waited while the Chief Constable added: "A bit of blotting paper would do the trick, wouldn't it?"

"It would, sir. Or a coffee filter paper."

"Ah! Yes! I'd forgotten those things are fairly common these days."

"Wait a moment" said Rainford. "Sixty per cent alcohol is pretty potent stuff. Would vodka or gin be that strong?"

"The same thought had occurred to me," admitted Masters, "and I will deal with your question in a few moments, if I may—purely for the sake of continuity, and bearing in mind that I said earlier that when this particular tincture is being prepared as a medicine, amounts of ingredients, their strengths and proportions are critical. But when being prepared in secret as a poisonous substance, such niceties are not important.

"What I would like everybody to realize is that many of the herbal glycosides I have mentioned have been used for hundreds, perhaps thousands of years. They had not been isolated and named, of course, but country folk knew that digitalis, for instance, was good for certain heart conditions and sufferers would chew the leaves or concoct simples of their own. Convallaria was—and is—particularly popular and widely used in Russia and Eastern Europe for heart conditions. Nowadays, perhaps, such medicines are prepared by the local pharmaceutical manufacturers, for the Polish, Russian and German pharmacopoeias certainly feature them and they specify that only the aerial parts of convallaria should be used in manufacture. But I am sure you will appreciate that in the large rural areas of these countries, the local people are not well supplied with modern medicines and so frequently brew their own herbal remedies. Particularly is this true of the elderly people.

"You will have noted that I mentioned Poland, Russia, East Germany and Eastern Europe in general."

"Just the areas," said the Chief Constable, "where they make such a thing of May Day and grow lily of the valley to celebrate it."

"Just so, sir. So you will appreciate, gentlemen, that my thoughts turned to those people now living round about here who originally hailed from those parts."

"Two of them," said Bennett. "Josef Kisiel and Mimi Hillger."

"Three, chum," said Green. "Old Elke Carlow herself was Prussian."

"Of course. But if you include her you are still entertaining the possibility of suicide."

"We were at the time his nibs is talking of."

"I see. Sorry."

"Not at all," said Green graciously.

"Shall we say that by the time we came to concentrate on murder there were two?" asked Masters. "You will all of you—with the possible exception of the Chief Constable—remember that everybody I spoke to at first strove to avoid telling me that Josef Kisiel had been a bitter enemy of Elke Carlow for more than forty years. So great was your concern to protect him that you, Theo, accepted a palpably false argument of suicide caused by rejection, you Mr Bennett, in company with Dr Whincap, did your damnedest to head me away from Kisiel, as did his son, and Mrs Marian Whincap accused me of suggesting she was guilty of some criminal act when I attempted to elucidate the standing between Mrs Carlow, Mr Josef Kisiel and all the other members of the family group."

Whincap and Bennett looked suitably contrite, but Rainford said hotly: "Because you've got a bloody devious way of going about finding your facts and impressions."

"You mean I ask the wrong—or unexpected—questions?"

"Yes."

"What would you rather I did? Subject the people I spoke to to long gruelling hours of interrogation, gaining a few crumbs of information by attrition?"

213

"Well . . . no, not exactly."

"Remember, Theo," said Green, "that you were allowed to be present when we spoke to your missus and your daughter. Everybody had somebody else present even though the doc got het up because he mistakenly thought we were grilling his practice nurse."

"I did apologize," complained Whincap.

"So you did. All I'm saying is that we didn't put anybody through the hoop. Because his nibs asks unexpected and, therefore, awkward questions and then puts his own brand of interpretation on the answers doesn't mean he's browbeating anybody. Just the reverse, if anything. You've got to make allowances for egg-heads like him. They're always full of bright ideas."

Rainford shrugged. The Chief Constable asked him: "You were present at some of the interviews, Theo. Have you any specific complaint about the way Masters conducted those you heard?"

There was silence for a moment, and then, to his credit, Rainford said: "No, sir. All I'm sore about is the fact that I couldn't do what he does and because my immediate family was on the receiving end."

"Thank you. Can we now get on, please?"

"Josef Kisiel, then," resumed Masters. "A known and implacable enemy of the deceased. A grower of lily of the valley, a Pole and, I assumed, a man with a knowledge of herbal remedies. He seemed the obvious suspect. Could the matter be brought home to him? He had the motive and the means. What about opportunity?

"For the benefit of Dr Whincap and Mr Bennett I should mention that when investigating a case of murder we look for, and hope to prove, three things. Means, opportunity and motive. The last is not mandatory, but it helps all round and particularly when a case comes to trial because juries can accept and understand a motive.

"I have said Kisiel had a motive and the means. We did not establish the necessary opportunity. It was necessary, therefore to ascertain whether there could be another person who fulfilled the criteria.

"Can I just interpolate here that when I mentioned means, I was referring to possession of a crop of convallaria. I was not referring to the physical act of feeding the toxin to the victim. That—the mechanics of the job, if you like—would be a subsidiary point which you might consider could equally well be a part of the opportunity which, at its simplest, is usually considered to be synonymous with proximity. By that I mean that the suspect could be proved to have been, at the critical time, in the vicinity of the victim.

"In considering that a knowledge of herbal remedies seems to be a feature of those who are born and brought up in Eastern Europe—certainly more so than in this country, for many decades at any rate—I was obliged to consider Frau Hillger who, until a year or two ago, had lived her entire life to the east of Berlin. She, as a girl child of yesteryear, would have been taught all the house-wifely habits of her forebears—or so I assumed. So I visited Frau Hillger at her home. Mrs Rainford was at the house and was in the act of pouring a glass of sherry for Frau Hillger when we arrived. Frau Hillger was sitting in the sunshine in the garden, so we were conducted through the house by Mrs Rainford to talk to her. As I said, Mrs Rainford was busy pouring drinks in the dining room. As we passed through I noted that bottles of gin and vodka were openly on view.

"Whilst Mr Green and I spoke to Frau Hillger in the presence of her niece, I asked our two sergeants to stroll down the garden for two reasons. First I did not wish to overwhelm Frau Hillger by the presence of four large policemen, and second I wished to ascertain whether there were lilies of the valley growing in the garden. There were."

Rainford grunted. "So you reckoned Mimi had the means and the opportunity, but no motive."

"Quite right—if by opportunity you mean simply proximity."

"That's what I did mean."

"I now come to an incident of which I think none of you, other than members of my team, is aware. This morning, while I was talking to Josef Kisiel, I was told that Mr Patrick Dean had received a phone call from a woman who called herself Mrs Leafe but who was, in fact, unknown to him."

"An anonymous phone call, you mean?" asked the Chief Constable. "What was it all about?"

"The gist of her message was that somebody was trying to cover up the fact that Mrs Carlow had been murdered by Josef Kisiel who had always vowed to see her in hell."

"Nice," murmured Bennett. "And, I suspect from what little I know of you, helpful to you. Theo, here, says you can make any titbit fit into your jigsaw. What deductions did you draw from that call to Dean? That Josef Kisiel was guilty of murder?"

Green gave him a pitying look. "Come off it, mate. We don't jump to hasty conclusions."

"Sorry. I merely asked."

"Because murder had not, at the time of the inquest, been established, it had not been mentioned publicly. The inquest took only a minute or two and then Dean deferred the hearing. Consequently no public interest had been aroused. I imagine very few people knew that Dean was sitting instead of Mr Bennett. And yet our unknown caller mentioned murder and Josef Kisiel and a cover-up."

"What sort of a woman was she? Could Dean tell?" asked Whincap.

"His secretary accepted the call and put Mrs Leafe

216

through because 'she sounded like a client.' I took that to mean it was not an uneducated voice. Dean himself described the voice as articulate and just the opposite from what he had imagined anonymous callers would sound like. From those two observations we deduced that she could be a woman whom one might meet in the circles in which people like you gentlemen are accustomed to move. Lest you should feel slighted at the idea of any of your acquaintances stooping to such depths, I will remind you of what I mentioned a few moments ago. The woman mentioned murder, Josef Kisiel and his hatred of Elke Carlow and a cover-up."

"Crikey," said Bennett, "she must have been one of us. I mean, murder had been mentioned as a possibility among us; nobody outside a fairly small circle would know about the enmity Josef had for Elke; and I doubt whether anybody not known to us would—or could— have unravelled the family convolutions which might lead one to suppose—or suggest—that a cover-up could take place."

"Quite," said Masters. "So having arrived at that point I had to decide which—if any—of the articulate women in your circle would phone a message like that to Dean."

"I reckon you're wrong," said Rainford. "None of our womenfolk would try to implicate old Josef."

"Even though the menfolk tried to protect him from us?"

"That's the opposite of what I've just said."

"In one way, perhaps. But both could be considered efforts to bamboozle the investigation."

Rainford turned in despair to Whincap. "I told you this chap can see both sides of a coin at once."

"You're not thinking well, Theo. There are two sides to every coin and you can't blame George for seeing them. But to get back to what you said about none of the women you know wanting to implicate Kisiel. His

217

nibs recognized that fact, so what's the other side of that particular coin? I'll tell you. If not to implicate Kisiel, then the call must have been intended to steer suspicion away from herself."

"Rubbish. You didn't know who she was."

"We did, you know. She was one of the very few women—and that doesn't include the lasses like your daughter, otherwise the typist and Dean would have known it was a young voice—who are in some way intimately connected with your family circle. His nibs assumed—and I agreed with him—that Kisiel's wife and daughter-in-law would not say he was a murderer. We reckoned Mrs Whincap senior wouldn't say it about her son-in-law's father. That only left Mrs Bennett, Mrs Rainford and Mrs Hillger. Now, I've been a copper long enough to know you can't discount anybody, but I reckon you, Theo, and Bob here, would excuse us for not considering your respective wives too closely."

"Most certainly," agreed Bennett.

"And don't forget," continued George, "that the phone call was from a woman who spoke precise English. Mrs Hillger fills that bill quite nicely."

Whincap nodded his agreement to this. Masters waited a moment as if to ascertain whether Green intended to continue and then continued: "I think, sir, that as a serving policeman you would also not have overlooked the lesson of statistics which tells us that members of the victim's immediate family are more often than not guilty of domestic murder—as opposed to gang warfare and violence of that nature."

The Chief Constable coughed. "Quite right, Masters. Quite right."

"So we thought of Frau Hillger as the unknown caller who had so unwisely indicated to us that the murderer was more likely to be a woman than a man.

"And so we concentrated our efforts on trying to support this belief. With this in mind, I visited Mr

Kisiel a second time, to get to know how the Eastern Europeans had been accustomed to making their medicinal tinctures." He turned to Rainford. "This is when the proof strength of gin and vodka came up."

"I can never understand this proof strength business," said Bennett. "The percentages they put on bottle labels mean nothing to me."

"It is a little complicated," admitted Masters. "But if I could digress for a moment, I'll tell you the origins of it, and you might then understand it a little better."

"I'm hazy about it myself," admitted the Chief Constable.

"In that case, sir . . . way back, in the old days of Excise Officers and Customs Houses, any drink such as brandy had to be proved to be spirit for duty to be levied. The way the Customs men did it was to dampen a little gunpowder with the liquid to be proved. They then applied a match. If the dampened powder still burned, it proved there was a goodly percentage of alcohol in the liquid. If it failed to burn, then the percentage of water was greater. The proof figure was known. It was slightly under half of alcohol by weight and slightly over half by volume. Both figures run to several places of decimals. But that is where these rather ungainly standards came from, and we still stick to them today. So gin or vodka of, say, sixty-five per cent proof would, in fact, contain only about thirty-two or -three per cent alcohol."

"I knew there was something funny about it," said Rainford. "So gin or vodka would not do the trick."

"It would, actually," said Masters. "When I mentioned this to Kisiel he told me that you simply put the spirit through several lots of the dried herbs, and just as if you were to make coffee stronger by putting it through several new lots of grounds, so you can make the convallaria infusion stronger. But perhaps Dr Whincap would confirm that."

"Right enough," said Whincap. "The alcohol would still retain its properties until you got to a saturated solution. And I imagine that would be considerably more potent than a single infusion with a stronger spirit."

"Thank you. That clears up the point about strength of spirit and also tells us how the people of Poland went about making the tincture with the potable alcohol they had in their houses, rather than resorting to a stronger industrial spirit which would, I suspect, have been dangerous to use."

Masters took a sip from the untouched glass of beer in front of him.

"How did Aunt Mimi get old Elke to take the stuff?" demanded Rainford gruffly. "You said that discovering that would be an important subsidiary to the means of poisoning her sister."

Masters inclined his head. "Did Mrs Rainford speak to you about the visit we paid to your aunt?"

"She told me it all."

"Then you will recall that Frau Hillger prepared cold bortsch for lunch on the day her sister died."

"She mentioned it, yes."

"I wondered what she'd had," said Whincap. "I didn't ask at the time, but when I was dealing with..."

"Must you?" demanded Bennett. "We all know bortsch is made from beetroot and we can guess what the vomit looked like."

"Shall we say," said Masters, "that soup of that particular colour would provide excellent camouflage for a small fatal dose of slightly greenish-brown liquid."

"You mean she spooned the stuff into her sister's plate?"

Masters shook his head. "I'm sorry to tell you, Mr Rainford, that your wife's aunt showed a great degree of cunning at this point. Or, at least, that is my reading of her actions."

220

"Mind reading, now, are you?"

"Theo," said the Chief Constable firmly, "you can ask questions, but not..."

"That was a question, sir."

"A mean one, asked in a mean voice. I can understand that you are upset by all this, but it is hardly Masters' fault that something nasty has cropped up within your family circle."

"Sorry," grunted Rainford, apparently making the one word suffice for both his senior officer and Masters.

"Go on, please," said Harrington.

Masters continued his narrative. "The cardiac glycosides are very unstable. So much I learned by reading. Heat destroys them. That is why the infusion is done with a cold drip—unlike coffee where boiling water is used.

"Frau Hillger must have been aware of this, to have served a cold soup that day. I say that because I believe bortsch is usually served hot."

Rainford seemed to have recovered his equanimity. "I must say that Margarethe always serves it hot. Not that we have it all that often."

"The second thing which caused me to mention Frau Hillger's cunning was the fact that in the Carlow household, chilli wine is always put on the table to take with soup."

"By jove!" said Bennett. "Chilli wine, eh? We always used to have that in the mess when I was in the army. It was the only thing that made some of the stuff they lobbed up even drinkable."

"We use it," said the Chief Constable. "I always look after it—topping it up with dry sherry and so on. Those chillis last for years. They lose their red colour and go brown... good heavens! Are you saying she put this convallaria tincture in the chilli wine?"

"Just so, sir. But then, having done that, she had to make sure her sister used it—or enough of it to bring

221

about the desired results."

"How on earth did she manage that?"

"Cunning again," said Masters. "She played on her sister's known irascible nature. The Scots are more accustomed to using the adjective contumacious than we in England are. Frau Hillger, I believe, regarded her sister as contumacious in that Mrs Carlow was stubbornly perverse. All of you gentlemen have assured me that this was so."

"And how!" said Whincap.

"Frau Hillger on her own admission..." Masters spoke directly to Rainford. "This came out in the course of conversation in the presence of Mrs Rainford. Frau Hillger stated that when they sat down for lunch that day, she drew her sister's attention to the fact that the chilli wine bottle was almost empty, and then added that nevertheless there would be enough for her sister. I believe Frau Hillger knew that Mrs Carlow would immediately disagree and demand that the bottle be topped up. Frau Hillger, of course, complied and then had the satisfaction of seeing Mrs Carlow sprinkle more and more of what she believed to be chilli wine into her soup—just to be contumacious in view of her sister's supposed rationing of the condiment."

"Good God!" said Rainford. "You mean she played on old Elke's weakness to ensure that the poor old girl took enough of the stuff to kill her?"

"That is my belief and that is why I said I thought her to have used a high degree of cunning. And, incidentally, we have recovered two or three tablespoons of used chillis from a small plastic bag of rubbish inside the large black sack waiting at the house for collection by the dustmen."

"That seals it then?" asked Rainford.

"The beans will have to be tested forensically."

"Of course. But I heard you'd brought Mimi in for

questioning. You've established means and opportunity, so I suppose you won't have to bother about motive."

Masters picked up the paper which lay face downwards on the coffee table. As he turned it over, he said: " This is Frau Hillger's confession. It was made voluntarily after she had been cautioned and after she had been advised not to make such a statement before seeing a solicitor. Both those points are noted at the beginning of the statement. It is signed by Frau Hillger." He turned to the Chief Constable. "Do you wish to keep this, sir, or shall I tear it up?"

"Tear it up? Why?"

"I don't like confessions of murder, particularly from elderly ladies, even less from foreign elderly ladies who have not had the benefit of advice from a solicitor."

"Well ... er ... I mean, I see your point."

"If we were to use it, her counsel would retract it, and he could suggest that we extracted it by less than fair means—for the reasons I have already stated."

Rainford said: "You're really prepared to tear it up?"

"I would prefer to do so, but it is the Chief Constable's property."

Rainford looked from one man to the other. "I can't ask you to destroy it, sir, because no matter what anybody says, Mimi is family as far as I'm concerned. But I'd like to say I've never before heard a police officer make a more generous gesture. I know he can prove the case quite easily without it, but getting rid of a confession to murder! That's unbelievable."

The C.C. hesitated a moment and then said: "If we use the confession, the whole case is sewn up. But I'll bow to Masters' wishes if he can produce a motive. For my part, in spite of what he says about means and opportunity being enough to prove a case I believe that in a situation like this, motive will be of paramount

223

importance. Little old ladies have to be shown to have motives before juries will accept them as bloodthirsty villains."

"Didn't she say why she'd killed her sister?" asked Whincap. "In her confession, I mean."

Masters shook his head.

"What about it, George?" asked Rainford. "It's up to you."

"I realize that, unfortunately."

"No motive?" asked Bennett.

"I believe I have one to satisfy my own mind," said Masters. "But I must confess that the compilation of the factors which go to the making of it is more a matter for the shrinks than for me."

"Tell us," said the C.C.

"Right, sir. But when I said earlier you might be able to help me, I was referring to what I am about to say now. Dr Whincap, I think you are the most likely to be able to add a few words of guidance."

"I'll do what I can, of course."

"Thank you. I shall be out of my professional ground now, so I shall try to make my points in as few words as possible." He looked round his listeners. "First of all, I would like to speak about Elke Carlow. With the exception of the Chief Constable, you all knew her. I shall attempt to describe her personality as we who have listened to many of you on the subject—imagine her to have been.

"I mentioned to Dr Whincap the possibility of mental illness in Elke Carlow. Basically, as I understood him, what he had to say was that he had never treated this patient for mental disorder not because he was convinced she was free from mental illness but because of the degree of the disorder if, indeed, it did exist.

"Mental illness has a great number of causes and exists in all manner of forms. But so long as individual peculiarities of any mental illness do not result in conduct or behaviour markedly at variance with accepted social custom, society—in the shape of doctors—does not interfere with that person.

"So there are all grades of such disorder from slight peculiarities up to legally certifiable behaviour. It follows, therefore, that there are among us a fair number of people who are not sufficiently abnormal as to be regarded as certifiable but who are, nevertheless, by ordinary standards, eccentric or peculiar.

"Delusions, for instance, play a part in paranoia, a condition which is just one of the many mental illnesses. Some paranoiacs have delusions in which they believe themselves to be the subjects of annoyance or persecution by other people. Such delusions cause the persecutions to be attributed to actual known persons. By that I mean that the annoyance is not caused by some imagined or unreal source, but by specific persons who can be named by the mentally ill person.

"Psychopaths—for this is what such people are—are essentially people who seem completely unable to live on normal ordered terms with normal ordered society."

"Quite right," said Whincap. "They are usually explosive personalities who either cannot or will not conform to existing standards of behaviour. They display tantrums or sulk and generally make life uncomfortable for other people."

"Thank you, doctor. Would you agree with me if I were to say that Mrs Elke Carlow fulfilled many of the criteria we have mentioned and, as a consequence of her inadequacy in social relationships, could be regarded as having been a sufferer from mental illness?"

"Oh come on," said Rainford. "She wasn't that bad."

"No?" asked Green. "You've all said she was stubborn, unpleasant, she sulked when she wouldn't go to the Christmas party, she tried to commit suicide, she had a maniacal hatred of Kisiel and a mania about him having shopped her to the wartime authorities. And she presumed by wanting to foist herself on your daughter and even sending a carpenter round there. If that wasn't anti-social behaviour, what is? And for who else, other than a crank, would the doc make the arrangements he saw fit to introduce for keeping her medicine on an even keel?"

"Put like that..."

"I would agree with you, Mr Masters," said Whincap quietly. "Elke Carlow was definitely a mental case. But before anybody asks why I didn't do anything about it, I plead that it was sub-clinical. In other words, I don't believe that her inadequacy was the sort of disability that warranted medical interference unless and until her friends and relatives actively complained that her life-style was affecting their lives adversely. She was, in my opinion, neither insane nor criminal, nor was she approaching either state."

"Thank you. Am I also right in assuming that such psychic stresses as she suffered may also have helped to produce a gradual mental disorder? I refer specifically to the fact that as a young woman she suddenly found her native Germany at war with her adopted country. That she was confined for some years away from husband, child and home, with all the grief and trauma such events cause."

"This has always been my view," said Whincap, "and I suppose because of it I made allowances for behaviour which might have caused me to be a deal stricter with another patient."

Masters nodded his appreciation of this point. The C.C., however, asked impatiently: "Where is all this leading, Masters? Why discuss the dead woman's mental illness when you're supposed to be explaining the motive that drove her sister to kill her?"

"Please bear with me, sir. I am reporting my thought processes concerning reasons and motives. As I said earlier, I am having to feel my way."

The C.C. grunted, which Masters took as permission to proceed.

"As we have already discussed, the causes of mental disorder are various, but usually they are considered to be either inherited or acquired, or both. There may be some congenital nervous or mental defect which is peculiar to the family of the affected person.

"We normally call this heredity. And the weakness shown by one member of a family may also show itself in other members of the same family by various nervous diseases allied to mental instability."

"Quite right," said Whincap. "Sometimes it's epilepsy or hysteria..."

"Wait a minute," growled Rainford. "Are you suggesting that my missus has inherited some mental instability? Because if you are, I'd like to tell you you're wrong."

"No, no, Theo," said Whincap. "Nothing like that at all. It's a terribly complicated business and usually springs from the marriage of two people with like neurotic tendencies. The offspring of such marriages sometimes show characteristics which are natural enough in the parents but which are apt to be more exaggerated in the children. Your wife—Margarethe—had a perfectly normal and delightful father, as you well know. There was nothing neurotic about him, so she is, herself, perfectly normal and well adjusted. And the same goes for Marian. You are her father and, as far as I can tell, you are not neurotic either. So don't take what Masters is saying as a slight on your missus."

"Thank you, doctor." Masters turned to Rainford. "My point is, Theo, that Mimi Hillger inherited some of the nature of her sister. She controlled it much better. Where Elke Carlow was irritable, jealous, wayward, unreasonable and so on, Mimi Hillger was a gentler, more controlled person. But—and this is my point—

in spite of her gentleness she was already predisposed by birth to mental disorder of some degree.

"Now, in persons so predisposed, other factors can trigger off a breakdown. Doctors call them exciting factors and they may cause sudden trouble or be slow in building up to the breaking point. Like her sister, Mimi Hillger has suffered great stresses in her life. She lived in Prussia which, as you know, was cut off behind the iron curtain. She suffered privation not only during the war but for many years afterwards. And then—after she was widowed—she got the almost unheard of chance to be let out of Eastern Europe and to come to Britain with all its freedoms of thought and action and so on.

"The prospect, so long awaited, must have been of heaven. But when she arrived, what did she find? An overbearing, unreasonable elder sister who had not availed herself of our freedoms and who seemed hell-bent on ensuring that neither would Mimi. Even family relationships were soured. Mimi couldn't come to the Christmas party because of Elke. Mimi couldn't visit Helewou because Marian and Adam wouldn't have Elke...and so on and so forth. You will know better than I do what the atmosphere was like in that house. But what I submit is, that mild-mannered Mimi reached her breaking point. The mind she had kept such careful control of for so many years finally rebelled. The contumacious sister was robbing her of the looked-for life. She gave in. Her sister would have to go. The means of getting rid of her were to hand. She used her knowledge of herbal remedies and the cunning invoked by her mental instability to plan the death. Once it was accomplished, and after a further little flurry of cunning when she rang Dean, her mind settled back to gentleness in preparation for the quiet life to come."

There was a moment or two of silence, then the C.C. said: "But if she is normal now, won't that invalidate her defence? The general principle is that if an accused person suffers from a delusion but is not insane in other matters, he or she is held responsible for the offence."

"I did not intend to imply that she is normal now, sir. Merely that she is quiescent. In order to establish a defence on the ground of insanity it must be proved that at the time of committing the act the party accused was labouring under such a defect of reason as not to know the nature and quality of that act. I shall report that in my opinion this was so. Of course, I am not an authority, but there is nothing to stop me claiming, quite truthfully, that it was a knowledge of her inherited predisposition to mental illness that led me to suspect Frau Hillger of, and consequently to charge her with, murder."

"With such support from you," said Rainford, "the defence would walk it on a plea of insanity."

"I hope so. And that is why I would prefer to tear up the confession and give her counsel a fighting chance of pulling it off."

"What's the difference?" demanded Whincap. "She'll still be locked up."

"Not in quite the same way, doctor. I can assure you that Broadmoor is, on the whole, a more pleasant residence than the Scrubs."

"And she could be let out quite quickly," said Rainford, "if she shows she really is quiescent and responds well to any treatment she is given."

"Tear up the confession," said Harrington. "Doctor Whincap, Mr. Bennett, I'd like you two to do what you can in your individual professional fields to help her and ease her through what has to come. I don't want the stress to cause her to go permanently over the top."

"After Masters' magnanimity, it's the least we can do," said Bennett. "I'll arrange the defence."

Harrington got to his feet.

"Well, that's that. Thank you, Masters, Green and

you sergeants. A good job. Now I must rush away."

As they left the C.C.'s office, Rainford said: "I want to thank you, too. For myself and Margarethe."

"Think nothing of it," said Green. "But don't tell your missus everything George said. Just tell her Mimi confessed but Bob Bennett has told her to withdraw the confession. It'll be easier that way."

Rainford nodded.

"We've got wives, too, you know," went on Green. "But I don't think I'll be buying mine any more lilies of the valley."